W9-CFL-218

DESERT FIRE

Tor Books by David Hagberg

Countdown
Critical Mass
Crossfire
Desert Fire
Heartland
Heros
Last Come the Children
Without Honor

Writing as Sean Flannery

Counterstrike
Moving Targets

DAVID HAGBERG

A TOM DOHERTY ASSOCIATES BOOK
NEW YORK

This is a work of fiction. All the characters and events portrayed in this book are fictitious, and any resemblance to real people or events is purely coincidental.

DESERT FIRE

This book is printed on acid-free paper.

A Tor Book
Published by Tom Doherty Associates, Inc.
175 Fifth Avenue
New York, N.Y. 10010

Design by Lynn Newmark

Library of Congress Cataloging-in-Publication Data

Hagberg, David.
Desert Fire / David Hagberg.
p. cm.
"A Tom Doherty Associates book."
ISBN 0-312-85496-X
1. Hussein, Saddam, 1937- —Fiction. I. Title.
PS3558.A3227D47 1993
813'.54—dc20 93-17048
CIP

First edition: July 1993

Printed in the United States of America

0 9 8 7 6 5 4 3 2 1

FOR LAURIE

1

SADDAM HUSSEIN al-Tikriti stood at the open flap of his desert tent some miles west of Baghdad, the skirts of his flowing galabia ruffling in the cool evening breeze. He was alone for the moment, which he seldom was, and it gave him a curiously disquieting feeling. As if he were the very last man on earth. Cities were empty. No one worked the land. No one lived across the sea. Emptiness.

Far to the southeast he picked out a slow-moving pinprick of light against the brilliant backdrop of the stars. His advisers told him that it was the CIA's latest spy satellite, the KH-15, sent up on the tail of an infidel rocket to watch them.

He edged a little deeper into the darkness of the tent. This night he felt as old as the desert hills and wadis around him, almost one with the spirits of the ten thousand years of history here. This was the Fertile Crescent. The valley of the Tigris and Euphrates rivers. The birthplace of a dozen religions, of civilization itself.

Like Mu'ammar al-Qaddafi, Hussein had begun coming to the desert to find solace among his ancestors after his defeat over the reclamation of Iraqi homelands in Kuwait. The Revolutionary Command Council was still his to control, and therefore the nation was his. Western forces had, for the most part, finally withdrawn from the region. And once again his oil was flowing, bringing his people the much-needed revenue so long denied them by the infidels.

And yet it wasn't enough. A people could either grow and prosper, or wither and die. Iran to the east and Israel to the west would have to be defeated. Decisively. But the Gulf War, as the Western media called the battle, had taught him an important lesson. One of patience. One of cat and mouse.

"General," the voice of one of his bodyguards called from the darkness.

Hussein's hand went to the pistol in the pocket of his felt jacket. "*'Ay-wa,*" Yes, he said, softly.

"He is here." The guard was visible now just beyond the ten-meter proximity detectors. A dark figure stood behind him.

The man was an old friend and comrade in the *jihad* against the West. Munich, Hama, Beirut. A dozen places, a hundred times, he'd proved himself. And yet there was something different about him in the past months since he'd gone to Germany. Hussein had seen it in the man's eyes, and he wanted to see if there'd been any change.

He reached to a panel on his left and flipped a switch that would interrupt the elaborate protective alarm system for ten seconds.

"Come," he said, and his grip tightened on the pistol. So much was at stake, and they were so close this time, that he could not afford to take any chances. This time there would be no Desert Storm.

The dark figure came forward, his hands spread outward in a gesture of humility and peace. Seconds later the alarm circuits tripped back on with an audible snap.

"I serve at your command," the man known to the world only as Michael said graciously.

He was taller than Hussein and just as thickly built. His features, which, unlike Carlos's, were in no police or intelligence file anywhere in the world, were dark and handsome, his hair only slightly gray.

They embraced; left cheek, right cheek, and left again, then separated. Hussein managed a slight smile. All was right with Michael. Some tension, perhaps, but nothing was amiss.

"How was your trip?" the Iraqi leader asked, taking Michael's arm and leading him into the more secure rear room of the tent.

"Tedious, in part because of the security precautions I had to observe. But it is good to be among friends. Believe me."

"You are not tiring yourself out? The strain is not too much?"

Michael shook his head in sadness. "Germany has deteriorated since the reunification. Nothing is the same. Nothing will remain the same. They watch us continuously."

"It is why we must be victorious," Hussein said.

"Yes, my general. There is no God but God."

Hussein thought of Michael as his soldier of Allah. The righteous fist of God will come down and smite mine enemies dead. It was written.

"Now, come and tell me what progress you are making," Hussein said, motioning Michael to take a place among the cushions at a low table laden with food and drink. Of all the men and women he'd sent to Germany on the project, Michael was the best. Michael would be the tool of Iraq's salvation.

2

BONN LAY under a thick fall overcast that covered the night sky. Streets glistened from the rains, shops were closed, traffic was heavy and angry. The Rhine flowed impassively, darkly, through the city.

Occasionally, a mournful barge whistle rose above the clamor along the Hauptstrasse or beneath the Konrad Adenauer Bridge, but there had been no pleasure boats on the river all day, and certainly none this night. If a city could be said to be holding its breath, waiting for something to happen, then Bonn was doing it now.

The killer felt it too. But he had the patience of a desert Bedouin, willing to wait, to watch, to stalk his prey. His time would come, as it had before and before that. He was one of the *fedayeen* . . . of the ones willing to sacrifice themselves.

"Insha' Allah," Praise God, he muttered.

He waited in his dark gray Mercedes away from the violet sodium-vapor lights on tall aluminum stanchions in the west parking lot of Kraftwerk Union's Research Facility Nord. The early shift had left hours ago and now only a few engineers and midlevel managers trickled out of the courtyard gates to their cars in the rain. They hurried, heads bent low, faces hidden beneath umbrellas, coat collars hunched up. No one noticed him in the darkness.

He'd been watching the girl for weeks now, ever since he'd spotted her downtown. She was just like the others. Chance encounters at a time when he felt as if he were going to explode with rage.

He'd known immediately that she would be the one, so he had followed her to her apartment. He'd watched as she parked her yellow Opel on the narrow street, its wheels properly up on the curb. He'd watched as she let herself in, and a half-minute later as the third-floor windows suddenly showed light.

Understanding full well what he was risking, he'd remained parked in front of her apartment building until well after midnight, when the lights in her window went out. Still he remained. If a passing police unit had spotted him, there would have been questions impossible to answer. But the blood lust was on him.

Hours later, perhaps around three, he'd seen the glowing tip of a cigarette at her window.

"Can't sleep, little girl?" he whispered to himself. "The demons are getting you. Satan is near. Night sweats? Legs cramping up? Breath coming short? Heart pounding in your chest?" He knew all those feelings. And there was only one cure for them, and that was death.

Now, at the research facility, a man and a woman passed the lighted security booth, pausing under the canopy that extended over the driveway, and then the man scampered across to the parking lot, leaving the woman behind.

The killer studied her, how she held herself, how she waited. Though she too was obviously an infidel, she was the wrong type. She was tall, and even beneath her raincoat he could see that her figure was slight. Not suitable at all, though her kind would be much easier to kill. He could snap her neck with little effort. There'd be no fight. The thought gave him no pleasure.

A car came up one of the rows and pulled beneath the canopy. The woman got in and they left. The killer watched in his rearview mirror as the taillights disappeared down the ramp that led to the Autobahn. Once more the parking lot was still.

He got out of his car and hurried past four rows of cars to where the girl's yellow Opel was parked. The driver's side door was unlocked, as he knew it would be. He opened it, and from inside released the hood latch. Around front, he lifted the hood.

Working in the dim light from a distant stanchion, he pulled the wire out of the ignition coil, then replaced the rubber tip a scant half-inch back down into the connector so that though the coil was now unplugged, it looked to be properly connected.

He closed the hood and walked back to his own car, the entire operation taking him barely forty-five seconds.

He was shaking when he got behind the wheel, and he had to force himself to calm down, to take deep breaths. It wasn't fear, it was excitement tinged with rage. The whore. The infidel. Satan's imp. He shuddered as he started his car and headed out of the parking lot back toward the city.

Control, that was everything. It was the lesson they'd learned at the Munich Olympics, at Hama, at Yemen, at Lockerbie, at a hundred places in the past twenty-five years. Even in insanity, control was important if he was to survive to continue doing Allah's work.

The killer knew he was insane. He'd known that for a number of years. And he understood his condition with a cold, clinical certainty. Cure was impossible. Survival meant maintaining control until his personal demons became so overwhelming in the night that he had to strike.

He took care with his driving, going with the traffic along the Köln-Bonn Autobahn, past the airport southeast of the plant, into the city. At times the urgent desire to hurry came over him, but he resisted. There was time. Plenty of time, he told himself.

Crossing the river at midtown on the Konrad Adenauer Bridge, he took the busy Friedrich-Ebert Allee into Bad Godesberg, arriving fifteen minutes later on the narrow street where last night again he had parked until nearly dawn. This time he stopped in the middle of the next block, shut off the car and sat back in his seat, adjusting the rearview mirror so that he could see her apartment building.

Time now, he thought, to wait. But not long. Not much longer, *Insha' Allah.*

He began to chant softly the Shahada. *"Allah-u Akbar; Allah-u Akbar; La illah illa Allah . . ."* God is most Great; God is most Great; I testify that there is no other God but God and Muhammad is His Prophet; God is most Great; God is Most Great . . .

3

IT WAS after 10:00 P.M. when Sarah Razmarah was finally finished with work and ready to leave her office for home. She shut down her computer terminal and pulled a dust cover over the monitor and keypad. She pulled on her coat and got her purse. At the door she switched off the lights, but she remained standing in the dark as tears began to slip down her cheeks.

At five feet four she was attractive in a buxom, Middle Eastern peasant way, with thick, shimmering black hair, large, jet-black eyes and a dark complexion. She'd been raised in the United States, but her parents never stopped talking about the paradise that was Iran under the Shah.

"Oh, Ahmed," she whispered.

It was the spying, of course. She had become a BND whore, but she hadn't counted on falling in love. "Watch him, Sarah," her controller had told her. "He is lonely, Sarah. He will tell you things in the night. He will trust you, they always do with their trousers down."

It was so goddamned cold and calculating. But then her life in the United States had been no bed of roses. It was a question of loneliness, of drifting. Where one day (except for her work as a nuclear engineer) was exactly like the day before. She wasn't accepted by her peers in a male-dominated field. Nor did she have female friends. They thought she was an egghead. And in California's Silicon Valley they took her dark looks for Hispanic, which isolated her even further.

"Knowledge is all we want, Sarah," Ludwig Whalpol had told her. "The truth, as simple as that. Nothing dishonorable in such an endeavor."

No there wasn't, in Sarah's mind. At least there hadn't been until she got the specifics.

"Ahmed Pavli," he'd told her. "About your age, perhaps three or four years older . . . thirty-five. This man is the chief engineer on the team. Very influential. Of much importance. Are you listening, Sarah?" He leaned forward for emphasis. "Let me tell you that this man Pavli is a walking compendium of everything we must know. At least he will be a start for you. With this man I want you to begin your concentration. He will be your first important conquest."

She hadn't counted on falling in love with him. Not that. She pulled herself together and left her office, taking the elevator down to the ground floor and signing out with the night guard.

"Have a good evening, Fräulein," the older man said. "But drive carefully, it's a bad night out there."

"A good night to curl up with a book," she said over her shoulder. Outside, she held up for a moment beneath the canopy. It was raining in earnest. "Damn," she muttered. She pulled her coat collar around her neck and strode into the parking lot.

Within fifty feet she was soaked to the skin. Her raincoat was old, its waterproof qualities long gone, but then in California she hadn't needed it often.

Reaching her car, she yanked open the door and climbed inside. Within seconds the windows began to fog up. She fumbled her keys out of her purse and in the dark searched for the ignition. When she turned the key the engine cranked, but did not start. She tried again and again.

"Damn," she cried. "Damn . . . Oh, goddamnit to hell!"

There seemed to be plenty of battery power, but the engine simply wouldn't catch. She turned on the interior lights, found the hood release and pulled it.

Outside, it took her a couple of seconds to find the safety catch on the hood and open it. In the dim illumination from the parking lot lights she tried to see if anything was obviously wrong. She was an engineer, after all. An automobile engine certainly was much simpler than the control systems she designed for nuclear-powered electrical generating facilities. But she was no mechanic.

After a moment she looked up toward the entry courtyard fifty yards away and shook her head ruefully. She wanted a hot bath, a stiff drink and a damned good cry, preferably in that order.

She lowered the hood, retrieved her purse and sprinted back across the parking lot. It would be nearly impossible to get a cab out here at this hour, but one of the other engineers might be leaving soon and she could catch a ride.

4

THE LAST person in the world she wanted to see this night was coming down the corridor when she reentered the building. His feral grin faded when he realized something was wrong.

"Why aren't I surprised to see you here, Ludwig?" she said to her control officer.

"What's wrong, Sarah? You look all in." Major Whalpol spoke with as much genuine concern as he was capable of.

"My damned car won't start."

"Shall I call a mechanic for you?"

"I don't want to deal with it tonight. I came back to see if I could get a ride to town."

Whalpol took her arm. "I'm on my way out. I'll drop you off."

She didn't trust or like him, but she was too tired to argue. Besides, it could be hours before any of the engineers would be ready to leave, and she wanted to get home to be alone.

"Just no questions tonight, Ludwig. Please?"

He smiled. "But we're in the wrong business for that sort of attitude, my dear."

He brought his car around and she climbed in beside him. They headed to the Autobahn a half-kilometer down the hill. As darkness closed around them, she felt she was encased in a cocoon. But the feeling wasn't one of safety. Around Whalpol there never could be safety.

When he had come to her in California with his proposition, the timing had been right. She was lonely and frustrated and miserable, and despite the fact that she was a U.S. citizen, she didn't fit in. She was an Iranian. Among other things, Iranians were stupid, lazy, deceitful and fanatical. Her parents were dead, and she had no sisters or brothers. There were some cousins in Tehran, but even if she could get there she doubted that she would be able to find them, or if she did, that they would accept her.

"We would like for you to help us," Whalpol had said. He had picked her up after work, telling her he had known her father very well in the old days. They stopped at a small coffee shop just north of the Van Nuys Airport. There were only a few other customers, and Whalpol led her to a booth in a far corner. He was a tall, thin man with a hawklike face. His suit was dark green wool, with narrow lapels set high on the jacket.

"My father never mentioned you," Sarah said over their coffee.

Whalpol shrugged. "Those were difficult days. The Shah's regime was coming apart, and your father, bless his heart, went through a difficult period with the Colonel."

Colonel Massedegh worked for SAVAK, the feared Iranian secret police. He was the bogeyman in her house, and as a little girl she'd been very respectful of the name because whenever it was mentioned she could see fear in her father's eyes.

"It was I who interceded on your father's behalf to get him and your mother safely out."

"You're not Iranian."

"I'm German. I've been sent here to ask you to come to Bonn. We'd like you to take an engineering position with Kraftwerk Union. You would be a project supervising engineer."

Sarah was startled. Kraftwerk Union was Germany's largest manufacturer of nuclear-powered electrical generating systems. The company was at the forefront of international concern and debate. Some years ago the huge firm had built a nuclear generating plant in Brazil, despite world opinion that Brazil almost certainly would use the technology to construct nuclear weapons. She wondered what the company was involved with now.

Whalpol beamed. "I can see that you are definitely interested."

"There must be dozens . . . hundreds of engineers better than me who are currently available. Why have you come here?"

"You would be the dark horse. The unknown."

"What?"

"Your job, Fräulein, would be two-pronged, in a manner of speaking. On the one hand, you would work directly for me."

"You?"

Whalpol reached into his jacket pocket for a thin leather wallet, which he opened and passed across the table. It contained an official identification card. The German eagle, its wings spread, was embossed on the card. For a moment she was afraid to reach out for it. She had a visceral feeling as to what it would be. Whalpol had helped her father and mother with SAVAK, and now he'd come to America to see that the debt was repaid.

The card identified the bearer, by photograph, as Ludwig Herbert Whalpol, Bonn, a major in the Bundesnachrichtendienst, the BND, the German Secret Service. She dropped the wallet.

He smiled as he stuffed it back in his pocket. "We would ask that you keep an eye on certain foreigners on the KwU engineering team."

"I am to spy?"

"Yes."

"Why me, Major? Why not a fellow German? I'm an American."

"You're an Iranian, Sarah. A nuclear engineer. And a woman. A rare combination."

"Are you building a reactor for Iran?"

"No."

"Then for who . . . Iraq?"

Whalpol nodded.

"You people are insane. The UN has finally cleared out the last of Saddam Hussein's nuclear research facilities . . . and my God, how long has that taken? . . . Now you bastards want to start it all over again?"

"Iraq cannot remain in the Dark Ages, Sarah. A strong, modern Iraq will be a stabilizing force in the region. Iran is poised to strike. You must know that."

"Hussein will build bombs."

"That's what you and I will prevent."

She laughed out loud, and Whalpol caught her meaning.

"Not just us, Sarah; there are many others, of course. But you are in a unique position to help us."

"I could tell my government."

Again the German major smiled. "They would not believe you. Please, Sarah, your life is nothing here. Make something of it. Do some good in the world. Your father would understand this, Sarah. Do you?"

Had she known what it would be like, she reflected now, morosely, she still would have taken the assignment.

There had been moments with Ahmed when she had felt alive, happy, finally in love.

"I thought you would be with him tonight," Whalpol said, pulling her away from her thoughts. "Nothing has gone wrong, has it, between you two?"

"No," she said softly. "He's worked very late all this week, and he's tired, that's all."

"The two of you should go away for the weekend. I have a place on the Wied River you could use."

"Wired for sound, no doubt," Sarah said.

Whalpol shrugged.

"You're a dirty voyeur, Ludwig. I suppose you get a big kick out of this. Your little arrangements."

"The bloom is off the rose," Whalpol mumbled. "It's time, I think, to give you a new assignment."

A bolt of fear shot through her. "What?"

"You are burned out, Sarah. You are no longer being completely honest with me. Or yourself, for that matter. In fact, I think you have fallen in love with poor Ahmed Pavli. Is that it, Sarah?"

"I'll handle it," she said miserably.

"It's my job, I can handle it for you."

"He's a good man," she cried. "Leave him alone. Leave them all alone!"

"No."

"Let me tell him."

"Tell him what, Sarah? That you have slept with him on orders from the German government to find out if Iraq is stealing even more nuclear technology than we are already selling them?"

"I'll tell him that I no longer love him."

"You aren't capable of that type of lie. Not that."

"Let me tell him that!" she shrieked. "He deserves that much. I deserve it. I've earned it."

Even as she was saying it, she wondered if she meant it, or if, as Whalpol suggested, she was incapable of such a lie. She did love Ahmed, but their relationship could not go any further without the truth between them. A truth she could not share with him.

"Easy," Whalpol was saying.

"Let me deal with it," she said, calmer now, taking a deep breath. "I don't want him hurt, Ludwig."

"Neither do I," Whalpol answered gently. "Let me think about it, and tomorrow we'll talk, just you and I. We'll work something out. Despite what you think, I'm not an ogre."

"I understand."

"I don't think so, but we'll talk tomorrow."

"Tomorrow," she said, but she was drifting again, watching the lights of the oncoming traffic as they neared town, and wondering where her life was going.

5

THE THREE-STORY apartment building was thick, brooding, in the chill, wind-driven rain. The windshield wipers of Whalpol's car provided a rhythm to Sarah's efforts at keeping herself together.

"Would you like me to come up with you?" Whalpol asked her.

"No, I'll be all right." She got out of the car, crossed the sidewalk and let herself into the building without looking back. Inside, she leaned against the door. It wasn't supposed to be like this. She half expected Whalpol to come after her, but she heard the car pull away. She was soaked and cold. When she reached the third floor she was winded and shivering. Finally she found her keys at the bottom of her purse, and unlocked her door.

She closed the door behind her and snapped the locks, fearful of making any noise. You dare not disturb the sleeping ghosts lest they awake and devour you. It was a line from something, but she couldn't remember what.

Her apartment was long and narrow, well furnished. The living room was in front, a bathroom and the bedroom in the middle, and the kitchen in the rear overlooking a courtyard.

In the bathroom she pulled off her sodden raincoat and laid it over the drying rack at the foot of the tub. She kicked off her shoes as she unbuttoned her blouse, peeled it off and dropped it over the edge of the tub. She felt like a robot, like one of the remote handling machines for nuclear materials at the research facility.

Wrapping a towel around her wet hair, she went into the bedroom, where she pulled off the rest of her wet clothes, letting them lie where she dropped them.

She put on a thick terry-cloth robe and padded barefoot into the kitchen. She poured a stiff measure of cognac and drank it down straight, shuddering as it hit her stomach, but enjoying the afterglow.

One year she'd given herself to finish the KwU project and her dirty little job of spying for Whalpol, and then she would strike out on her own again. Her father would have been proud of her if he had been alive. He had served as a construction engineer in the Shah's army, but he lost an arm so the best he could do was clerk in a small hotel in Tehran until the opportunity came to manage the Four Seasons Hotel in Beirut.

Those were difficult times for everybody. The PLO was gaining strength, although nearly everybody in Iran thought Arafat was nothing but a joke. And Israel was putting a lot of pressure on the Lebanese, so her father had returned to Tehran, where he believed his family would be safer. He had not counted on SAVAK, which had become mistrustful of him. How was it that a one-armed clerk could be selected to manage such a prestigious hotel in Beirut? Whom had he paid off? Whom did he work for? What secrets had he sold to get such a position? Questions upon questions.

It was because of him that Sarah had gone to the United States for her engineering degree. But now he was gone, and at this moment she wished more than ever that she had siblings. A sister, perhaps to telephone and tell her troubles to. A brother, who would put his arm around her and tell her that it was all right, Sis. She was lonely.

The telephone in the living room rang, startling her out of her thoughts. At this hour, it had to be either Whalpol checking up on her, or Ahmed Pavli because she had avoided him all day. She didn't want to talk to either of them.

She put down her glass and went into the living room and took it on the fourth ring.

"Yes?" she said softly.

"It's me," Pavli said. His voice was deep and rich, his German precise.

She gripped the telephone hard but couldn't speak.

"Sarah? Is everything all right? Are you ill? Shall I come over?"

"Not tonight, Ahmed," she said, the words choking at the back of her throat.

"I missed you at work."

"In the morning, we'll talk."

"I could come to you now. I'm only a few minutes away."

"No." But she wanted to beg him to come and hold her in his arms, to put everything right.

"Is it to do with work?" he asked. "Has something happened that you can't talk to me?"

"We'll talk tomorrow, Ahmed, I promise you. *Insha' Allah.*" Tears welled up in her eyes again. She felt as if someone had kicked her in the gut.

"We'll have lunch together," he said. It was the Western thing to do. Nearly everyone on the Iraqi team had adopted the custom.

"All right."

When she hung up, her heart was beating rapidly, and it took effort to breathe.

She went back into the kitchen, where she put the teakettle on to boil. Then in the bathroom she started the water in the tub.

Someone knocked at her door. Ahmed already, she thought, as she turned off the water and went into the living room. It was like him. He'd heard the strangeness in her voice and had come to help.

She unlocked the door and opened it. The killer was much taller than she, and bulky. He wore dark slacks and a dark windbreaker, slick from the rain. A Greek fisherman's cap was pulled low over his eyes, and she noticed in the split second that he wore thick-soled, heavy shoes—brogans—and black leather gloves. She'd never seen him dressed that way before. The effect was ominous.

"What do you want?" she asked.

The killer smiled cruelly. "You," he whispered.

Before Sarah could react, his right fist smashed into her face, snapping her head back and driving her into the apartment.

She tried to scream, but nothing came, and it seemed as if she were falling forever, tumbling over the arm of the couch to the floor.

She could see the killer as he stepped into the apartment and locked the door behind him.

He unzipped his jacket and moved behind her.

She had trouble breathing, and realized that her mouth was filled with blood and bits of something hard. Her teeth, he had broken some of her teeth. She coughed.

She was able to move her head an inch or two so that she could see him. The killer stood with his back to her, looking into the kitchen, his gloved hands gripping the sides of the door frame.

The telephone. If she could get to the telephone before he turned around she could call for help. He had not come here to rape her, he had come to murder her. And she knew why.

She managed to roll over and gather her legs beneath her and push herself up to her hands and knees. Blood and bits of broken teeth dribbled out of her mouth. For several agonizing seconds she could do no more than remain where she was, one hip against the side of the couch, her arms shaking, her stomach heaving.

He was behind her. He grabbed the back of her thick robe and lifted her onto her feet and turned her to him. For a second her eyes were locked with the killer's—like a desert scorpion's.

"Why?" she whimpered.

The killer shook her like a rag doll, as if he wanted her to come out of her daze, wanted her to scream for help, to fight back. But she could not.

He pulled her away from the couch, past the low coffee table, dragging her effortlessly with one hand.

She could not make her feet work, and the robe cut into her armpits as he hauled her down the corridor to the kitchen. He slammed her against the counter, the sharp edge catching the small of her back, driving the air out of her lungs. Spots filled her eyes.

He faced her, pressed his body against her. She could feel his erection against her belly, and she thought that perhaps he would only rape her after all, and not kill her.

He pulled the robe open and looked down at her breasts and the curves of her belly and hips.

Rape. If that's all he wanted, she would give it to him. She spread her legs a little, and thrust her hips forward.

The action enraged him. He grabbed her pubis, and pain stabbed her. A gloved finger was inside her, and he lifted her off her feet by her vagina, the pain shooting through her body like nothing she had ever felt before.

"Whore," he whispered roughly. "Strumpet. Slut."

He jerked his hand away from her crotch and as she slumped to the floor he slammed his fist into her right breast. Even more pain burst in her. The air was driven out of her lungs in a spray of blood, and she felt another blow, then another, until mercifully she faded, drifting, her mind disconnected from her body, the floor coming up to meet her face.

6

PAIN COURSED through Sarah's body like molten lead. Her eyes fluttered open. She lay on her back on the kitchen floor. Her legs were spread and the killer knelt over her, hitting her with his fists: her breasts, her belly, her pubis.

He clamped his fingers around her throat, slowly tightening his grip and cutting off her air.

She felt as if her head would explode; this could not be happening to her.

She flailed her arms feebly to ward him off. He smiled, as if glad that she was fighting him.

Something was in her left hand. Something small and hard. It cut her palm. Something metal. Something of the killer's. She grasped it with her last strength.

The killer said something, but there was roaring in her ears. The teakettle was whistling above her on the stove, and the lights grew dim.

She was falling into a black bottomless pit, into nothingness, and finally she eased into a painless peace.

7

IT WAS a few minutes after midnight. The sky was still overcast but the rain had finally stopped. The temperature had plunged and a thick, icy fog covered the river valley, harking back to the Romanesque days of dark river fortresses.

A well-built man, good-looking in a thick, Germanic way, stood on the balcony of his Oberkassel apartment looking out across the slumbering city of Bonn. Heedless of the cold, he wore only trousers and a light pullover as he smoked a cigarette. His thoughts flitted across ten dozen childhood memories, few of them pleasant.

Only of his father, now dying in a sanatorium near Bern, were his memories fond. Now it was nearly over for the old man, and he found himself wishing that the waiting would be over, the end would come, the pain would end. And he felt guilty for it.

Look to the future, our only salvation, his father was fond of saying, forced into such a dreamer's philosophy as the only logical alternative to the insanity of the forties.

But the future was here. The Germanies had reunited. And Roemer did not feel saved.

The telephone in the apartment rang and Gretchen answered it. She came to the balcony door.

"Walther?"

"I'm not in," he said softly.

Behind him, he could smell her fresh lilac scent.

"It is the Chief District Prosecutor. He says it is very important he speak with you. Walther?"

Roemer would forever remember that exact moment, for it was the watershed of his life.

8

WE WERE told to wait, so we've waited," Bonn Criminal Police Lieutenant Rolf Manning said. "But no one has told us what interest the Bureau has in this case. Can you tell me?"

It was chilly in the third-floor corridor. Police had been coming and going for several hours, the downstairs door left open most of the time, the apartment building's heating system stingy against the cold weather.

Roemer looked down the stairwell. Bonn Kriminalpolizei Laboratory men were dusting the banister for fingerprints. Somewhere in the building a television or radio was playing, even so late. And from within the apartment came the muted hum of cop talk.

Manning was much shorter than Roemer. An ever-present Marlboro dangled from the corner of his mouth, making him look like a cop in an old American detective film. There was an angry glint in his wide Westphalian eyes. Although Roemer had never worked with him, he knew of Manning's reputation as tough, territorial and steady, with a long list of accomplishments under his belt. Manning had not been picked for elevation to the Federal Bureau of Criminal Investigation, because presumably he lacked imagination . . . whatever that was.

Blood was tracked on several of the steps leading down

from the third floor. The footprints had been outlined in white chalk and covered with clear plastic.

"As far as you and your people are concerned," Roemer said, turning to him, "I was never here."

"I was told as much, but that doesn't mean I have to like it, does it?" Manning said.

Don't make waves, Roemer had been told. Just get in, see what there is to see and get the hell out. Orders from on high. He'd taken them all his life. *Ordnung.* It meant everything, actually, if there was to be a stable society. But order with compassion.

Gretchen did not understand why it had to be him. "Because we make our own choices," he had told her. "Because all of us are either a part of the solution or a part of the problem." His father's philosophy he had taken to heart a long time ago. But Gretchen, like his ex-wife, had tried to narrow that sense of a wider responsibility in him. They had both mistaken his empathy for people for a weakness, for a pliancy. Both had tried to mold him into something they imagined he could or should be; neither would accept him for what he actually was. Gretchen had used the same argument tonight that his wife might have used in an effort to persuade him to pass on the assignment.

"Let someone else take it," she cried. "Why you? Why always you?"

He had made his way in without recognition by the newshawks gathered outside. Manning had briefed him. An anonymous telephone tip had been received at 22:53 hours, and a radio unit had been immediately dispatched. The body was discovered and Manning was called. After a very brief look, he called the Kriminalpolizei van with its complement of detail people, as well as the coroner.

Then the lightning strike had come, according to

Manning: Hold everything until the BKA arrives. Don't touch a fucking thing until the Bundes people get a peek. And Manning had begun to wonder just what sort of a case he had on his hands.

"I'd like to look inside now," Roemer said.

"Can you tell me what you're looking for?" Manning asked hopefully. "Perhaps we can help."

"I just want to look."

The uniformed Landpolizei were all downstairs. Inside were only the plainclothes specialists: the coroner, a police photographer, two fingerprint men, a forensics laboratory expert with bottle-thick glasses perched on the end of his nose, four detail men who had been taking the place apart until the call had come to hold up, and Manning's young sergeant, who seemed bored. The living room was filled with cigarette smoke. Conversations died when they saw Roemer.

"Look lively now," Manning said. "We are going to do a quick run-through for the nice man, and then he'll get the hell out of here and let us do our jobs."

There were a few appreciative chuckles.

"No forced entry, we're sure of that much," Manning said. "She either left the latch open, or she let her murderer in. Recognized him, perhaps."

"What's your preference?" Roemer asked softly.

"She let him in, I'd say. Lady downstairs in Two-B seems to think that our girl always kept her door locked. Lady said our *Fräulein* was secretive from the beginning, though she had her men friends."

"Any sense of the number?"

"Two in particular. One medium height, on the husky side, dark, sad-looking, she said. And the other tall, thin, like he'd been marooned on a desert island and just returned to civilization."

"How long had this been going on?"

"Since fall for the thin one, a bit before Christmas for the other."

Roemer inspected the door. There was a deadbolt and a slip chain in addition to the tumbler lock. The deadbolt looked new. She had been security-conscious.

They hadn't told him much on the telephone. They said they wanted him unburdened by preconceived notions other than the possibility that the murder could have a political significance, possibly even an international meaning.

"Nice apartment, arranged for her by her employers, we're told," Manning continued. "She was an American. We have her passport."

"Nothing touched in the living room?"

"It started in the living room. We found blood and bits of teeth on the rug. But it was finished in the kitchen. She was probably raped. Dr. Sternig says as much." Manning lowered his voice. "Possibly after she was dead. Fucking pervert."

Several bloody footprints on the living room carpet had been outlined in chalk and covered with clear plastic like those on the corridor stairs.

"If she let him in, they definitely knew each other well," Manning said. "Invited him in for tea."

"How do you know that?"

"She was wearing nothing more than a bathrobe. You don't let strangers in dressed like that. And the teakettle had been on. At least we think it was at the time of death."

The living room was well furnished, but there were no personal touches anywhere. No photographs. No paintings, other than a poorly done print of a Bavarian mountain scene. An ashtray on the table was filled with smoldering cigarette butts. Last month's issue of *Stern* magazine lay next to it.

"Care to see the body now?" Manning asked. "We'd like to get on with it."

"The ashtray. Was it clean or dirty?"

Manning glanced at the coffee table, clearly embarrassed.

"It was clean, sir," Jacobs, his sergeant, volunteered.

"Was it dusted?" Roemer asked.

"Yes, sir," the young man replied, puffing up a little. "We didn't let anyone in until that was finished. Standard operating procedure in our office, sir."

"That'll be enough, Sergeant," Manning said crossly. He didn't like the federals cross-examining his people, but he didn't like disrespect, either.

"The killer wasn't already in the apartment when she arrived?"

"Not unless he was well hidden," Manning said. "She came home, laid her wet raincoat over the rack in the bathroom. Took off her shoes and her blouse, which she laid over the tub. Took a towel, and while she was drying herself, walked into the bedroom. She got undressed—her clothing is lying on the bedroom floor—put on a robe and went into the kitchen, where she had a drink of cognac, and put on the teakettle."

"Then the murderer came calling?"

"It's the way we see it at the moment."

Roemer went to the bedroom door and looked at the wet clothing on the floor. A small bed, a dressing table in one corner, and along the opposite wall a substantial-looking *Schrank.* The big wardrobe had been moved out from the wall. There was a lingering odor of perfume.

Manning came up behind Roemer. "We moved the *Schrank.*"

"Why?"

"It had been moved before. We saw the marks on the carpet. But whatever may have been behind it is gone."

"If there was anything," Roemer said absently. He stepped into the room. The small wastepaper basket beside the dressing table was empty. The skirt on the floor was wet; so were the bra and panties.

"Has your office been investigating this girl?" Manning asked.

"No."

Manning stood aside as Roemer came out and went next into the bathroom. A soaked raincoat hung on a drying rack, and a white blouse lay over the tub. A pair of low black pumps lay by the toilet. No bath towel on the bar.

"The towel is in the kitchen," Manning volunteered.

The bathroom, like the living room and bedroom, seemed devoid of personal touches, as if this place had been used as a hotel, not a real home.

Why had the Chief District Prosecutor asked him here?

"I'll see the body now," he said.

Manning, relieved, stepped back. "This way."

Roemer moved down the hallway to the kitchen. The devastated body of a young woman, possibly in her late twenties or early thirties, dark hair, large breasts, lay flat on its back, legs spread, between the refrigerator and a small dining table. There was a lot of blood around her head. Her face had been crushed. Her bathrobe was open. There were large, dark bruises around her breasts, and angry white welts and blisters covered her belly and thighs.

"Her name was Sharazad Razmarah," Manning said from behind. "She was thirty-two. Lived here since October. Apparently she was an engineer at the Kraftwerk Union research facility."

"You said she was an American?"

"American passport. Gave her place of birth as Tehran, Iran."

A teakettle lay on the floor next to the body and there was a lot of water on the floor.

"We didn't disturb anything," Manning said.

Her left arm was bent back at an odd angle, apparently broken. Her right arm was outstretched, the fingers of her hand spread apart as if they too were broken.

Along with the metallic odor of a lot of blood, there was something else that Roemer could not define. A natural odor, not a pleasant one.

He stepped around the table to look more closely at her right hand. There seemed to be a bruise in her palm. Her left arm had been badly burned, flesh peeled away. Her jaw was broken. Most of her front teeth had been shattered.

Roemer closed his eyes. He could not help imagining her last moments of life, how it must have been.

"Dr. Sternig," Manning called.

The coroner appeared in the doorway. He wore a three-piece suit, the tie snugged up tight, a watch fob and chain in his vest. His lips were pursed, his eyes narrow.

"I'll have an autopsy report to your office this afternoon, providing I can have the body in the near future," he said.

"What can you tell me now?" Roemer asked.

"For now I'm placing the time of death between twenty-one hundred and twenty-two hundred hours. Cause of death, massive cerebral hemorrhage."

"There's more damage here. How do you see it?" There was a copper taste in Roemer's mouth, and his stomach was knotted.

"She was in the living room. Probably opened the door. The killer struck her in the face. I'm assuming he used his fist. It was a strong enough blow to shatter her lower mandible, breaking seven teeth and knocking her back against the couch."

"She didn't cry out," Manning said. "No one heard a thing."

Roemer held himself from looking at the body.

"She was probably unconscious, or semiconscious at that point, because there are no defensive wounds other than the impression on her right palm."

"She may have grabbed something from her killer," Manning said. "A button, a tie clasp, a cuff link. After she was already dead, the killer realized she had something in her hand and pried it loose, breaking three of her fingers in the process."

"We may be able to lift an image from her palm," the coroner said.

Roemer was suddenly cold. He always reacted like this. It was another of the reasons his wife, and now Gretchen, complained to him that he should get out of the Bureau.

"I can only guess at the order beyond that point," Dr. Sternig said. "He hit her many times, possibly even tortured her. We know that he dragged or carried her here into the kitchen, where he continued beating her. The tea water was hot. At some point he poured it over her. He kicked her too, in the back, the side, in the breasts. You can see the large hematoma. And then he stomped on her face, at least three times, crushing her forehead, causing her death."

"And he raped her," Roemer said after a long hesitation.

"Either just before or just after her death. I can't be absolutely certain until after the autopsy. But I'm seeing what I presume to be ejaculate on her inner thighs."

Roemer stared at Sarah's body.

"He was in a hurry," Manning said. "He killed her and it excited him. He couldn't wait to fuck her."

"A boyfriend?" Roemer asked. There was a buzzing in his head.

"Perhaps." Manning was agitated. "If you could just tell me why you're here, we wouldn't be operating in the dark. *Verdammt,* we could catch the dirty bastard who did this."

"Did she have a car?"

Manning sighed. "Apparently. She had a valid driving license, and we found a copy of the registration for a 1986 Opel. But we haven't found the car yet. There is an outside chance that she was driven home. One of the people below thought they heard a car pull up and the victim come in alone."

Roemer shook his head. "I've seen enough for now. If you would be so kind as to send along your reports as soon as possible . . ."

"Yes, sir," Manning said, and he and the coroner stepped aside as Roemer left the way he had come: quietly and anonymously.

9

ROEMER HAD been to the Chief District Prosecutor's Königswinter home before, but this time there was no butler. Ernst Schaller himself opened the door, took Roemer's coat, hung it on a hook and showed him to the study in the back, uncharacteristically apologizing right off.

"Sorry we had to call you out so late. But then murder never is very convenient, is it?" Schaller sat him in a wingback chair by the blazing fire, and poured him a stiff cognac. "Such a terrible thing, death, especially in one so young, so vital and alive, don't you agree?"

Roemer nodded absently. He was weary, and the young woman's smashed face wouldn't leave his mind. There were three locks on her door, all of them open. The murderer had been angry, yet there had been no other signs of a struggle in the apartment.

"Just one other thing to attend to, then we can get started," Schaller said. "If you'll just excuse me."

He left, and Roemer sat back, snifter in hand. The room was large and smelled of burning wood and pipe tobacco. There was one wall full of books, floor to ceiling, which surprised Roemer. He had never thought of the Chief Prosecutor as a learned man. Perhaps they were for show.

Along two other walls was a large collection of photographs showing a younger Schaller with the American president Kennedy, with Reinhard Gehlen (the founder of the postwar German Secret Service), with Willy Brandt, Konrad Adenauer and other German and international leaders.

It was past four in the morning, and though tired, Roemer was wide awake. A young woman's murderer lurked somewhere (presumably still in the city), and the Chief District Prosecutor had something to say about it. Roemer felt as if he were watching a stage play; he desperately wanted to know the ending so that he could go home without having to endure the middle. Every case he'd ever been assigned to, he took personally. His ex-wife would say he couldn't take on the entire world's problems. But he couldn't be stopped from trying, one at a time.

The carpet seemed old and obviously expensive. It probably cost more than everything Roemer owned. But then Schaller was a political animal, while Roemer was not. Schaller had the right connections, knew the right people, traveled in the right circles, while Roemer was nothing more than a cop with a penchant for irritating people, especially ex-wives, lovers and supervisors.

The cognac was very good, very German. Probably Asbach-Uralt. Roemer sipped it, then sat back and closed his eyes.

Sharazad Razmarah was an Iranian-born American, according to her U.S. passport. What had brought her to Germany? The job? A friend? A lover? A lark? A murder investigation was like meeting a new person. There were the first impressions that gradually resolved themselves into real opinions as time went on, until in the very end the nasty bits finally presented themselves in a sad commentary on what one person could do to another.

The house was very still at this hour of the morning. Roemer supposed Schaller's wife and the house staff were all asleep, as good people should be. Yet he could hear a murmur of distant conversation. He glanced over at the massive leather-topped desk, where one of the buttons of the executive telephone was lit. Who was Schaller speaking to, and what was he saying that could not be said here?

The murderer had been careful to pry some object out of a dead girl's hand, and yet careless enough to step in her blood and track it through the apartment and down the stairs. Carelessness, or arrogance, Roemer wondered. And where was her car?

Schaller appeared in the doorway. He was shorter than Roemer, but with the same huskiness to his frame, and similar, but older, meatiness to his face; large nose, firm lips above which perched a Prussian mustache. He was dressed in gray trousers and an open white shirt, over which he wore a gaudy brocaded smoking jacket. He reeked of pipe tobacco and cognac.

"Was it terrible, Roemer?" He leaned against his desk. "Was she terribly mangled?"

Her jaw was broken, Roemer thought. Her face was smashed. Her breasts bruised, her body scalded. And she had been raped afterward. Schaller got to the cases after they had been investigated. He never had to root about in the gruesome mess.

Schaller, eyes bright, stared at Roemer as if waiting for a bit of gossip. But he was frightened too, Roemer could see in the rigid set of his shoulders.

"It'll be just a few minutes now, and then we can get started," Schaller said.

"A few minutes for what, Chief Prosecutor?"

"Someone else is coming along. Shed some light on the

mystery. Give you some much-needed information to go on. You'll need it, believe me. Delicate."

Roemer sat forward. "Can you tell me why she was murdered, sir?"

Schaller looked aghast. "Good God, no! What must you be thinking?"

"You called me out in the middle of the night. You said that this murder could have political ramifications. Yet the City Criminal Police Division knows nothing of this."

"I'm just the go-between, believe me, Roemer. I was advised of the poor girl's murder and was asked if I could provide an investigator—the very best in all of Germany for the job."

"Lieutenant Manning has already begun . . ."

"The Kriminalpolizei have their own case. This is another matter." Schaller reddened.

"It is the same murder."

The telephone rang and Schaller hopped away from the desk and picked it up before it could ring again. "Yes?"

Roemer watched the Chief Prosecutor, who turned away.

"He's here now, sir," Schaller said.

Roemer wondered who the Chief Prosecutor called "sir" in such an obsequious manner; whoever Sharazad Razmarah was or why she had been killed, she had to be very important.

"No, sir, Major Whalpol will be here momentarily for the briefing. I just spoke with him by mobile telephone. He was on his way."

Was this a crime involving the military, then? Was Major Whalpol some army prosecutor here to establish a liaison with the Federal Bureau of Criminal Investigation, with Schaller as the conduit? Perhaps Sharazad Razmarah had worked on military secrets. Then what was Roemer needed for?

"Yes, sir, I promise I will let you know as soon as," Schaller said. "Yes, sir," he said again, and he hung up. For a moment he stood still; then he turned around.

He had just received another scare. Roemer could see it written on his face.

"Do you mind telling me what's going on, sir?" Roemer asked quietly.

"In due time," Schaller said. "Before this night is over, you'll be privy to all the grubby little secrets. This isn't fun and games, you know. There is real concern here from on high. On high, I'm telling you. Christ!"

Yes, Christ, Roemer thought. Christ in heaven. He remembered when Gretchen took him to the baroque Jesu Church—for months afterward he'd been concerned that he hadn't had any reverence while facing the altar with its hand-carved statue of Christ on the cross. In such a world as this, religion meant very little to him.

"You're going to have to understand from the outset that this is a very difficult, very delicate matter."

"Who was this girl?"

"An engineer, Roemer. A very good nuclear engineer, from what I'm told. But none of this should have happened. It's just awful. The repercussions could be . . ." He seemed to search for the word. ". . . could be simply shattering. One minute she is alive, and in the next she is a shattered lump of lifeless flesh and bone. It makes no sense."

"You knew her, sir?"

Schaller gaped at him. "You think that I'm some cold fish here, dealing merely in numbers. In case histories. No personalities. Well, Investigator, that couldn't be further from the truth."

Roemer had a hard time accepting the man's sincerity. Cynicism will kill us all. His father's line. It was painful, but he couldn't accept the statement from his father any more than he could from Schaller. What was missing? Was life passing him by? Or was it that he didn't care? Or cared too much? The two Germanies were reunited. Be careful what you wish for, the adage went. You might get it. Not many in Germany were happy.

"I'm sorry," he said.

"No need to be." The Chief District Prosecutor pushed away from his desk. At the sideboard he poured a drink, knocked it back, then set the glass down. "I know about you, Roemer. You're a good German. You, among all people, are like us. You understand."

A chill passed through Roemer. "Sir?"

Schaller spun around. "Don't make this more difficult than it already is. You cannot believe . . ."

Headlights flashed on the study windows and moved toward the front of the house.

"You selected me because I am discreet," Roemer suggested.

"Your past is bound with Germany's."

"Yes, sir."

Schaller nodded hesitantly. "You understand nationalism? Loyalty?"

"That, sir, as well as truth."

Schaller flinched. "Truth, tempered with wisdom. Truth, tempered with an understanding of the real world."

"Murder is its own truth," Roemer said. "If it is not war, then it is murder."

"Your definition of war and mine may be different."

"I think not. Especially not in the final analysis."

The heavy brass knocker sounded loud and hollow. For the moment Schaller seemed like a cornered animal. Clearly he wanted something settled here, and yet his tension indicated his uncertainty.

For the first time this morning, Roemer was of no mind to help. He looked down at his large, powerful hands. In *Gymnasium* he had played soccer. He'd been told that his speed, combined with his rugged frame, made him an awesome force on the playing field. There had been talk at the time of his going professional. He had opted instead for the Police Academy at Westphalia. Among her other complaints, his ex-wife always said he was too serious. "Have more fun in life," she told him.

Schaller hurried out of the room, his impasse unresolved, leaving Roemer to sink back into his own thoughts, made more morose by Schaller's implication that one's national loyalty took precedence over murder. And he wondered: If it came down to hurting his father, would he do it? Presumably no one knew that the old man was finally dying, and would soon be out of reach of the zealots. Did it matter any longer?

He heard them out in the stairhall, talking in low voices. Then the front door closed with a heavy thump, and moments later Schaller appeared with his other guest, a tall, very thin man, dressed in a dark, old-fashioned southern suit.

Roemer put his brandy snifter down and got to his feet as Schaller and the other man came in.

"Walther Roemer, Ludwig Whalpol," Schaller said breathlessly.

Roemer shook the man's limp, damp hand. "Herr Major," he said.

Whalpol's left eyebrow rose, but he smiled. "Let me tell you, Investigator, that I've heard a lot of good things about you. Believe me, really tremendous things. It's good to have you with us."

"He's already been out to the apartment," Schaller said.

Whalpol shook his head. "A terrible business. We never thought . . . never dreamed it could come to something like this. We're all shocked."

Whalpol was not military. He was a bureaucrat. It showed in his bearing, so obviously that Roemer made the only other connection possible.

"I wasn't aware that the BND had an interest in this case," he said. "It certainly would be much easier for you to liaise directly with Lieutenant Manning rather than have me in the middle."

Whalpol grinned. "I told you that this one was sharp as a tack, Ernst. I knew it the moment you suggested him. With this one we cannot pull the wool."

"Don't patronize me, Herr Major," Roemer said sharply. "It is late, I am tired, and there is a young woman lying dead and raped in Bad Godesberg. What exactly is my part in this investigation?"

Whalpol shot back, "You are to find Sarah's murderer. As simple as that."

"Sharazad Razmarah."

"We called her Sarah. It's the name she preferred."

"What about Manning and the Bonn Kriminalpolizei?"

"They will satisfy the news media," Whalpol said.

"I am to be given privileged information. I'm to find her murderer and turn him—or her—over to you. No trial. No justice?"

"That is correct, Investigator."

"Why?"

Whalpol nodded. "I like you. You are a direct man. It means that I can speak directly with you."

Roemer said nothing. He was angry. He didn't know the facts, and yet he was ready to judge.

"There is a lot at stake here, let me tell you."

Sarah was an engineer at KwU, one of the largest exporters of German high technology. "Money?"

"Perhaps more than eight billion marks. A prodigious sum. But beyond that, it is possible that Sarah was murdered by an Arab. By an Iraqi."

A connection was made in Roemer's head, and it sickened him. A light turned on, illuminating a vast cavern filled with tens upon tens of thousands of people all looking at him. He understood, or thought he did, why he had been called this night; why they were going to allow the Kriminalpolizei to publicly continue with the case while he would be given all the help he required. But like a hound that plays with a bone even though he's not sure he wants it, Roemer refused to make the final link in his conscious mind. He knew that if he did he might not be able to control himself. Instead he focused on the other aspect of this business that bothered him.

Sarah Razmarah had been an engineer for KwU. She was an American, but exactly why had she come to Germany? Whalpol had the answers.

"You are giving me carte blanche?"

"Within reason," Schaller replied.

Roemer nodded to Whalpol, but addressed his remarks to the Chief Prosecutor. "What about his crowd, why don't they simply take over? National security. It's within their province."

"For reasons that will become quite clear before we're finished this morning," Whalpol said.

"We simply want you to listen," Schaller said in an obvious attempt to mollify him.

"Then I have a choice?"

Schaller flinched.

"Why don't we just sit down here," the BND major said. "Why don't we just have a little chat. Let's see if we can put our heads together and figure out what is best for Germany."

10

THEY WERE an odd, dangerous trio, Roemer thought. Schaller, the political animal. Whalpol, the agent provocateur. And Roemer, the investigator.

"I'll just start off here," Schaller said. "And then Major Whalpol can bring up the details for you."

"It's important that you understand everything, Investigator. Absolutely everything."

"You don't have a charter to work within Germany, Herr Major," Roemer said.

"That is correct," Whalpol said.

"Has the American Consulate been informed?"

"No."

"Why was I selected for this case?"

"Because," Whalpol said crisply, "I believe you are a man with his head firmly planted on his shoulders, and his feet firmly planted on German soil."

"Is it because of my father's past that you think you can control me?" Roemer asked.

"I won't even dignify that remark with an answer." Whalpol leaned forward. "What the hell do you think we are here, Roemer? We're more eager to find Sarah's murderer than you are. But there is much more going on here than murder."

"We want you to find the fiend, you have to believe that. And it cannot go public," Schaller said. "The media must never find out what has gone on."

"Then let Lieutenant Manning find her murderer."

"Manning may find a suspect, but he will never have the proof to make an arrest. Sarah's body will be quietly flown back to America, where it will be buried."

"I will find her murderer."

"Yes, Investigator, you will bring this madman to justice. You will avenge poor Sarah's death, and you will do it with no publicity, no medals, no notice."

"Are your hands clean?" Roemer asked them.

"You weren't called up for this," Schaller said sharply.

Roemer held his silence while he listened to the crackling fire in the grate. He felt an odd awareness of his own mortality. His father was dying in a Swiss sanatorium, and he had viewed the body of a murdered young woman. A snatch of something from Dryden crossed his mind from his school days: *None would live past years again / Yet all hope pleasure in what yet remain / And from the dregs of life think to receive / What the first sprightly running could not give.*

"In 1982, early spring," Schaller said, "in the middle of the Iraq-Iran war, our government was approached by the Iraqi government. This was on high, above the ministerial level, you understand. One power to another, one state to another. I want you to grasp the historical perspective here, Investigator. Germany was in trouble. There was unemployment, unrest, strife. No one knew which way the wind was going to blow.

"Germany had nuclear technology for export. The government of Iraq wanted this technology, and we agreed to sell it, subject of course to limitations."

"The Kraftwerk Union is in the business of designing

and constructing nuclear-powered electrical generating systems," Whalpol said. "The State of Iraq has been in the market for just such a system ever since the Israelis destroyed their Osiraq reactor in 1981, and especially since the post–Gulf War dismantling of their nuclear energy program. Our government has agreed that the KwU would be granted the license for such a sale provided certain conditions were met, among them Iraq agreeing to an aggressive inspection program. An ongoing inspection program."

"Sarah was an engineer for KwU," Roemer said. "Was she working on the Iraqi project?"

"She was much more than that," Whalpol said.

"She worked for you as well?" Roemer asked, an angry edge in his voice.

Schaller stepped between them again. "Understand, Roemer, that such a project does not happen overnight. There are years of research and design, at not only the technical level but the political level as well. There have been more than one hundred Iraqi citizens living and working here for the past year. Scientists, technicians, engineers, as well as lawyers and economists and bureaucrats. The project is vast. You have no conception."

"It's been kept very quiet, I'll give you that much."

"The Americans, not to mention our own EC neighbors, would crucify us," Schaller cried.

Roemer smiled at Whalpol. "The Germans selling Saddam Hussein nuclear technology. The ramifications are endless."

"Don't kid yourself, Investigator. Hussein already has his arsenal of nuclear technology, which he's managed to keep hidden from the UN inspection teams. We're giving him nothing more than an electrical generating plant. But that's not what we've been talking about here."

"What then?"

"Murder."

The telephone rang and Schaller picked it up. "Yes?" he said. "Yes, sir, they're both here."

Whalpol wore a hawkish, feral look. The stage was set, Roemer thought. It would be the BND major's turn next.

11

SCHALLER FINISHED on the telephone. There was a slight sheen of sweat on his brow. He seemed distracted. "In heaven's name, I cannot understand what they expect of us," he mumbled.

"Anything from the other camp yet?" Whalpol asked quietly.

Schaller shook his head. "Not a thing. But they are expecting results already. Pull the rabbit out of the hat. I believe they are petrified up there in Berlin. Simply quaking in their boots. It's dangerous."

Roemer was surprised at the Prosecutor's irreverence. But then there had been a lot of surprises already this night.

Whalpol held out his glass, and Schaller poured him another brandy. Roemer declined. His stomach was acting up.

"I was called into this business in February, when the preliminary negotiations had just gotten under way," Whalpol said. "I was to head up a watchdog committee. Try to make sure no one went astray, and the like."

"Why not the BfV?" Roemer asked. "All this happened on German soil."

"Division of labor, as simple as that," the BND major replied. "We didn't want to be stumbling over each other's boots. We were involved in a very touchy situation. One in which there was the possibility of a major international incident, and one in which there was a distinct possibility that the Iraqis were playing us for fools." Whalpol smiled. "You should have been witness to the absolute chaos when the old boy himself showed up here."

"The 'old boy'?"

"Saddam Hussein, of course. Keeping it straight and secret was no easy chore. There are certain technical aspects that would indicate that the Iraqis were indeed planning to use our technology to create nuclear-weapons-grade material. It was our job to watch for such signals."

Of the two federal agencies involved with security matters, Whalpol's BND normally dealt with threats from outside the country, and the Bundesamt für Verfassungsschutz (the BfV) dealt with threats from within. It had been decided at high levels, Whalpol explained, that the BND would take charge of the overall project, leaving the local security matters to the District Prosecutor's office. One federal security agency and one federal police agency. Clean and simple.

"I was to take care of security and intelligence, and Ernst, through his good offices, was to pick up the odd bits: the traffic ticket, the stray drunk-and-disorderly. All of these people, remember, are here in secret and with full diplomatic immunity."

"The murder."

"When that occurred, I came to Ernst and asked for his recommendation: Who simply is the very best investigator in the land? He mentioned your name, and I agreed wholeheartedly."

"Were you watching her?"

"There was no need."

"How did you find out so quickly that she had been murdered?"

"I discovered her body."

"You were the anonymous telephone caller?" Roemer asked in wonder.

Whalpol nodded. "She was having car troubles, so I drove her home around ten. After I left her off I began to worry about her. Her mental state. So I went back. But I was too late."

"What was wrong with her mental state?"

"Please, Roemer," Schaller said. "There will be time for all of those questions."

"We're not trying to hide anything here, Investigator. Before we're done this morning, you will know everything. I promise."

Roemer held his silence. Was it axiomatic, he mused, that the higher one went the dirtier the jobs became?

"This all began on a need-to-know basis, and the list is still quite small. The Iraqis are here working out the technology and engineering for the construction of a twelve-hundred-megawatt neutron source reactor and isotope separator. Naturally we are extremely interested in just what their intentions are. Honorable or dishonorable."

"Can there be any doubt, Major?" Roemer asked.

"That's politics, my dear Investigator. Whereas I deal with security."

"So you sent spies after them to find out if they were developing weapons technology out of what we were selling them?"

"It's more complicated than that, actually, but in essence that was one of our charters for which the supervisory staff at KwU was admirably suited. But a lot of work toward that end can be done in such a fashion that it simply cannot be detected by normal workaday methods. From what I understand, certain mathematical techniques necessary for plutonium-refining methods can be worked out under apparently innocent guises. One scientist talks with another. Friendly competition, if you will. Fireside chats."

German guilt, Roemer thought. "But such an effort would be directed. It would have to be preplanned."

"Exactly." Whalpol beamed. "Now you have an understanding of the problem we have faced. Keeping a tight rein on the technology is one thing; keeping track of the personalities and their relationships with each other is another, certainly much more difficult business."

The Iraqis almost certainly knew that the Germans would set out spies, and would in turn bring in their own intelligence teams.

There were four scenarios. In the first, the Iraqis were not interested in weapons technology, and had sent no spies. In that case the BND would have nothing to do. Security would belong entirely to the Chief District Prosecutor's office.

In the second scenario, the Iraqis were not after the illegal technology, but had nevertheless sent watchdogs to make sure their people were treated properly. The BND's job would be only to identify Iraq's intelligence operatives and isolate them.

In the third, least likely scenario, the Iraqis were after bomb technology, but cold, with no Secret Service backup.

And in the final scenario, the one with the highest likelihood, the Iraqis had come to Germany to grab anything and everything they could, and had mounted a highly sophisticated intelligence operation, using not only the team members, but a few well-chosen Mukhabarat operatives.

Roemer felt another chill. In all of Whalpol's cold,

dispassionate account there was no regard for the people involved. For the human element. A young woman lay dead in Bad Godesberg. He couldn't get the vision of her ruined body out of his head.

"Weeks before the main body of the Iraqi team arrived, we received a list of their personnel, who would all travel on diplomatic passports. A few were rejected for various security reasons. Most, however, were allowed to come to Germany. We investigated every team member who would be working on the project."

Roemer had been caught up in his own thoughts as Whalpol talked. He suddenly sensed he had missed something important.

"Just a minute, Herr Major, please."

Whalpol fixed Roemer with a steady gaze. "Yes?"

"You knew ahead of time which of the Iraqi team were Secret Service . . . Mukhabarat?"

Whalpol smiled dryly. "It is more complicated than even that, Investigator. We have identified a number of the Mukhabarat officers, including their field chief, but others on the team . . . damned near every member of the team was and is a potential intelligence operative."

"But you did say you recruited Sarah Razmarah."

Whalpol nodded. He seemed smug, as if he were a teacher allowing his prize student to work something out that, while difficult, was obvious.

"You recruited her because you needed some skill that was unique to her. Not merely her engineering ability, but perhaps her looks? Perhaps her loneliness? These are Arabs."

Whalpol glanced over at Schaller. "Simply stated, Sarah was recruited because she was a good engineer, she was Arab, she was quite good-looking and she was an unknown. Someone from outside the German engineering establishment. A dark horse."

"Plus she was Iranian-born, she had no love for the Iraqis."

Whalpol shrugged.

"But you must have had something or someone very specific in mind for her."

"Ahmed Pavli," Whalpol said. "One of their chief engineers."

"A weak link?"

Whalpol nodded.

"Sarah was to get close to him—in his bed—and find out what he knew?"

"She was very good."

"This fellow, he is a man of medium height, husky, dark, perhaps even sad-looking?"

"Yes."

The woman in Two-B had told Lieutenant Manning that Sarah had two regular visitors. Pavli, husky and dark. And the other, tall and thin. Whalpol.

"Did Ahmed Pavli kill her?"

Whalpol took a long time to answer, and when he did he wasn't as sure of himself as he had been earlier. "It's a possibility which I've given serious consideration." He looked down at his hands. "But I don't think he did it. I wish it were that simple, you know."

"You and Pavli were her only regular visitors?"

"Presumably."

"You for your regular reports."

Whalpol nodded.

"And Pavli . . . because he was in love with her."

Whalpol's eyes glistened. "I didn't give a damn about this man. Only Sarah concerned me. I felt a certain responsibility. I researched her background. I recruited her."

Roemer waited.

"Pavli was in love with her, all right. But she fell in love with him. In the end she wanted to quit."

"You sonofabitch," Roemer said softly.

Whalpol went on as if he hadn't heard. "I gave her a list of people on the Iraqi team whom I wanted her to get close to. Pavli was to be her first . . . but not her only one."

"She hid your list behind the *Schrank* in her bedroom."

"It didn't take me five minutes to find it."

"Did you kill her, Herr Major?"

Schaller gasped.

Whalpol's head jerked up. "No! What in God's name do you take me for? What sort of person do you think I am?"

"I honestly don't know," Roemer said.

"I knew there was trouble," Whalpol continued woodenly. "I've known it for weeks. I tried to talk to her, make her see the futility of it, but she wouldn't listen."

"Did you try to pull her off the project?"

"I did not. It was too important. Besides, we were beginning to suspect that the Iraqis were feeding Pavli disinformation, knowing that it would get to Sarah."

"I didn't think they were that sophisticated."

"They learned a lot from the Gulf War."

"Did they have her spotted?"

"We think so. If Sarah had been pulled out, another pipeline would have been shut off. They would have placed someone else in the loop. An unknown. Someone we might not have been able to control."

It was a different world in which these sorts of people lived and operated, Roemer thought. A world devoid of . . . he searched for the word . . . devoid of compassion for the human results of their manipulations. This seemed to be his night for revelations.

"I met with her on a regular basis. Sometimes at her

apartment, at other times in town, or even at KwU. On the chance that she was being watched, we were very careful. Always."

"Then her watchdogs may have seen her killer," Roemer suggested.

"If that is the case, and if she was murdered by someone on the Iraqi team, you will be working against a double handicap."

Roemer could think of nothing to say.

"At first her product was quite good, you know. She seemed to take to her assignment. But then it began to fall off, and I suggested to her that she might have run her course with Pavli, that perhaps she should move on. But she kept putting me off. She kept hinting at bigger and better things."

"You were wild for what she was bringing you . . . big or little."

"When I realized that she had fallen in love, I tried to discourage her. But I didn't want to upset something. By then she herself was becoming unstable."

"What'd you expect?"

Whalpol made no answer.

Roemer got to his feet.

"Don't go, Investigator," Whalpol said. "We do need your help. Honestly."

"To clean up the mess you've created?"

"No. In actuality very little has changed. The Iraqis will remain on the project. We are talking about eight billion marks here. They will continue to spy on us, and we will continue to spy on them. We want the murder resolved."

"But delicately," Roemer said.

Whalpol nodded. "Is it so difficult for you to understand?"

"On the contrary, Major, I believe that I understand more than you want me to understand."

"Then you'll help?"

Roemer looked at him. "Did you have something on her, or did she volunteer?"

"We had nothing on her," Whalpol said.

"What about me? You have something on me?"

"Heavens no," Schaller blurted.

"Yes, in a manner of speaking, we do," Whalpol said softly.

Roemer turned on him. "A refreshing dose of honesty from the BND. What is your lever on me, Herr Major? My father?"

"If I said yes to that, Investigator, would it satisfy you that indeed I am a bastard?"

Roemer held himself back from sarcasm. He felt off balance. He was being manipulated. But Whalpol was very good, and in the final analysis, Roemer wondered if he cared.

"You were selected because you are a good cop, but even more than that, because you are honest, conscientious, and no matter who might try to sway your investigation, you would not be moved. And in the end you will find Sarah's murderer . . . people, policies or governments be damned. And that, my dear Investigator, is the lever I hold. Your own honesty is the fulcrum."

The bastard was right, and Roemer found himself nodding.

"Now." Whalpol picked up his briefcase, set it on Schaller's desk, opened it and withdrew two fat file folders. "Are you on the case?"

Roemer returned his gaze. "I will find her murderer."

"You will report directly to Ernst and . . ."

"I will report to no one, Herr Major. If I need

assistance I will call the Prosecutor or you. Other than that you will not hear from me until I have the killer."

Whalpol considered that for a moment, then nodded. "Fair enough, but you understand that my work will continue. Don't interfere."

"I'm only interested in Sarah's murderer."

"You will need these." Whalpol handed the files to Roemer. "One is a dossier on Sarah, the other a list of everyone on the Iraqi team, including those we've identified as Mukhabarat."

"Who is their field chief?"

"Her name is Leila Kahled el Zayn."

Schaller smiled. "You will do a good job for us."

Roemer saw that the man's hands were shaking.

12

THE HOUSE was dark, Teutonic in its foreboding heaviness, with its thick wooden beams and tall, smoking chimneys. It looked down on the Rhine and the city of Bonn, just now coming alive with the chill, desultory dawn.

In a third-story bedroom, Leila Kahled woke with a start, her heart thumping and perspiration on her forehead. She glanced at the bedside clock, then lay back and closed her eyes.

It was just seven. The same dream again. *Insha' Allah,* how she hated it here. During the daytime she was usually all right, but at night, the memories came flooding back and she relived the horror that had forever changed her.

Too much responsibility for one so young, her Uncle Bashir might say. But at thirty-two she had seen and done more than most men twice her age.

She was worried about the girl, Sharazad Razmarah, and Ahmed Pavli. Their relationship was disintegrating. But the BND would never let the poor woman go. Not until the project was finished.

She had to laugh. Colonel Mikadi was worried about the U.S. or Germany's EC trading partners finding out about the deal. He was rabid about security. In reality the

Germans were more interested in security than the Iraqis were. The Germans would make sure it stayed within the country.

In her last report to Baghdad, she'd recommended that Pavli be pulled off the project. Despite the German cooperation, he was becoming a danger. Her request had been denied. Pavli was too important now that the BND was targeting him. What the Mukhabarat wanted the Germans to learn, they would funnel through him.

But Allah in heaven, there was more going on than they had told her. Something else was happening here. Something sinister that most of the time she did not want to think about.

"Find out what they are doing and what they are thinking, but do not antagonize anyone. This is not Lebanon," Bashir Kahair, the deputy director of the Mukhabarat, had told her. Uncle Bashir, though not really an uncle, was an old family friend.

No, she thought, her eyes closed in the darkness, it was not Beirut. It was Germany. But again the dream came to her, the same awful memories.

She'd been just eighteen and full of idealism, working for Yasir Arafat's Palestine Liberation Organization. Everybody worked for the PLO in those days. You didn't even have to be Arab.

One night a Phalangist patrol caught her in the hills above Beirut, where she had gone to spy on one of their camps in which it was suspected that some Shiites had been tortured and killed. One by one, all fifteen of the young men raped her.

That night she managed to escape, and she found and killed them all by slitting their throats as they slept. It was the Arab punishment. The one certain to make them and their brothers understand.

But the memories refused to fade. At times the brutal

rape haunted her. At other times, like this morning, it was the killing of the fifteen young men. It had taken her most of the night. As they strangled on their own blood, the gaping wounds in their throats made horrible gurgling sounds. She would never forget.

The experience had left its indelible mark on her soul.

"You are too hard on yourself, my little one," her father, General Josef Assad Sherif, had told her some years ago. "You need to care for a man, perhaps a child."

By then they had left Beirut and enlisted in Saddam Hussein's growing movement. The PLO would never win the struggle against the Zionists, let alone the West. But with a strong Iraq, the region might come back to the law of Allah. The reasonable law of Allah, not the Ayatollah Khomeini's vision of the Koran.

"I can't care for myself, let alone anyone else," she had cried. "There's nothing left inside of me, can't you see that?"

When Leila was ten, her mother had been killed in an Israeli air raid on the camp where they'd lived outside Beirut. Her father, who was often absent for long periods, took over the raising of his only child with the help of his good friend Bashir Kahair and the local camp women. She loved her father, but she realized she'd never really known him. He was, in some ways, even more distant a relative than her Uncle Bashir.

She opened her eyes. She pushed back the covers and got out of bed. She slept nude. Her skin shimmered in the early-morning light as she padded across the large bedroom to the windows, where she pulled back the curtains and looked out. She was a tall woman with a slight, almost boyish body and long legs. Her complexion was olive, her hair long and jet-black and her eyes wide and intense.

It had rained heavily in the night and the city looked

fresh and clean. Below, in the cobblestone courtyard, her father's chief of staff, Lieutenant Colonel Mahmud Habash, was stowing a suitcase in the trunk of a gray Mercedes. He closed the lid and looked up.

Leila did not move. For a long time they stared at each other. Of the dozen men here on her father's staff, she liked Habash least. His eyes were cold and dispassionate, yet whenever he looked at her she got the impression that he was imagining her nude body—but clinically, without lust.

The old Beirut, before the fighting, had never seemed so far away from her as it did at this moment. She shivered but remained where she stood. She would not back down, despite how silly and dangerous for an Arab woman this was. Let the bastard have an eyeful! He answered to her father.

The happiest days of her life had been when she was a little girl, her mother was alive, and her father would take them to a fancy restaurant downtown, overlooking the water, or perhaps they would stroll along Hamara Street looking in the windows of all the fancy shops. She felt nostalgia for something she'd never had for long: a sense of belonging with another person, shared emotions.

Habash finally lowered his eyes and disappeared into the house.

For another minute Leila stood by the window, her eyes drifting to the city and the river that wound its way through the plains and hills. She could not imagine Germany as a place of lightness and contentment, even though this country had been their ally from time to time. Germany for some reason was to her a dark, brooding place.

"The Germans have their hands full, Uncle Bashir, they're not the enemy," she'd argued the afternoon she'd been handed this assignment.

"You're not going there to make trouble, Leila. You're going to make sure there is none. Nothing more."

"And if there is—what then?"

"You report the problem and we will take care of it. You're to be nothing more than an observer for us. A little desert mouse in the corner."

"The BND will know who and what I am."

"Almost certainly. They will have their people watching us. Their efforts will be sophisticated, no doubt. It is to be expected."

Uncle Bashir had come to her apartment near the Tariz Air Base, and they went for a walk in the pleasant evening. He'd come not only to tell her about her assignment in Bonn, but to talk to her about her father, who'd been working too hard. A lot of people on the Council were worried about him, at his age.

"He won't listen to me," Uncle Bashir said. "Calls me an old woman."

Leila laughed. She could hear her father saying it. "But he's not an old man, Uncle Bashir. He's just fifty-four."

"The president has taken a personal interest in his well-being."

"I'll go over and slow him down, if that's what you really want. But you know how he's always been."

"This is so important to us, Leila. Your father may have discussed it with you, considering your . . . position."

She shivered. Since she had separated from her husband, she'd taken care of her father's household. She had become the son he'd never had, and assumed the responsibility of mistress of the household for a man who was rarely home.

"You know how delicate this is," Uncle Bashir went on. He was a tiny, birdlike man with a mind as sharp as anyone's in Iraq.

"The Germans are selling us nuclear technology and

no one must know about it. I'm not completely lost in the forest," she said.

"If it gets out, there will be a lot of trouble for us," Uncle Bashir said. "In Washington, in Tel Aviv. Everywhere."

"I understand."

"Your father is a presence."

"I'll slow him down, Uncle Bashir."

"There's been criticism from the Council because your father was not born in Iraq, yet he's chief negotiator."

"Have there been questions about his loyalty?"

"Some," Uncle Bashir admitted. "But President Hussein is behind him for the moment. So long as no mistakes are made."

"I see what you mean," Leila said, and she was sick at heart. But these were horribly strange times for all of them since the war. She wasn't even sure that they were doing the correct thing.

They started back up the hill toward Operations. Uncle Bashir looked at her shrewdly, and smiled. "You need a vacation from the foreign desk in any event, I suspect."

Leila had to laugh. "It shows?"

"It shows."

Six months, she thought. All during that time her father had shuttled back and forth between Bonn and Baghdad, and sometimes he disappeared for days at a time. Just like the old days. Now, in Germany, she was left behind again to maintain the household they had borrowed from one of the Krupp steel magnates across the river. And always there was the secrecy.

She turned away from the window and went to her desk, where she switched on a small lamp. Papers and files were strewn everywhere. Last night she'd gone to bed early, ignoring the report to Baghdad. First she wanted to speak to Pavli before she made another, stronger recommendation that he be removed from the team.

The telephone on her desk buzzed and she picked it up. Her father was on the house line.

"Good morning, little one, you're up?"

She smiled. "Just. Are you leaving again?"

"I'll be back tomorrow afternoon. You'll have to cancel our dinner engagement tonight . . . unless you want to host it alone."

"It's no one important," Leila said. "I'll reschedule for next week. But just a moment, I'm coming down."

"Don't bother," her father said. "I have an airplane to catch. I'll see you when I return."

"I'll be just a moment . . ."

"No." Her father cut her off harshly. "I'm leaving immediately. But listen to me, Leila. I don't want you parading around at the windows . . . naked."

Leila stifled a laugh. Habash had told on her. What a bastard. Her father was, for all his world travels, still an Arab.

"Yes, my father," she said at length. "*'As-fa,*" I'm sorry.

"You can never tell about the bastards in this country," he said.

"Have a good trip, Father," she said. "With Allah."

He hung up. A moment later Leila put down her phone and stared at it. Her father sounded exhausted. He was working too hard, just as Uncle Bashir had warned her. She would speak to him about it when he got back. Not that it would do any good. She felt further apart from him than ever before.

She went back to the window, now parting the curtains only a crack, and looked down. Her father and Habash came out of the house. They seemed to be arguing. She could see that her father was angry.

They got in the car, and a minute later they were down

the long driveway and out the gate, hidden from view by the trees that lined the avenue down to the Ronner-strasse.

She felt a sudden, overwhelming sorrow for her father, and for herself. Neither of them had anyone except the other. He'd lost his mate, and she had never really had one.

Turning away from the window, she could almost envy Ahmed Pavli and Sharazad Razmarah. At least they thought they had love.

13

IN THE palatial bathroom, Leila took a quick, hot shower, then dressed as a Westerner in a white blouse, short, dark wool skirt and medium heels. She pinned up her long hair, put on a little makeup, and at her desk stuffed a few things into her thin, soft leather briefcase.

Before she went downstairs she opened her purse, took out her Beretta .380 automatic and cycled a couple of rounds out of the breech, making sure the action was smooth. Then she ejected the clip, reloaded it and snapped it back into the butt, her motions quick and efficient.

Her passport and identification proved she was an Iraqi federal police officer. She had a permit to carry a concealed weapon, and was known by Interpol throughout Europe. Uncle Bashir thought it best to temper a big lie with a smaller one. That way the Germans could at least pretend it was all right for her to be in Bonn, armed.

Downstairs she was met in the hall by one of the domestic staff provided by the owners of the house. There were a dozen on her father's military staff, but they kept to themselves in a far wing at the back.

"Good morning, Madam Kahled," the maid said.

"Good morning," Leila replied. "Just coffee, and the

newspapers." She set her briefcase on the hall table. "And have Dieter bring my car around."

"Very good, madam," the older woman said, her English heavily accented. (Leila's father, though fluent, refused to speak German most of the time. As a consequence they all spoke English with the house staff, Arabic with one another.)

The breakfast room overlooked what in the summer was a pleasant garden of flowers, fountains and statuary. This morning, even in the uncertain autumn light, it looked lovely, neat, fresh.

Her coffee and the newspapers came . . . Bonn, Frankfurt, Berlin, the Paris edition of the *Herald Tribune,* and Baghdad.

At first Leila had tried to warm up to the house staff, but she had gotten nowhere. The chief butler had asked that their relationship be kept on a strictly professional level.

Finally her father had spoken to her about it. "They don't like us," he said with a smirk.

The mood only served to heighten her sense of isolation here, more so this morning because of her disturbing dream last night.

She lit a cigarette and sipped the excellent strong coffee as she began to look over the newspapers; first the German, then the international and finally Baghdad, so that she could keep her perspective in place.

The telephone in the hall rang and was answered.

The maid came rushing down the broad corridor a few seconds later.

"Oh madam . . . *Fräulein Kahled, Gott in Himmel!"*

Leila jumped up. "What is it?" She thought immediately of her father. Had he been hurt?

"Das Telefon. For you!"

Leila pushed the woman aside, raced to the telephone. "Yes, hello? This is Leila Kahled."

At first there was nothing, but then there was a muffled cry of anguish.

"Who is this? What has happened?"

"Oh, God . . . oh, God . . . she's dead," a man cried in Arabic. "Do you understand?"

"Pavli? Is that you? Ahmed?"

"She's dead! Can't you hear me? They killed her, they murdered her! She's dead. I saw her body."

"Ahmed, listen to me!" Leila shouted at him in Arabic. "You must calm down now. Perhaps your life depends on it."

"My life . . ." He suddenly laughed maniacally. "What does my life mean now?"

He sounded drunk. "Listen to me, Ahmed, you must pull yourself together so that I can help you."

Pavli sobbed.

"Who is dead? You say you saw the body."

"It is Sarah . . . The Germans killed their . . . whore. She is dead. Dead! You were right . . ."

"Where?" Leila forced a calmness into her voice. "Where did you see her?"

"At her apartment," Pavli cried.

"Ahmed, where are you now?"

"At home!"

"Did you just come from Sarah?"

"It was hours ago. Yesterday. Last night."

"Where have you been since then?"

There was a terrible silence on the line.

"Ahmed?"

"It doesn't matter," Pavli said, abruptly calm.

"Please stay where you are, and I shall be there immediately," Leila said. "Perhaps Sarah is not dead.

Perhaps she is merely injured. We'll call a doctor. Please. *Min fad lak.*"

"She's dead, all right," Pavli said, still calm. "I saw her. There was a lot of blood. Cold, stone cold, don't you see? They were jealous of us. You all were." He laughed, the sound slicing through Leila. "I'm going with her. We'll be . . ."

"No! Ahmed, listen to me. Do nothing. I will be right there. We'll work this out together. Don't you want to see her murderer brought to justice?"

Pavli did not reply.

"Ahmed?" Leila could hear that the line was still open—a clock chimed the hour.

"Ahmed?" she shouted.

She slammed down the phone, grabbed her purse, coat and briefcase, and rushed out the door. The yardman had not yet brought her car around from the garage in the back, so she ran around the house, slipping on the wet cobbles, her coat flapping, her breath ragged.

Dieter was just coming from the staff's quarters when she reached the garage and yanked open the door.

"Madam!" he called in alarm.

But Leila was inside, sliding behind the wheel of her dark green Mercedes 400E; she started the engine and shot out past the startled yardman and down the long drive to the access road.

Her mind was racing. Sarah's death was not a Mukhabarat action, she knew that for a fact. Nor did she think the BND would have any reason to eliminate her. In fact, had she learned about Sarah's death from anyone else, she would have bet Pavli had killed her.

14

ROEMER HATED surveillance, that part of police work that entailed endless waiting. What he hated more, however, was driving very fast under poor conditions.

The dark green Mercedes fishtailed around the sweeping interchange from Siegburg onto the broad Königswinterstrasse, which paralleled the river through Beuel, and sped up, weaving through the early-morning traffic.

Roemer was tired from being up all night, and the tires on his aging BMW were not great, but he managed to keep up with the woman.

Sarah Razmarah had worked for Whalpol, with Ahmed Pavli as her primary target. The Iraqi intelligence service surely had that information. Roemer had decided to watch what would happen once the Mukhabarat team leader found out about the murder.

He'd had a near false start when the other Mercedes, gray, had emerged earlier from the Klauber estate, until he recognized in it General Sherif and another man.

Minutes later, the green 400E, Leila Kahled driving, had screamed down the road like a bat out of hell. Bound for Bad Godesberg, he was betting.

Roemer passed a large tandem truck, the sudden airstream pushing his car over on the wet pavement, and he fought the wheel to keep control, nearly missing the Konrad Adenauer Bridge turn.

The green Mercedes ducked around a trolley bus across from the Federal Parliament Building on the Gorresstrasse, then shot toward the Friedrich-Ebert Allee, another of Bonn's main thoroughfares.

As he drove, Roemer's mind worked. Who killed Sarah Razmarah? It was a toss-up between the Iraqis and the Germans. The Mukhabarat because she knew too much? Because she had been too effective against Ahmed Pavli? In which case it admitted a gigantic Iraqi conspiracy. And if so, how the hell would he handle it? Eight billion marks had a logic all its own.

On the other hand, the murderer could be a BND hit man sent to neutralize the woman because the Mukhabarat had been using her as a conduit for disinformation.

In either case, Roemer would be up against stiff odds. As a cop he was good. As an unraveler of international plots, he was way out of his league.

Nevertheless, it was murder. A crime he understood. And this one especially bothered him. This morning he had run through the dossiers Whalpol had handed him.

Sarah Razmarah was a poor Iranian girl who had desperately wanted to better herself. Perhaps she had seen in her father's fate her own. So she had emigrated to the United States to improve her lot.

On the other side was Leila Kahled, the Mukhabarat bitch, here to manipulate her charges; she with her smooth good looks, her fluency in a dozen languages. Christ, her type made him sick.

The Allee became the Kölnerstrasse past the Godesberg Fortress on the hill, then ran up beyond the ornate town hall and the Redoute on the Kurfürstenstrasse.

Roemer expected the Mercedes to turn onto the Schillerstrasse, off which Sarah's apartment was located. Instead it continued several more blocks, finally turning into a narrow alley, where it pulled up in front of a tobacconist's.

Roemer recognized the address from the dossiers. It was Ahmed Pavli's apartment.

He parked a block beyond the alley and trotted back to the corner.

The Mercedes was half on the sidewalk, the engine still running.

Pavli's apartment was on the second floor above the shop, which was closed at this hour. A side door led up to the short corridor. Even before he started up the stairs, Roemer heard the crying and shouting above.

He pulled out his gun and took the stairs two at a time.

The apartment door was open. Leila Kahled stood just within, her back to the corridor, her right hand outstretched as if in supplication. She was saying something in Arabic which Roemer couldn't understand. He did understand, however, the urgency of what she was saying.

Roemer moved away from the railing for a better line of sight into the apartment. He froze.

Ahmed Pavli, holding a large pistol to his head, was backed up against the far wall of the living room. His eyes were wild, and he was babbling.

Holding his own weapon down at his side, Roemer stepped into full view just behind Leila.

Pavli suddenly aimed the pistol at the doorway.

"Murderer!" Pavli screamed in German.

"Don't do it, Ahmed!" Roemer shoved Leila aside.

Pavli's gun went off, the shot blowing a big hole in the plaster wall inches from the door frame.

"Police!" Roemer shouted, dropping to his knees.

Pavli fired a second shot, this one catching Roemer in the left arm above the elbow. Two more shots went wild.

Roemer fired twice to the left of Pavli, hoping it would freeze him.

Pavli shouted, "Sarah!", then turned the pistol to his forehead and pulled the trigger.

His head slammed back against the wall, the rear of his skull erupting in a mass of blood, bone and brains. The pistol fell to the floor, and Pavli fell sideways onto a lamp table, his legs twitching.

Holstering his weapon, Roemer rushed across the room and pulled Pavli down onto his back.

"Call an ambulance," he shouted over his shoulder, as he started CPR.

Pavli's eyes were open, his eyelids fluttering. He was still breathing in huge, racking gasps. Sweat poured from his forehead; his complexion was deathly pale.

"Come on, kid, hang on!" Roemer shouted.

Pavli's body heaved and went slack.

Roemer put his ear to his chest. Nothing. The heart was still.

For a minute, Roemer pumped Pavli's chest, his hands locked, elbows stiff, blood from his own wound soaking his coat sleeve. But he knew it was no use. Too much damage had been done. Mucus clogged the boy's mouth and slid down over his blue lips.

"Verdammt," Roemer said softly, sitting back on his haunches. He hung his head. "Goddammit to hell."

"Who are you? What are you doing here?" Leila demanded in German.

Roemer turned tiredly to look up at her. She was pale, but controlled, no hysterics in her eyes.

"He must have telephoned you, Fräulein Kahled. What did he tell you?"

"Who are you?" Her right hand was in her purse at her side.

A gun, Roemer figured. "My name is Walther Roemer. I am assigned to the Federal Bureau of Criminal Investigation."

"This is a political matter over which you have no jurisdiction. Ahmed Pavli is an Iraqi national. He has diplomatic immunity."

Roemer shook his head. "No, Fräulein Kahled, he does not. He is dead. And so is an American girl, Sarah Razmarah."

"Insha' Allah," Leila said, lowering her head. She looked up a moment later. "Why have you come here?"

"This man was a suspect in her murder, diplomatic immunity or not."

"Ridiculous," Leila said.

"Perhaps."

"In any event, I must ask you to leave at once, until I can contact my embassy."

Roemer got slowly to his feet. There was a telephone on a narrow table beside the couch. He nodded toward it. "Please, Fräulein Kahled, telephone your people."

A siren sounded in the distance.

"You must leave now," Leila insisted. "At once."

Roemer's shoulder throbbed, as if it had been dislocated. He wasn't losing much blood, however. He suspected it was merely a flesh wound. "I'm afraid I cannot comply with your request."

Leila pulled an automatic from her purse and pointed it at him. "If I have to shoot you, Investigator, I will."

Roemer ignored her. God, why did he always have such rotten luck with women?

"Investigator!"

The sirens were coming closer. Someone must have reported the gunfire. "Leave, you bastard!"

Roemer went into the bedroom. Leila was right behind him. She grabbed his shoulder to pull him back. He spun and with his right hand yanked the gun from her grasp, then shouldered her away. "Don't ever point a gun at me, Fräulein Kahled." He thumbed the Beretta's safety on and handed the weapon back to her.

She looked into his eyes for a long moment, then took the gun, turned and went out to the telephone.

The sirens were just outside now, a lot of them. Roemer went into the bedroom. Even before the first footsteps clattered up the narrow stairs he found what appeared to be Pavli's diary, a small, leather-bound volume on the floor beside the bed. Beside it was a German schnapps bottle, nearly empty, and a glass sticky with the dregs of the liquor. Roemer pocketed the diary.

Someone out in the corridor shouted: "Police! This is the police!"

"In here," Roemer called back. "BKA."

A uniformed officer in a heavy green leather jacket, his service revolver drawn, appeared at the bedroom door. Others were crowding into the small apartment, while still more pounded up the stairs.

Roemer held his badge up to the cop. "Roemer, BKA. For the moment I am in charge."

"Yes, sir." The uniformed cop nodded. "Sir, you've been hurt."

"I'll get to the hospital on my own, Patrolman. As soon as a KP officer shows up, have him report to me. In the meantime, I want you people out of here and all entrances secured."

The cop was confused. "The man out there is dead . . . Shall we call for the coroner?"

"This is a simple suicide, for the moment. The victim is not German, and what's more, he has diplomatic immunity."

"The woman . . . she was armed."

"She too is not German. Return her weapon to her, with my apologies. She will be allowed to remain in the apartment."

"Very good, sir." The cop turned on his heel and began issuing orders.

Roemer quickly searched the bedroom, beneath the mattress, in the drawers of a large chest and in the *Schrank.* But there was nothing else of interest.

The apartment had quieted. Leila stood in the doorway, looking very angry.

"Have you called your embassy?" he asked.

"They are on their way." She held out her hand. "I want it."

"What?"

"Whatever it is you found in here. Letters. Notes. Files. They are of no concern to you, and in fact may contain information classified by the State of Iraq."

"A pretty speech," Roemer said.

"I demand . . ."

"You're in no position to demand anything, Fräulein Kahled. You are on German soil now."

"There will be a lot of trouble over this, Investigator."

"The name is Walther Roemer."

"How do you know my name?"

"You would be surprised at the extent of my knowledge."

Someone called his name from the corridor. Roemer walked out to the living room as Lieutenant Manning, a cigarette dangling from his mouth, his long tan overcoat open, charged through the open door.

"Guten Morgen, Lieutenant," Roemer said wearily.

Manning took in Pavli's body, Leila just behind Roemer and the wound in Roemer's arm.

"He's dead," Roemer said. "Self-inflicted gunshot wound."

"Has an ambulance been called for you?"

"I'll manage on my own," Roemer said. "The boy is Ahmed Pavli, an Iraqi citizen, with, I'm told, diplomatic immunity. However, he was, and this scene is, material to our investigation into the Sharazad Razmarah murder."

Manning looked at Pavli's body. "Did he kill Sarah?"

"I don't know."

Manning looked up. "The woman?"

"Leila Kahled. An Iraqi who also enjoys diplomatic immunity."

"You're a cop?" Manning asked her.

"Yes, Lieutenant," Leila said. "And I wish this apartment to be secured immediately."

Manning's eyebrows rose. "Has your embassy been contacted, Fräulein?"

"It has."

Manning looked at Roemer, then back to Leila. "Very well, we shall wait until the proper diplomatic authorities arrive. But I will have to ask you to remain on the scene. There will be questions."

"Naturally," Leila said gruffly.

"And now, Investigator Roemer, if you would care to step outside, I would like to have a word with you," Manning said.

"Sure." But before Roemer left he hunched down over Pavli's body.

"Do not touch him . . ." Leila started, but then she realized Roemer was just closing the man's eyes.

Roemer followed Manning outside. A crowd had already formed, and the uniformed police were busy dispersing it.

"Are you all right?" Manning asked. They stopped at his unmarked car.

"Just a superficial wound. Hurts like hell, though."

"What happened up there?"

"The man shot himself."

"What brought you here?"

"He was Sarah Razmarah's boyfriend. I came to talk to him."

Manning nodded. "And the woman?"

"I think Pavli telephoned her this morning."

"Iraqi Federal Police," Manning said. "You two should have a lot in common."

15

BONN WAS actually three cities in one. Premier among them was the former parliamentary metropolis of 300,000 people, with its Bundeshaus and other government buildings, as well as the secondary residence of the Federal President at Villa Hammerschmidt in the Adenauerallee. Then there was the ornate town with two thousand years of history: Ancient buildings competed with the modern; castles overlooked the Autobahns; the spires of baroque churches stabbed the same gray sky as radio and television towers. Finally, at the center was the middle city of libraries and gas stations, of supermarkets and the Sears store, of police barracks and the hospital.

It was not quite noon when Roemer was discharged from the hospital's emergency ward, three stitches just above his left elbow, his arm in a sling. His shoulder had been thrown out of joint by the force of the .357 magnum slug.

"You are lucky, Investigator, let me tell you," the doctor had said cheerfully as he stitched. "If it hadn't been a steel-jacketed slug, you might not have an arm."

"I feel very lucky by comparison with the one who did this to me," Roemer grumbled.

He was in a foul mood. He was tired and hungry, and

angry that he had been dragged into this business. Pavli's diary was still in his jacket pocket. It would be so easy to blame the murder on him and leave it at that. That would make Whalpol happy.

Manning would accept the verdict. The Iraqis might put up a little fuss. But Pavli had been using the girl as much as she had been using him. Soon the furor would die down, and even Gretchen would be pleased.

But he couldn't, could he? Whalpol had counted on it, just as Gretchen knew it was inevitable: his stupid sense of dedication. Or was it simply that he didn't like loose ends?

His jacket thrown over his shoulders like a cape, Roemer walked down the hospital driveway to his car on the street. There was a parking ticket on the windshield.

He grabbed the ticket, crumpled it up and threw it in the street. "Goddamnit to hell," he roared.

Two nurses who were passing by looked up, startled, and quickly crossed the street. He was being a fool. He had a choice here. He could walk away from this business. Lay it in Schaller's lap: "Here, Chief Prosecutor, I am not the man for this."

Whalpol had maneuvered him so easily. Of course they knew about his father. And of course they'd make use of the fact. It was a wonder Simon Wiesenthal's people weren't already camped on his doorstep. The sins of the fathers would be visited upon their sons. Wasn't that the line?

Perhaps this weekend he would drive down to see his father. There weren't many hours left.

Roemer went back to the hospital and took the elevator down to the basement, to the city morgue. He rang the bell at the security door.

The door was opened by the forensics man who had

been on Manning's team at Sarah Razmarah's apartment. Roemer knew of him. His name was Stanos Lotz and he was one of the best in Germany.

"Investigator Roemer, I wondered when you'd be showing up," Lotz said. His lab coat was dirty, and his thick glasses, which had slipped to the end of his nose, were flecked with blood.

"Is Dr. Sternig here?"

"At lunch, I suspect."

"Has he finished his report?"

"On the Razmarah girl?" Lotz smiled briefly. Then he shook his head. "You are too optimistic. Perhaps tomorrow, but then the weekend will be upon us. Monday would be more likely."

"I need it now," Roemer said. He felt dangerous.

"I thought as much. Come in."

Roemer followed Lotz down the corridor, through glass doors into a long, narrow operating theater. There didn't seem to be anyone else around. Two steel tables were illuminated by overhead lights. Next to them stood several instrument tables and equipment stands on rolling carts. At the center of the room were laboratory benches. One wall contained two dozen body boxes. The room was cold and smelled of antiseptic. White-tiled and stainless-steel sterile. Here, death was a business.

On one of the tables lay a body covered by a white sheet.

Lotz crossed to the table and took the edge of the sheet. "Was there something specific you were interested in, Investigator? Some fact, some bit of pathology?"

"I want to know who killed her."

"A strong, right-handed male military officer." Lotz flipped back the sheet with a flourish. "Sharazad Razmarah."

Roemer's stomach did a turn, and the room got warm. He used to confide in his wife, and later in Gretchen, about his squeamishness. He had learned to keep his mouth shut.

"Only a strong man could have broken her jaw with one blow," Lotz said.

The top of Sarah's skull had been sawn off, the cap laid back in place. An incision had been made from her sternum, between her breasts, all the way down to just above her pubis, and then had been sewn back up with long, looping stitches. She looked terribly mangled.

"I understand that, Lotz," Roemer said.

The little forensics man softened his expression. He replaced the sheet. "Sorry. I tend to get caught up in what I'm doing. They're like big anatomical models. No basis in reality—in life, if you know what I mean."

"A strong man or a dedicated, well-trained woman?"

"Not unless she was a woman with very big fists. The bruises are too large."

"Right-handed?"

"The angle of the fractures."

Roemer couldn't keep his eyes from the form beneath the sheet. She looked worse here than she had at the murder scene. Twice violated, he thought. Once out of passion. The second time out of curiosity.

"Why are you involved in this case, Roemer? Why the BKA?"

Roemer looked at the man, who, after all, was a personal friend of Manning. "I've got a job to do, just like you."

Lotz smiled wryly. He glanced down at the form on the table. "Right-handed, strong male. Now you want to know why I'm making the military connection." He reached beneath the sheet and uncovered Sarah's right hand and forearm. Her fingers were open, and most of the flesh in her palm was missing, exposing the muscles and tendons. "She grabbed something from her killer. A bit of jewelry. Held it tightly. So tightly, in fact, that the object was pressed into her flesh. She died like that."

Lotz covered her arm. "When we die, we stop sweating, of course. Everything, at least most things, are held then in stasis. Makes it easy for us. Silver nitrite, a little black-light photography, and we have lifted an impression. The American FBI taught us that little trick."

Lotz stepped around the table and went to one of the lab benches, where he rummaged through a stack of file folders. He pulled out a couple of strange photographs.

"The woman's right palm," Lotz said, holding up one of the shots. Three sets of points showed up, side by side, some of them connected with faint, blurry lines.

He laid the photo on the table, pulled a pen from his pocket and quickly traced lines between each of the points, making three small stars in a row.

Roemer nodded.

"A cuff link, probably," Lotz said. "Gold. We found the flecks of it embedded in her skin, which means it was probably twenty-four-karat. Expensive."

"Could these have been octagons?"

"No. Some of the connecting ridges were there as well. Her killer was a three-star general."

"What else have you got for me?"

Lotz replaced the photo in the file folder, then took off his glasses and carefully rubbed his watering eyes. "One last thing, Investigator. One last nasty, ugly, unfortunate thing. The girl was in her first trimester."

"What?"

"Sharazad Razmarah was pregnant. Seven, perhaps eight weeks."

"Shit."

"On a general's pay he could have done better by her, don't you think?"

But Roemer wasn't listening.

Sarah's killer may have been an officer, but not necessarily a general. Three small stars in a row was the national symbol of Iraq.

16

FROM HIS car, Roemer telephoned Manning at his office and asked if Sarah Razmarah's automobile had been located. Manning had just got back from Pavli's apartment, and, sounding angry, he asked Roemer to come over.

Manning's office was in a new wing of the Bonn Kriminalpolizei Building not far from the hospital. The Interpol office was just upstairs, and to the east was the City Prosecutor's office.

They were waiting for him when he arrived. A lot of the cops nodded in respect. Manning had a reputation, but so did Roemer.

His arm and shoulder were stiff and sore. He wanted nothing more than to go home, take a long, hot bath and go to bed for a few hours. The painkiller the doctor had given him made him nauseated.

"How is your arm?" Manning asked. "I understand they wanted to keep you for a day."

Ignoring the question, Roemer followed Manning into his office, which smelled of sweat and stale cigarette smoke. A cigarette was burning in a nearly full ashtray on the desk. By the window was a large chalkboard. A piece of white paper taped to the frame covered whatever might be written on it.

Manning poured them both a cup of strong coffee. Roemer slumped down in a chair. "I called about Sarah Razmarah's car."

"We found it this morning, no problem," Manning said, perching on the edge of his desk. "In the parking lot at KwU, where she left it the night she was murdered. Where she *had* to leave it. The coil wire was pulled loose. Someone sabotaged her car."

"The killer drove her home, then?"

Manning shrugged. "The thought has crossed my mind." He lit a cigarette. "Have you been to the morgue?"

"I saw the photographs."

"Of her palm? Of the impressions?"

Roemer nodded.

"What do you think?"

The coffee was bad. It was upsetting Roemer's stomach. He put it down. "May I have a cigarette, Lieutenant?"

Manning gave him a cigarette and impatiently held out his lighter. The first drag nearly made Roemer vomit.

Manning leaned forward. "An Iraqi killed her. One of the crew working at KwU."

"You're not supposed to know about that."

"Shit." Manning sniffed. "Who the hell are you trying to kid? You're the fair-haired boy, and I'm hamstrung here. I can't get a fucking thing done. Everywhere I turn I'm blocked. Diplomatic immunity is the term of the hour. I can't even get cooperation from my own prosecutor."

"Have you tried Chief Prosecutor Schaller?"

Manning laughed derisively. "He's not interested in the likes of me. But I'll tell you one thing, Roemer, I'll find that girl's murderer, no matter how many toes I have to step on. Even yours."

"That's commendable. Anyone at KwU see anything?"

Manning stared at Roemer. Finally he shook his head.

"Nothing yet, but my people are working on it. That is to say, we're being allowed to speak with a few supervisors. The Iraqis are off limits. They're not even there. Nobody will even admit that much."

"You don't like them."

"Frankly no, Investigator. But you probably do, considering who their primary enemy is."

Roemer was out of his chair. "You bastard."

Manning was taken aback. "Sorry, Investigator. I meant nothing by it."

"We both have a job to do, Lieutenant," Roemer said. He had overreacted.

"I understand my job, but I do not understand yours."

"Finding Sarah Razmarah's murderer."

"Ahmed Pavli," Manning said. "The girl's child was probably Pavli's. They were lovers."

"But I don't think he killed her."

"Neither do I, really."

"Then why did you say so?"

"That is the official line for now. It'll be in thc papers this afternoon."

"Schaller will block it."

Manning threw up his hands. He stepped to the chalkboard and flipped up the paper cover. Two columns of notes had been written on the board. It was efficient, unimaginative standard police procedure.

"You'll not share with me, so in the interest of justice, I'll share with you," Manning said.

The left column showed the strong leads; the right listed the basic topics.

AHMED PAVLI	BIRTH
TALL THIN MAN	SCHOOL
1986 OPEL	EMPLOYMENT
LEILA KAHLED	FRIENDS
AUTOPSIES	NEIGHBORHOOD

There was nothing new or out of the ordinary, except for Leila Kahled's name. She would be off limits to Manning's investigation, but crucial to Roemer's.

"What have you got on the Kahled woman?"

Manning tapped the chalkboard. "She was at Pavli's apartment. She knew Sarah Razmarah. Which brings us to you, Investigator. Goddammit, what are you doing in this business?"

"Investigating."

"Then help me."

"I will, if and when I come up with something I think you will be able to use. Believe me."

"Scheiss." Manning looked out the window. "I could have you followed, you know."

"Don't."

"Then you take the case. I'll turn everything over to the BKA. I'll personally bring everything we've come up with over to your office."

"It wouldn't be accepted. Find the murderer, Lieutenant. If I can help you, I will."

"In the meantime, what will you be doing? Cozying up to the Arabs, perhaps?"

Roemer went to the door.

"I just hope to God it wasn't one of them who murdered her," Manning said softly.

Roemer hesitated a moment. "If it comes out that way, I'll kill the bastard myself."

17

ROEMER PARKED his car in its usual spot in the alley behind his building on the Oberkassel, then walked around front and let himself into the first-floor vestibule. His building was in a row of similar, modern steel-and-glass buildings.

He would have much preferred a small house, or even a unit in one of the older, more traditional buildings downtown, but just now in Bonn, foreigners found the older sections of the city most charming. The price of anything decent, as a result, had been driven through the ceiling, even with the revalued mark.

Gretchen Krause, with whom he had been living for two years, preferred the new and modern in any event. And Roemer had learned not to argue with her.

He took the elevator to the eighth floor and let himself in. His apartment was bright and airy, with a balcony and several large windows overlooking the river and the city. A patchwork carpet covered most of the living room floor. In front of the stereo lay a couple of cushions, and on the wall hung several paintings by American artists. Gretchen had picked them out. Just now anything American was perfect with her. She complained that he was too German.

He tossed his coat on the couch just as Gretchen, in a

bathrobe, a towel around her hair, appeared in the bedroom doorway. She was tall and blond and pretty, with broad hips, a narrow waist and large breasts.

"Walther . . ." She noticed the sling on his arm. "Oh, Christ, you're hurt." She started uncertainly toward him, then stopped.

"I screwed up my shoulder a bit, that's all."

"Where? What happened?"

Roemer knew she wanted to mother him; it was her natural instinct. And yet she was mad that he had stayed out all night, and that he had been hurt in the line of duty.

"What are you doing home?" he asked.

"I called in sick. I was worried about you. You'll get killed one of these days, and then what am I supposed to do?"

Roemer could smell the coffee in the kitchen. "There was a murder last night. A young woman. It wasn't very pretty."

"We have to talk, Walther. We can't go on like this. Something is going to have to change."

This had been coming for months. But just now Roemer didn't think he could handle it. "I'm tired and sore, Gretchen. Let me get some rest, and we'll talk about it tonight. We'll go out to dinner."

"Now."

Roemer went into the kitchen, where he poured a cup of coffee.

Gretchen was right behind him. "Whenever it's time to talk, you ignore me. I won't be put off this time."

His back to her, Roemer hunched over the counter, the cup cradled in his hands, steam rising into his face.

They'd met in Munich. She worked for the American Provost Marshal on the army base. A young GI had killed a German B-girl and the Joint Forces Agreement required

German Federal Police involvement. The first time he talked to her he was struck with her sincerity.

"Why can't it wait until I have rested?"

"Because something will come up. It always does. You'll be called out on some emergency and I won't see you for another day or two or three."

"Then we'll talk, but I'm going to soak in a hot tub."

"I'll run it for you." She went into the bathroom.

Roemer poured his coffee into the sink, then opened a bottle of beer and took it into the bedroom, where he peeled off his clothes. There was some blood on his bandage; a large bruise had formed above his elbow, and his shoulder throbbed now that the painkillers had begun to wear off. He took a deep drink of the beer. For a moment he thought he would be sick, but the feeling passed, and he went into the bathroom.

Gretchen was sitting on the closed toilet seat, a thick bath towel on her lap. The water was running in the tub. Her eyes were wide with concern. "My God, you really are hurt. What happened?"

He thought about Pavli, the look on his face when he turned the gun to his own head.

"I was shot." He eased himself into the tub. The water was wonderfully hot. Maybe it was time for them to have it out.

He lay back, closed his eyes and held the cool bottle against his forehead. "It was a younger man. He didn't really want to shoot me. Afterwards he shot himself. Blew his own head apart."

"I don't want to hear it," Gretchen said softly.

Roemer opened his eyes. "You wanted to talk. I'm a cop. Isn't that what you wanted to talk about?"

"You could have been promoted long ago. You could be a chief district investigator. You have the background, the education, the experience."

"I'd be stuck behind a desk."

"Yes! Is that so terrible?"

"For me it would be."

"I won't put up with this, Walther. I simply will not stand for it."

"Your choice," Roemer said gently. He closed his eyes again. He had spent ten days in Munich that time. They went out together every night and in the end, when he finally did return home, he gave himself two weeks before he telephoned her to come to him. She had dropped everything and come running.

She got up and shut off the water and stood over him. His head was going around and around with the vision of Sarah Razmarah's ruined body.

"You've changed," she said.

"We all change." The footprints in the blood bothered him, but he didn't know why.

Gretchen left the bathroom. He heard her in the bedroom. It sounded as if she had pulled down the suitcases.

"There's a government affairs conference in Berlin over the weekend," she called to him. "Kai Bauer asked if I'd like to come along."

Bauer was her boss. He worked for the parliament, translating news summaries. He was a priggish little man who had left his wife several months ago. His job was quite safe and involved a lot of travel to the States. He had a wonderful apartment across the river and a chalet outside Garmisch-Partenkirchen, south of Munich. He'd be a perfect catch for her. The thought didn't sit well.

He opened his eyes. Gretchen had come back to the doorway. She had taken off her robe, and she stood there nude. Her nipples were erect as they always were when she was excited or angry. She was a beautiful woman.

"He thinks I should move out on you," she said.

Roemer didn't know what to say. But he felt bad.

"Do you hear me?"

"Is that what you wanted to talk about?"

Her nostrils flared. "You're impossible," she cried. "Fucking impossible."

She went back into the bedroom and Roemer listened to her packing while the warmth of the water soaked into his bones.

18

AN HOUR later, when Roemer roused himself enough to get out of the tub, Gretchen was gone. He dried off and crawled into bed. He slept fitfully for a few hours, the pain in his arm and shoulder half waking him with a jolt whenever he moved. He dreamed of how it used to be with Gretchen, and of Sarah Razmarah's body. Major Whalpol's visage kept floating in and out nightmarishly. And just at the edge of his awareness he thought there was something else he should know. A face, perhaps. A figure, dark and threatening.

The telephone woke him a few minutes after four and he painfully rolled over and reached to answer it. The caller was Leila Kahled, and the cobwebs instantly cleared from Roemer's head.

"Your office said you'd probably be at home," she said.

Roemer thought of his jacket still lying over the back of the couch. She'd be wanting Pavli's diary. "Has everything been cleared up between your people and Lieutenant Manning?"

"Yes. We've agreed to an autopsy; then Pavli's body will be flown back to Baghdad in the morning."

"I'm genuinely sorry for the young man. He must have been very troubled."

"How is your arm?"

"Painful."

"Listen, Investigator, I think it was a very brave thing you did, trying to save his life at the risk of your own."

"You should tell that to Gretchen."

"Pardon?"

"You didn't call to ask after my health, Fräulein Kahled."

"I'd like to talk to you."

"Talk," Roemer said.

"I meant in person."

"For what purpose?"

"You have a murder on your hands, and I have a suicide on mine. The two are certainly connected."

"We can meet at my office first thing in the morning. Say eight?"

"No," Leila said. "I think we should talk now."

Roemer stood up and took the phone over to the window. He looked down at the street. There were a few cars parked along the curb, but he recognized all of them. "Do you know where I live?"

"I could be there in fifteen minutes."

"All right, I'll see you then."

Roemer went into the bathroom and shaved, then dressed in slacks and a sweater. From his desk he took out a large brown envelope, which he addressed to himself at his office. He took Pavli's diary from his jacket pocket and thumbed through it.

Pavli's handwriting was small and precise. Each entry was dated, but most of the writing was in Arabic. Sarah's name, however, was in Latin script and appeared throughout most of the last third of the book, beginning in late October.

Roemer studied the entries. It was clear that as early as the twenty-eighth of October Pavli had been thinking about Sarah. That was probably when they'd met. And if all had gone according to Whalpol's scheme, it had probably been love at first sight.

He checked his watch, then sealed the diary in the envelope. Before he returned it to the Iraqis he would need a translation. There was no telling if the woman would bring help when she came, but he didn't want to take any chances. Leila Kahled was the Mukhabarat chief here in Germany. The Iraqi Secret Service had a very tough reputation. He wouldn't put it past her or her people to barge in and snatch the diary. He stuck a couple of stamps on the envelope and deposited it downstairs in the mail slot.

Back in his apartment, Roemer telephoned his office and spoke with Rudi Gehrman, operations chief for the district.

Unlike the Bonn Kriminalpolizei, the federal criminal office was more a clearinghouse than a nuts-and-bolts investigative agency. The BKA depended on reports from other police forces, much like Interpol. Individual federal investigators, such as Roemer, were called in only for cases that crossed county lines or involved national issues. Gehrman was the coordinating genius behind all those efforts.

"Someone from the KP called this afternoon and raised hell about you, Walther," Gehrman said. "Came out of the blue."

"Manning?"

"Right. Would you mind telling me what the hell is going on? The first I hear of this is you getting shot up. Are you all right?"

"I'll live. What'd Manning have to say?"

"He wants us to handle this case—officially. I naturally told him I didn't know what the hell he was talking about."

"It's a long story, Rudi. You can call Schaller on it. This is his baby."

"He was here. And by the way, the colonel wants to see you in the morning. And you had another call, from a woman. Iraqi Federal Police. She's involved at the embassy."

"I talked to her."

Gehrman was a short, thin man who wore steel-rimmed glasses. He was married and had six children who adored him. No other operations man in Germany could compare with him. But he got miffed when he was left in the dark.

"Give me a clue, will you? I don't know how to log this. Do we start a file? A case number? What about your time?"

"I've been detached. You'll get something on it."

"Detached," Gehrman said. "It has a wonderful ring. Will you be gracing us with your presence soon?"

"First thing in the morning. But listen, I want you to do something for me. But quietly."

"This doesn't sound good."

"I want you to pull the national security file on Ludwig Whalpol. He's a major in the BND."

"What are you talking about?"

"I want to know who he works for, and I want his background. Whatever you can dig up."

"You're playing with fire here, Walther. They don't take kindly to those kinds of inquiries down in Pullach. They'll want to know why."

"I don't want them to find out."

Gehrman hesitated. "What have you gotten yourself involved with? I'll have to clear this with Legler."

"No," Roemer said sharply. Colonel Hans Legler was the Chief District Investigator. Roemer's boss. "I don't want a fuss, Rudi. But if you can't do it . . ."

"You'll owe me a very large explanation."

"You'll get it."

"I'll see what I can do. But you'd better start thinking about how you're going to cover your ass if the right people start asking the wrong questions."

"I'll see you in the morning, maybe sooner." Looking out the window, Roemer saw Leila Kahled getting out of her Mercedes in front. "Oh, one other thing. There may be a large, brown envelope coming for me tomorrow. If you haven't heard from me by then, open it. It's a diary. In Arabic. Have it translated."

"And don't tell anyone about it," Gehrman said.

Roemer smiled. "You're catching on. You just might make a good cop yet."

"An unemployed cop."

Roemer hung up, and only then did he remember the files on Sarah Razmarah and the Iraqi team that Whalpol had given him. He had stuffed them under the front seat of his car and had forgotten to bring them upstairs this morning. They were still there.

19

ROEMER OPENED the door for Leila Kahled, and it struck him in that instant how like a pocket Tintoretto she looked. Her dark hair was up, her eyes were wide and her lips were moist. She was a painting. But clearly she was upset.

"Thank you for seeing me on such short notice, Investigator," she said in perfect German. She looked beyond him into the apartment. "May I come in? Or perhaps you have company?"

"No, please come in." Roemer stepped aside.

She brushed past him into the apartment, a faint odor of perfume wafting after her.

Roemer closed the door. "Would you care for coffee, perhaps a glass of wine, Fräulein Kahled?"

"This is not a social visit. I want what you took from Ahmed Pavli's apartment."

"I don't have it." Roemer turned and went into the kitchen, leaving her standing there.

"Then you admit you took something from the apartment," Leila said, coming to the doorway.

Roemer poured himself a small cognac. "Sure you wouldn't like a drink, or do you adhere to your religion?"

"I asked you a question, Investigator."

He took his time answering. He sipped the brandy.

"Ahmed Pavli was a suspect in a murder investigation."

"Don't be a fool, he didn't kill that girl."

"They were lovers, weren't they? They worked together."

Leila's eyes narrowed. "What gave you that idea, Investigator?"

Roemer smiled. "I'm curious about one thing here. Just what is an Iraqi national doing at KwU? Building nuclear reactors, perhaps? You were aware that Sarah Razmarah had been brought here from the United States to work at KwU."

"I wonder if you understand the significance of what you are saying," Leila said evenly.

She was beautiful. She didn't look like a cop or a spy. In fact, she could pass for a mannequin. French. Very chic.

"I understand the significance of murder," he said. "Did you know she was pregnant?"

Leila sucked in her breath.

"No, I did not know it. Was it Ahmed Pavli's child?"

"We'll know after the autopsy."

She took a deep breath and sighed. "I think I'll have that cognac now."

Roemer poured the German brandy, and they went back into the living room, where he took her coat and hung it in the vestibule. She glanced over the record albums by the stereo, his collection of classical music mixed with Gretchen's American and British rock.

"An odd combination," Leila said.

"For an investigator or a German?"

She turned to him. "Let's not be at odds here. Please. This is simply too important."

"Then we need some honesty between us," Roemer replied.

They sat down, Leila on the couch, her long, lovely legs

crossed demurely, and Roemer perched on the arm of a heavy easy chair.

"Evidently you have been briefed by someone in your government," Leila said.

"I understand essentially what is going on at KwU," Roemer said dryly.

"You were told about me?"

"Ostensibly you are an Iraqi Federal Police officer, here with your father. In actuality, I was told, you are chief of security on the Iraqi team."

Something flashed in Leila's eyes. Disbelief? She knew he had been briefed, but he had not mentioned the Mukhabarat, and she might not suspect that the BND had talked to him.

"What of Lieutenant Manning's investigation?" she asked.

"He understands that Ahmed Pavli and Sarah Razmarah worked at KwU, but he is not aware of the extent of your project."

"Which, as far as your murder investigation is concerned, is superfluous."

Roemer thought about the impression in Sarah Razmarah's palm. Had it been too obvious?

Leila sat forward, an earnest expression in her eyes. "Ahmed told me he was in love with her. I tried to discourage it, of course."

"Of course."

"It's not what you think, Investigator," she said sharply. "I knew that man. He came from a very good family. He was honest, sincere, bright."

"And troubled."

She nodded. "He had a conscience."

Roemer suspected that Leila, like Major Whalpol, was an expedient person. It was part of the business. "Was Sarah sleeping with anyone else on your team?"

"Not that I was aware of," Leila said carefully. "Do you believe someone from our team killed her?"

"Pavli."

"Other than him."

"When her body was discovered, we went looking for her car. We found it at the KwU parking lot. It had been sabotaged not to run. Someone drove her home."

"That is a large company. There are more than ten thousand Germans and other nationals working there."

"She worked on your project, with your team." He kept thinking about the footprints in the blood.

Leila got up. A strand of hair had come loose and lay across her forehead. It made her seem fragile.

"I'd like my coat now, and whatever it was you took from Pavli's apartment," she said.

"It was his diary, but I don't have it."

"You have read it?"

"It's in Arabic."

"Where is it now?" she demanded.

"It is off for translation. I will personally see that you are provided with a copy."

She stared at him in disbelief.

"It may be material to my investigation," Roemer said.

"That book very likely contains sensitive Iraqi state material."

"This is not Iraq, Fräulein Kahled. This is Germany, and it is my investigation."

"We'll see," she snapped, and she turned on her heel and went to the vestibule, where she grabbed her coat.

Roemer did not move from the arm of the chair. He raised his glass. "Nice seeing you again," he said softly. She was beautiful, but she was a bitch.

She let herself out without looking back, and Roemer finished his drink in one swallow. He put the glass down, went to the window and watched her drive away. She might try to pressure Ernst Schaller for the return of the diary, but he doubted it. She would, however, undoubtedly warn the Iraqi team members that a German police investigator suspected one of them of murdering Sarah Razmarah. Or at least he hoped she would.

Meanwhile, there was Gretchen. He turned away from the window. He should feel bad that he was losing her. But he did not. They'd had a few good years. In a way he felt relieved.

20

ROEMER PICKED the lock on the downstairs mail slot and retrieved the envelope containing Pavli's diary. Then he drove downtown, arriving at his office well after six. Gehrman was getting ready to leave. He walked across the quiet operations room into Roemer's office.

"You don't look much the worse for wear," he said.

"Is Colonel Legler still here?"

Gehrman shook his head. "He left early, some dinner function somewhere. But he still insisted on seeing you first thing in the morning."

Roemer took off his jacket and hung it over his chair. "How about you, Rudi, are you up to some overtime?"

"I was afraid you were going to say something like that," the operations chief said, but his eyes were bright. He loved a mystery. The more complicated the better. He had once said: "I should have been a scientist. Figuring out the universe has to be a hell of a lot easier than unraveling human motivations."

"Anything yet on our friend Major Whalpol?"

Gehrman laughed. "What the hell, Walther, it's only been two hours!"

Roemer waited.

"Shit. I could never hold out on you. It came up twenty

minutes ago. It's locked in my desk. Manning's report came over too." Gehrman went across to his office as Roemer opened the envelope he had addressed to himself and pulled out Pavli's diary.

The entries started nine months ago, presumably when Pavli had been assigned to the KwU project, and continued until the night before his suicide.

Throughout the book Roemer caught references to Sarah Razmarah, as well as to a lot of other people by initials. Near the end, however, another name was spelled out in the Latin alphabet: Ludwig Whalpol. Pavli knew Whalpol.

Gehrman returned with two file folders, one thick and the other quite thin.

Roemer looked up. It was stunning. Pavli had known about Whalpol for at least two months.

"What is it, Walther? Christ, are you all right?"

"Who can we get up here right now to translate from the Arabic?"

Gehrman's eyes went to the diary in Roemer's hands. "Janet Hölderlin, downstairs in research. She was here as of half an hour ago."

"Get her up here," Roemer growled. He was suddenly having a bad feeling that he had been set up. That he, and not Manning, had been dragged into this thing as window dressing.

Gehrman left to make the call, and Roemer opened Whalpol's dossier in the thin file folder. There were only two sheets of paper: one listing his vitals, including his date and place of birth, his height, weight and blood type (O positive), his educational history, his employment background and his present assignment and addresses. He had houses in Munich and here in Bonn—in Bad Godesberg. He had set Sarah up there so that he could be close to her. It was very cozy.

The second document, marked "Confidential," contained a more extensive outline of Whalpol's background, with emphasis on friends and acquaintances. This was a summary report of Whalpol's background investigation at his time of entry into the BND.

None of it was any help. Whalpol was who he presented himself to be, a loyal, hardworking German who had spent most of his career with soft assignments. No assassinations, no battlefields for him. He was an agent runner specializing in industrial espionage.

"She's on her way up," Gehrman said at the door. "What else have you got?"

"I want you to put a flag on some passports. I want to know if and when they leave the country."

"How many of them?"

"One hundred and twenty-six." Roemer handed over the dossier on the Iraqi team.

Gehrman whistled when he opened the folder and looked at the names. "I think it's time for that explanation now. This is a BND file. A lot of trouble could come from this."

"A young girl spying on the Iraqis for Whalpol was murdered."

"One of these Iraqis killed her?"

"It was made to look like that, Rudi."

"Then this assignment belongs to the BND."

"It was given to me by them. By Whalpol himself."

Gehrman's eyes went automatically to Whalpol's dossier, then to the diary. "The one who killed himself?"

"He was spying on us for the Iraqis. He and the girl were lovers."

Gehrman shook his head. "Listen to me, Walther, we don't belong on this mountain. Dump it in Colonel Legler's lap. Let him make the right noises."

"We're already involved in it, don't kid yourself."

"I don't know."

"Don't fold on me now, Rudi. I need you. With any luck this will be all over by tomorrow."

"Do you know who killed her?" Gehrman asked. "The Iraqi?"

"Get the flag on those passports. But under no circumstances are any of those people to be detained. I just want to know when they come and go."

Gehrman shrugged. "I think you are crazy, but what the hell, so am I."

21

JANET HÖLDERLIN was a shirttail relative of the German poet. She was in her late thirties, mousy, a little dumpy, never married. But she was very bright. She could read and write in fourteen languages.

"I want you to listen very carefully to me, Janet, because this matter is of extreme importance," Roemer began once she was seated.

Her glasses slipped down on her nose. She pushed them up and nodded.

Gehrman brought in a tape recorder and Roemer turned it on.

"I have something that I would like you to translate from the Arabic, orally. But when you are finished, you will leave everything you have seen or heard in this office. You will take no notes, and afterwards you will speak to no one about this. Do you understand?"

The woman looked from Roemer to Gehrman, who stood by the door, and then back again, before she pushed at her glasses. She nodded. "It is a police matter?"

"Exactly," Roemer said. He picked up Pavli's diary. "This is a diary of a man who committed suicide recently. The man may also have been involved in a homicide. There may be clues here material to the investigation."

The woman nodded again, nervously.

"I must warn you of one other thing, Janet. There will be information that may be quite startling to you. Perhaps confusing. That should not be your concern. I merely want you to be a translator."

"Anything I can do to help, sir."

Roemer handed her the diary, then sat back and lit a cigarette.

Perched on the edge of the seat, her knees primly together, she opened the leather-bound book and scanned the first couple of pages. "A lot of this is in code, sir," she said. "Initials and things like that."

"For instance?"

She indicated the first page. "The very first entry says: 'P. was at it again, and we've only been here two weeks from seven.'"

"That's all right," Roemer said. "Just go through the book for me. We'll figure out the code later."

22

ROEMER SAT alone in his dark office, smoking a cigarette. He looked out his window at the deserted streets. He was tired again, and his arm was aching.

He was disgusted. He had listened to parts of the tape three times now. There was little to be gained by going over it again. Nothing would change.

Ahmed Pavli had known about Ludwig Whalpol. Sarah or someone had told him everything. About how she had been recruited, and how she had been brought in to spy with Pavli as her main target.

Roemer inhaled deeply and coughed, the smoke burning his raw throat. He felt like hell.

Pavli wrote in his diary that he had not understood Sarah until he had spoken with LK . . . Leila Kahled? Afterward he had gone back to Sarah and told her everything, including the fact that he too was a spy.

And a few days later Sarah was dead. The spy gone bad had been murdered, and then raped after she was dead. A pregnant woman brutally battered. Where was the motive beyond the obvious?

Gehrman had reluctantly gone home a couple of hours ago, after he had confirmed that flags had been placed on the Iraqi passports. The further they got into this business the unhappier he became.

"We're playing with fire, Walther," he had said after Janet was gone. "Leave it for Legler in the morning. He'll know what to do."

"You worry too much, Rudi. Go home. Your supper will be cold and your children worried. There's nothing left to do here tonight."

Gehrman shook his head. "You dumb bastard. Why don't you and Gretchen come for dinner on Sunday?"

"I don't think so."

"Are things going badly again?"

"Gretchen is gone for the weekend. Some conference up in Berlin." He thought about Kai Bauer, who'd be fucking her. It embarrassed him more than it hurt.

"How about you, then? Marlene and the children would love it if you came."

Roemer smiled. "No thanks, I'd just as soon be alone this weekend. I have a few things to do."

"I understand." Gehrman went to shut off the lights in his office. Before he left he stopped back. "Listen, Walther, if there is anything you need, give me a call at home. I'm not going anywhere tonight."

Roemer nodded.

"I mean it," Gehrman said. "And for God's sake, don't stay here all night."

Roemer went through Manning's police report, page by page. There was a lot of detail from the search of Sarah's apartment, testimony from her neighbors (including the observation that her only two regular visitors were men, Pavli and Whalpol), the preliminary forensics results, as well as several photographs of her body and of the bloody footprints, with the comment that they had been made by a man and that the right heel of his shoe was worn down.

The telephone rang.

It was Manning. "There was no answer at your apartment, so I figured you'd be in your office," the KP cop said gruffly. "Sternig brought up the autopsy reports. The child was Pavli's. We're ninety-five percent sure."

"How about the semen on the girl's legs. Pavli's?"

"No. Wrong blood type. His was A negative."

"Then Pavli didn't kill her."

"It's not likely."

"Anything else?"

Manning hesitated. "I could ask you that, Roemer, but I don't suppose you'd offer much."

"I may have something for you tomorrow."

"Yes?" Manning said eagerly.

"Tomorrow," Roemer said firmly. Manning would be feeling the squeeze now. He had tried twice to dump the case onto the BKA, and had failed both times. They'd be getting pretty desperate over there, wondering what the hell they had gotten themselves into. But it was murder, and they would have to go through the motions. Knowing Manning, the motions would be extensive and methodical, if unimaginative.

"We still haven't found out where he got the pistol. It is a three-fifty-seven magnum. American-made. Unusual."

"It wasn't registered?"

"No." Manning laughed derisively. "You saw the impression on her palm. How many Iraqis are running around Bonn just now that she would know, besides that bunch at KwU she was associated with? Don't worry, Roemer, I know goddamned well where I'm going to find her killer. Only I can't get to them. Not through ordinary channels."

"I might be able to help with that," Roemer said.

"Yes?"

"Tomorrow."

Roemer sat at his desk for a long time, staring at the photographs of the bloody footprints they had found in Sarah's apartment and on the stairs. Poor Sarah, he thought. Was it possible to tell in advance which people were doomed by their own natures to such endings? Most murder victims had one thing in common . . . at least the non-random victims did. They lived dangerous lives. They surrounded themselves with unstable, violent people. They got themselves involved in dangerous situations in dangerous places. But they never really knew it. It was like the man who complained he had been robbed. He could not understand why it had happened to him. He had walked down a dangerous street late at night, alone, wearing expensive clothes and carrying a lot of money. He was a mark. So had Sarah been a mark.

23

It was nearly one in the morning by the time Roemer drove to Bad Godesberg, finding an address off the Hinterholerstrasse in an area of narrow, tree-lined streets. A lot of the foreign diplomats working in Bonn lived in this section. And there was a lot of old money here.

He parked his car across the street a half-block from the two-story brownstone house. No lights shone from the windows.

For a long time Roemer just sat there, watching the house. With the car's heater turned off, it was cold. But not as cold as the grave.

He smoked a cigarette, and when he was done he picked up the telephone and gave the mobile operator Whalpol's number. He stared at the house as he waited for the connection to be made. Whalpol lived alone. He did not have a house staff. But he had two homes, which meant if he was in residence in Munich at the moment (which supposedly was the case), this place would be empty.

The telephone rang a dozen times before Roemer hung up. Ernst Schaller had seemed frightened of Whalpol, and of whomever he had spoken with on the telephone the other night. Why? He wasn't a stupid man. There was a lot of this business that the Chief District Prosecutor knew but that had not been presented that night.

Roemer got out of his car, hunched up his coat collar against the chill wind, crossed the street and, keeping within the shadows, walked up to Whalpol's house. He let himself in the gate and went to the front door.

The door was secured by an ordinary tumbler lock. Roemer studied it a moment in the dim light, then took a thin leather case out of his jacket pocket, opened it and selected a long, thin stainless-steel pick. A number six. The lock was stiff with the cold, so it took him nearly two minutes to get it slipped. He pushed the door open a few centimeters with his foot.

The house was quiet. There were no lights, nor were there any audible alarms.

Roemer slipped inside, closed and locked the door, then moved silently through the vestibule into a narrow stairhall. The living room was to the right.

Walking on the balls of his feet, Roemer went up the stairs, which opened onto a short corridor, two doors on either side. A faint odor of perfume, cologne or soap lingered above a mustiness. This house was not used very much, but someone had been here. Recently.

The first room appeared to be a guest room; two chairs and a table, a bed, a chest of drawers and a *Schrank,* empty. The second contained boxes of books stacked in one corner. The third, at the end of the corridor, was a small bathroom, and the fourth, on the right, was the master bedroom, with a wide bed, a big chest and a very large *Schrank* against the far wall.

Roemer went to the window, which looked out over a rear courtyard, and pulled the heavy curtains tightly shut. Then he turned on the light and opened the *Schrank.* Several shirts and trousers were hung on one side, two of Whalpol's old-fashioned suits on the other. On the floor of the big wardrobe were three pairs of shoes, two pairs black and one brown, all of them substantial oxfords with heavy soles and thick leather heels.

One pair of the black shoes was nearly new, but the other black pair and the brown ones were much older. The right heel on each pair was worn down.

Roemer took both right shoes out of the *Schrank* and held them up to the light. The brown shoe was clean, the black was dusty. The brown shoe had been recently cleaned. The sole and heel had been scrubbed.

Sarah Razmarah's face had been crushed as if someone wearing heavy shoes had stomped her to death. Christ, Roemer thought. Why had they asked him to investigate? What had they wanted him to find? How much control had they expected to exert over him?

He set the brown shoe aside for the moment and, no longer giving a damn how much noise he was making, began searching the room, ripping drawers open.

Quickly he found the jewelry box in the top drawer of the chest. For a moment he just looked at it, as if the thing were diseased. Whalpol was arrogant, but was he stupid?

The jewelry box contained a half dozen sets of inexpensive cuff links, a few tie tacks, a gold cigarette lighter, a thin silver chain.

The cuff links were not here, only the shoe. The damning, arrogant shoe.

By the time he left, at nearly three-thirty, it had begun to snow. The roads were slippery, and the Königswinter Bridge over the Rhine was beginning to ice up. Below, the dark river was choppy in the wind, the snow disappearing at an angle into the broad, black maw. The sins of the fathers shall be visited upon the sons; the line kept drumming in his head. Bonn suddenly seemed a dark, frightening city.

24

CHIEF DISTRICT Prosecutor Ernst Schaller, dressed in a bathrobe and slippers, his hair mussed, his eyes still clouded by sleep, answered the door.

"You," he said.

"You'd better let me in," Roemer said ominously.

"What's this, for God's sake, Roemer? Have you any idea of the time?"

"Ludwig Whalpol killed that girl because she fell in love with an Iraqi spy."

"Good Lord." Schaller staggered backward.

Roemer followed him into the house and closed the door. Schaller seemed genuinely frightened of him. His eyes were wide and he seemed suddenly unable to talk.

"Do you understand what I am saying to you, Chief Prosecutor?" Roemer had a harsh, flat edge on his voice. "I have your murderer for you, and now I wish to be withdrawn."

Schaller glanced toward the head of the stairs. "Keep your voice down."

"I shall present my evidence, and then I shall leave."

Schaller shook his head. "It's quite impossible, you know. Ludwig Whalpol is not a killer . . ." He broke off, a sheepish expression crossing his face, as if he had said something stupid.

"This is a BND matter," Roemer said. "It was from the very beginning. It is not something for me."

Schaller noticed that Roemer was holding several files and a shoe. "I don't want any of that."

"Neither do I."

"Have you got enough evidence for me to go to trial?"

Roemer laughed. "This will never go to trial. You know that. You and the good major sat in your study and told me as much."

"Don't be absurd, Roemer. A murder has been committed. If . . . if an officer of the government, or anyone for that matter, is implicated we will go to trial. It's the very reason you were picked for this assignment. I knew you would find your man."

"But not Whalpol?"

"I don't think so. I can't imagine it, under the circumstances."

"If it were true, what then, Chief Prosecutor?"

"Then he would be arrested and placed on trial, as a matter of procedure, of course."

"Why me?"

"The very question I was about to ask you," Schaller said. "If Whalpol had killed this young girl, why in heaven's name would he ask for the premier investigator in Germany?"

"Because he's an arrogant bastard who believes he can't be found out."

Schaller was becoming more sure of himself. "What is your evidence against him? This shoe?"

"I took it from his closet. It will match the footprints at the young woman's apartment."

"And if it does, so what? He discovered the body. He recovered the file." Schaller shook his head. "Even if he were the murderer and I knew it for a fact, I still could not go to trial on the basis of a heel print."

"I wasn't asking for a trial, Chief Prosecutor," Roemer said. "I merely asked that I be withdrawn from the case. It is clearly a BND matter . . . unless, of course, you want me to pass my information along to Lieutenant Manning."

"Don't be a fool!"

"There may be another problem."

"Yes."

"Leila Kahled, who is chief of security for the Iraqi team at KwU, came to my apartment to see me. She is the Mukhabarat chief here. Major Whalpol's counterpart."

"Go on," Schaller said, grim-lipped.

"She knows who and what Whalpol is, and she knows he recruited Sarah Razmarah to spy on them."

Schaller seemed to consider it for a moment, but then he smiled. "I don't think you will have too much of a problem with Fräulein Kahled. I'll speak to her personally. I'm having dinner with her and her father on Sunday evening. It was scheduled for last night, but he was recalled to Baghdad unexpectedly."

"I don't understand. Do you know who this woman is?"

"Yes."

"And that there is a very good possibility that Whalpol murdered Sarah Razmarah because she was giving away our secrets?"

"I know that you've made that wild accusation."

Roemer didn't think he could dislike anyone more than he disliked the Chief Prosecutor at that moment.

25

It was noon by the time Roemer managed to get away from the city. A couple of hours of sleep and a light breakfast had refreshed him enough so that the six-hour drive to Bern was not impossible.

Colonel Legler had postponed their meeting until Monday (Roemer suspected Schaller had spoken with him); Gehrman was in conference and Manning was busy, so Roemer had left.

The snow had stopped, the sun had come out and the Koblenz Autobahn was clear, though traffic was heavy. Roemer gassed up at the B9 entrance ramp just outside Bonn and, keeping to the left lane, sped up to 150 kilometers per hour. Radio Luxembourg was playing a Tchaikovsky symphony; it made him think of his father, who had loved Tchaikovsky even when loving things Russian was unpopular, in fact dangerous.

By rights he should have hated the old man for all the things his mother had told him. But he did not. It was genetics; like father, like son.

His first memory of his father was after the war. They were living in a large basement apartment in what was left of Munich. He could clearly see in his mind's eye a photograph of his father in a black uniform, twin silver lightning bolts on the lapel. He had been one of the administrators at nearby Dachau. It was work he was proud of.

Then his father disappeared, escaping with a lot of gold, jewels and artwork to Switzerland, leaving his wife and young son behind. Those next years were incredibly difficult. Roemer still vividly remembered being cold and hungry, though he wasn't yet four years old. He remembered that even the rats had deserted the city—the ones the people had not trapped and eaten. He remembered sickness, and he remembered the American school that he and the children of other SS officers were made to attend. They were taught in detail, every day, about the horrors of the Final Solution. They were shown photographs and were made to listen to speeches about God and America and guilt. Mostly guilt.

For several years, investigators would come every week to talk with his mother about the whereabouts of her husband. They were living in Augsburg. After each visit his mother would rant about what a bastard his father had been. About how he had deserted them. How the Russians had captured him, and had tortured and killed him, and how he had finally gotten what he deserved.

Money began to arrive from Switzerland and their lives became easier. Roemer was placed in a boarding school and then the police university. Before his mother died, she told him that his father was alive and well in Interlaken, a small city in Switzerland. From then on, once or twice a year he drove down to see the old man. Each time he came away unfulfilled. He was searching for a father, but all he ever found was a distant, bitter stranger. Yet despite the old man's terrible past, Roemer felt something for him.

His father's health began to fail, and in 1976 the old

man went into a private sanatorium outside Bern. His sergeant remained at the Interlaken house.

"Here is where I die," he wheezed. "Not at the end of some Jewboy rope."

And now he was truly dying. Cancer. Kidney failure. A dozen maladies of old age in which the body simply gives up.

Roemer was glad for it. The pain and guilt could finally be laid to rest.

The sanatorium was a few kilometers northwest of Bern on a large wooded tract in the hills along the River Aare. A lot of snow had fallen; the trees were heavily laden, and the air had a crisp, ethereal feel. As usual, the place seemed deserted. There were never many visitors here. This was a dying place, mostly for the well-to-do old men who preferred anonymity, as only the Swiss could provide it.

It was past six when Roemer came up the long, looping driveway and parked just beyond the main entrance overhang. He got out and stretched his legs. His shoulder hurt like hell and he had a headache.

The large and ornate building had once been a resort hotel, but had been converted into a hospital after the war.

He walked slowly across the driveway and entered the expansive, tasteful lobby. An older woman in a starched white uniform rose behind a long counter.

"Good evening, Herr Walkmann," the woman said coolly. Here everyone had an alias.

"How is he doing?" Roemer asked quietly.

"He has his days, but before you leave, Dr. Klausen would like to have a word with you."

"May I go up now?"

"Of course. Will you be staying the weekend?"

"I'm not sure yet. I'll let you know."

Roemer took the elevator to the third floor. The nurse on duty at the floor station was just hanging up the telephone.

"Good evening, Herr Walkmann. You may go right in, though he may be dozing."

"Thank you." Roemer walked to the end of the long corridor and knocked at the door before going in.

His father was propped by pillows in an easy chair in front of the window. The room smelled of urine and alcohol. A small wooden crucifix hung on the wall over the bed. The only other adornment in the room was a small vase of cut flowers on the bureau.

For a moment Roemer stood at the doorway staring at his father's frail form, his wispy white hair in disarray, his gnarled, blue-veined hands folded in his lap, his arms and legs beneath his pajamas hardly more than brittle twigs. The old man had faded since the last time Roemer saw him, three months ago. He'd lost weight. The skin hung in ugly blue-tinged folds at his neck and jaw, and he had developed a slight palsy.

Roemer pulled up a chair next to his father. The old man was awake, staring out the window, his eyes moist and clouded by cataracts.

"So you've come again," the old man said.

"Hello, Father."

"I suppose you want more money. Or perhaps your mother sent you to tell me what a tough time she's having."

"No, I just came to say hello. See how you were doing."

The old man turned to look at his son, his thin purple lips mean. "I feel *für Scheissen.* I can't piss, I can't shit, I can't eat. Max has left me, and I'm stuck in this filthy prison."

Roemer lit a cigarette and gave it to his father, who

held it backward, like a Russian, with his thumb and forefinger. He coughed each time he inhaled. Roemer lit one for himself.

"You can do me a favor while you're here," the old man said between coughing fits.

"Sure."

"Get them to give me my schnapps. They've cut it out."

"I'll talk to the doctor."

"Fuck the *Schweinhund Juden.* I want you to talk to Frantz. The administrator. I've given that old bastard enough money."

"I'll speak with him tonight."

"See that you do. It's all I ask." The old man sank back into himself and turned so that he could again look out the window. It was getting dark already.

Whenever Roemer came to see his father he was taken back to the early fifties, when there was still a genuine mystical belief in the old ways; in the old gods, the *Nibelungen,* who lived underground with their riches; in the Valkyrie, the warrior maidens of the Norse god whom the Germans had borrowed to look over their fallen warriors; and in the tragedy of heroes cut down in their youth. It was an atmosphere that seemed to hang around his father. The danger about the man was damped now only because he was very old, and dying. He was the Butcher of Dachau. How many men and women and children had he killed? How many screams had he heard, how many pleas for mercy? Yet here he was, the tragic old hero for whom a place waited in Valhalla.

"I hate this goddamned country. I want to go home."

"It's not there anymore," Roemer said.

The old man shook his head. "The atomic war is going to start over the Jewish state. The Arabs are pissed off. The Russkies will supply them with the bombs and the rockets and they'll wipe the kikes off the map."

"The Israelis have their own nuclear weapons now."

The old man laughed, the sound brittle. He coughed. "I'm goddamned glad the bastards didn't have the bomb in forty-two."

Roemer wondered why he kept coming here. It was like this each time.

"How is your mother doing?"

Roemer closed his eyes. "She's all right."

"Maybe I should send for her. Wouldn't that be a good idea?"

"Perhaps."

"Shit, don't do me any favors," the old man mumbled. After a while his head nodded forward and his body slumped sideways. He dropped his cigarette in his lap.

Roemer took the cigarette and his own and put them out in the ashtray on the table. He gently lifted his father out of the chair and laid him on the tall hospital bed. The old man's body stank of rot.

"Don't let them get me, Walther," he said with intensity. "It won't be long now."

Roemer covered him with the sheet and thin blanket and lifted the side rails. "You're safe here, Father."

Roemer stood at the bedside for a time watching his father sleeping, hearing his labored breathing. For a terrible moment he had the urge to take the pillow from beneath his father's head and press it over the old man's face. It would be a peaceful end.

Dr. Emile Klausen, the resident physician, was at the nurses' station. "Ah, Herr Walkmann." The doctor was a shambling bear of a man with thick brown hair. "Is your father still awake?"

"He's sleeping now. I put him to bed."

"Good."

"You wanted to speak with me before I left?"

The doctor sighed. "You understand it will not be long. Perhaps two months at the most."

"Is he in any pain?"

"Not in any ordinary sense. He is pretty much in his own world now, most of the time."

"Call me at the end, please," Roemer said.

"By the way, Herr Walkmann, your friend has arrived. She is waiting for you downstairs."

A cold hand clutched Roemer's throat. "Friend?"

"Fräulein Kahled?"

Roemer ran to the elevator. He couldn't believe the bitch had followed him here. She wanted something on him, some lever to use against him. Well, she had it now.

26

LEILA WAS in the lobby looking at a large painting of a Swiss alpine scene hanging above the fireplace when Roemer emerged from the elevator. He fought to control himself. After all these years he was finally going to be confronted.

He crossed the lobby. "What are you doing here?" he demanded when he reached her.

Leila turned. "I could ask you the same thing, Investigator," she said coldly. "But I've already figured it out."

So goddamned close. Just another couple of months and it wouldn't have mattered.

"Your father is here. The Butcher of Dachau."

"He is dying. There are only a few weeks left for him."

"The Justice Department in Berlin would find interesting the fact that he's still alive. The Wiesenthal organization in Vienna might be grateful to learn that he's here."

"I wonder what the Americans would say if they knew what your people were doing in Bonn?"

Leila smiled. "You would become a traitor? I think your own government would have you shot."

"I'll do whatever it takes to protect my father."

Leila appraised him. "Yes, I can see that you are the son."

Roemer tensed. He wanted to lash out, smash her face,

knock her down. He was at the raw edge. "I'm not a Nazi," he said softly.

"You had a good teacher . . ."

"I never knew him until long after the war."

"And your mother, Investigator, was she a Nazi bitch?"

God in heaven, he couldn't take much more of this.

"I want to know," Leila said relentlessly. "Was she there on the torture squads in Dachau? Did she make lampshades from human skin?"

Roemer's right fist came up slowly.

"Touch me, you bastard, and I'll kill you."

The nurse behind the counter stood up. She was looking at them. She picked up the telephone.

"Leave," Roemer said. "He'll be dead very soon."

"In Berlin, at the end of the hangman's rope."

He lunged and shoved Leila back against the wall, his right forearm across her neck. Her eyes were wide with fear; she grappled for her purse.

"I'll break your fucking neck the instant you touch your gun."

"Herr Walkmann!" the nurse was shouting.

"Not a day goes by that I don't feel guilt," he spat. "Not a night passes without nightmares. But he is my father!" Tears streamed down his cheeks.

Rough hands were on his shoulders, tearing him away. Suddenly spent, he allowed himself to be shoved aside by the hospital's security men.

Leila gaped at him, wide-eyed. But there was something else there too. Sadness? Pity?

"This woman is armed," Roemer said calmly. "She is here to kill my father."

27

THE POWERFUL overhead klieg lights went out moments after the red transmission light on camera one winked off, and Joan Waldmann bundled up the news feature script she had just read, sat back with a sigh and lit a cigarette. It was late Sunday night and she was tired. It had been a hectic week. Time to go home to bed.

She was a pretty woman of twenty-eight with a big-city polish on camera and a wholesome look off. She was short and sensuous, with dark hair, wide eyes and a firm body.

Her director, Rolf Dürer, called her "the answer to every man's dream." The station manager, Kurt Bruckner, who was in love with her, called her his greatest asset. And the German National Television Board in Berlin persistently tried to lure her away from Bonn.

"Nice job, Fräulein Waldmann," a cameraman said, hanging up his headset.

Joan flashed him a warm smile and got up from behind the desk. She felt very good about this story. A lot of heads would roll. Euro-television would certainly pick it up, and after tomorrow morning's airing they would send a tape over to the American networks.

She glanced up at the director's booth as the studio intercom came on.

"A smashing job as usual, darling," Dürer said. "Before you go, Bruckner would like to see you in his office."

She frowned. It was nearly eleven. Unusual for Kurt to be here this late, especially on a weekend, unless he was after something. Namely her. He'd been trying to get her into bed for months now.

Perhaps tonight would be the night to straighten him out. She walked down the corridor to her desk in the newsroom. She locked the script she had just read in her desk along with the files and notes on the Kraftwerk Union story, got her purse and coat and took the elevator up to the fourth floor.

Bruckner's office was through a set of glass doors at the end of a broad, carpeted corridor. Joan walked through the empty outer office, knocked once on the door and went in.

The station manager was seated behind his desk. He was a tall, stolid man in his late forties, with gray hair. Seated across from him was a thin, stern-looking man wearing an unstylish wool suit. The television monitor was playing the tape she had just made.

"There is no question among trade unionists that Germany can and should export its technology." Her voice came from the monitor. Her onscreen image looked into the lens of the camera. *"We must ask . . . what technology will we export? Who shall get it?"*

Bruckner flipped a remote control switch on his desk. The television monitor clicked off, and the office lights came up slowly.

"Hell of a report, Joan," he said, standing.

The thin man rose. He was very tall. "Fräulein Waldmann," he said. "Really, I have to concur with Kurt."

This man had "government" written all over him. But she returned his smile. "Thank you, Herr . . ."

"I am Ludwig Whalpol."

"Major Whalpol wants to talk to us about the KwU story," Bruckner said in a subdued tone.

"Please, won't you have a seat, Fräulein Waldmann?" Whalpol asked pleasantly.

Joan looked sharply at him. "What's going on here, Kurt? Is it what I think it is?"

"Be reasonable, sweetheart. Just listen to the man. We may have jumped the gun here."

"No." She remained standing. "My story will air in the morning. I told no lies, no inaccuracies. And, *Scheiss,* it's a story that has to be told."

"I'm afraid not, Fräulein," Whalpol said sadly, as if scolding a naughty child.

"This is still a nation of laws!"

"If need be I will have a Z notice brought over within the hour. I would much prefer we do this one on a friendly, volunteer basis."

"*Verdammt!* Is my story airing in the morning, Kurt?"

"Just listen to the man, for Christ's sake," Bruckner said.

"We *are* a nation of laws, Fräulein. But you can also understand that information vital to a nation's safety and well-being must be kept confidential."

"Don't give me that shit, Herr Major, whoever the hell you are. I'm not some little schoolgirl here. Legitimate defense secrets must be kept. But when a government begins to do something that endangers the lives of its citizens and perhaps world safety, something must be done to stop it."

"And how are we endangering world safety, in your opinion?"

"By exporting nuclear technology which could be used for bombs."

Whalpol smiled. "KwU does not build atomic bombs, I assure you. Nor does it export the technology to do so."

"It sells nuclear reactors," she said, infuriated at being patronized.

"Just so."

"And it sells reprocessing technology. Weapons-grade plutonium from spent reactor fuel rods could be the end result. Anyone could make the bomb. Even someone like Saddam Hussein."

Whalpol turned to Bruckner. "Your Fräulein Waldmann is a strong-willed young woman."

"Will my story air in the morning, Kurt?"

Bruckner lowered his eyes and shook his head.

"Then I'll take it to the American networks."

"You will be charged under the Secrets Act, with espionage," Whalpol said softly.

Joan stepped back. She couldn't believe this was happening. "Then I quit as of now!"

"There will be no job for you in Berlin, nor in Frankfurt," Whalpol said.

"My God . . . you've been spying on me!" She turned and barged out the door, emerging into the corridor just as her director was getting off the elevator.

He stopped in his tracks, a bundle of files and papers in his arms. For just a moment, Joan refused to believe what they were. But she knew. They were her files and notes and the script for the KwU story. He'd taken them from her desk.

"You too, Rolf?"

Dürer shrugged. "Sorry, *Liebchen.* Orders. You know how it is."

28

A LINE OF six Russian-built Tu-117a fighting vehicles topped a ridge in the desert 125 miles west of Baghdad, and on Saddam Hussein's signal they stopped.

It was the middle of the night, and they'd been traveling since before nightfall, straight across the desert, keeping well away from population centers. Hussein was paranoid, and the security measures designed to protect him were extraordinary. Whenever he left his command bunker in the capital city, he traveled in mufti and in secret.

He got out of the third vehicle, five of his armed bodyguards surrounding him, and walked a few yards along the ridge, a smile creasing his jowly features.

Below, nearly filling the valley, was a mammoth construction project. Even at this hour thousands of lights illuminated the spires and scaffolding and thousands of miles of pipes and gridwork. A continuous stream of trucks and earth-moving equipment went in and out. High-voltage transmission lines came across the desert from Baghdad in the east, from Turkey in the north, from Syria in the west and even from Saudi Arabia in the south.

Peace was upon his nation. And this place would

become the jewel of Iraq. "Flowers will grow where even the cactus failed to bloom," he told his people on State Television.

But coming here in secret, like a desert warrior in the night, even Hussein was awed. This time, he thought, they would not fail. The world would cower before the sacred rage of Islam.

Minister of Defense General Ihsan Hajjaj came over from the lead vehicle, a cigarette cupped in his left hand. "It's tremendous, Mr. President. But we must maintain secrecy for two more years. That is a very long time."

"Yes, it is," Hussein said.

"Please pardon me, Mr. President, but your presence here is very dangerous. Not only for you, but for the sake of secrecy."

"The United Nations inspectors have crawled over every centimeter of construction like the dung beetles they are. It is what it is. *Insha' Allah.*"

"Yes, Mr. President, but with you here they may take a new interest."

"What will they see, Ihsan? The largest desalinization plant ever constructed anywhere in the world. They will see water pumped from three thousand feet beneath the surface of the desert. And they will see thousands of German engineers and specialists. Five thousand miles of pipe. Fifty thousand miles of copper and aluminum wire. A million tons of concrete. Steel. Brick. Glass."

"Perhaps they will dig even deeper than that."

"What would they see?" Hussein asked. He felt powerful. He felt as if he'd never had so much strength as he did at this moment.

To the northeast he could make out a broad flat spot on the valley floor. When this site had been selected for what was being designated as the All-Iraq Desert Agrarian Reform Project, the village of Qasr al Khubbaz had occupied the upper corner of the valley. Now the village was gone. Its 750 people were dead of a mysterious coliform bacteria in their water supply. The settlement had been bulldozed flat and the entire place paved with crushed stones.

In 1982 Syria's President, Hafiz al-Assad, had done a similar thing at his fourth-largest city, Hama. He killed twenty thousand of his people, flattened every building, and paved the entire area. He was *President* of his people. No one had forgotten it.

Because the Hama project had been masterminded and arranged by Michael at Hussein's bidding, Syria owed Iraq a very large favor. One that had been only partially repaid by Syria's neutrality in the Gulf War. There would be other payments. Many others.

"What would they see if they dug even deeper, Ihsan? What?"

"What we are constructing in the salt caverns."

"Water pumps." Hussein smiled, warmth spreading through his veins. There is no God but God. He felt as if he could fly up into the night sky, to the stars.

"And other things," Hajjaj replied nervously at the look on Hussein's face.

"I don't know what you are talking about. Can you explain this to me?"

"The neutron-source reactor, Mr. President."

"Iraq has no nuclear program. We have forsaken all such projects. General Hajjaj, you were at my side when I made this announcement more than two years ago."

Some of Hussein's other staff officers had gotten out of their vehicles, but kept their distance.

"I understand what we have told the Israelis, and the Coalition."

"Am I a liar, Ihsan? Before Allah, is that what you think of your president?"

General Hajjaj began to sweat. "I am simply concerned about security, Mr. President."

"But I lie. Therefore I am unfit to lead my people. I think it is safe to say that is your line of reasoning."

"Before Allah, no, my president . . ."

Hussein pulled out his nine-millimeter SigSauer automatic and fired one shot point-blank into Hajjaj's forehead.

The general fell backward like a marble statue, dead before he hit the sand.

"Colonel Zahedi!" Hussein shouted.

His guards stood at a half-crouch, their weapons drawn.

"Zahedi!"

"Yes, Mr. President," Colonel Nayef Zahedi, chief of operations under General Hajjaj, answered from the back of the column.

"I am promoting you to brigadier general, effective immediately. Will you serve as my Minister of Defense?"

Hajjaj had been Hussein's personal friend since the mid-seventies. But, like others in the past, he had misjudged Hussein. Zahedi was not going to make the same mistake. "Of course, my president," he called out. "I will be honored to serve as your Minister of Defense!"

They were all fools, Hussein thought. Zahedi, Hajjaj, Tariq Aziz. All of them fools, except for Michael, who was the only man in the entire world he could trust.

29

THE DRIVE to her apartment in Bonn-Putzchen across the river seemed to take Joan Waldmann forever this night. It was very cold. No stars shone. It would probably snow again soon, though it really didn't matter. The fight had gone out of her when she'd seen Dürer with her files.

The story had been an uphill battle from the beginning. She wondered why she cared so much. When she was a child her father used to chide her: "You are too serious, *Liebchen.*" It was true. In *Gymnasium* she frightened boys off with her intensity. Now she felt more alone than ever.

She parked her Volkswagen Jetta in the lot behind her high-rise building and took the elevator up to the tenth floor, where she let herself into her large, modern apartment.

Closing and locking the door, she leaned back and shut her eyes. Ordinarily she did not mind living alone. Sooner or later the right man would come along, and she would have two babies. One boy, one girl. They would have a summer house in the mountains and take vacations in the winter to the coast of Spain, perhaps even to America. Just now, though, Joan wished for some companionship. Any companionship.

She smiled wanly. If Kurt had stood up to Whalpol, she would have taken him home with her. To bed.

After a while she undressed, ran a bath and poured a glass of white wine. The one thing that had bothered her in the KwU story was that she had not been able to find out whom the huge company was selling its technology to. She would find out the rest of the story, and then Major Whalpol and his cronies would sit up and take notice.

The door buzzed as she walked nude into the bathroom. *"Verdammt,"* she swore, putting down her wine. She knew damned well who it was. She grabbed her robe from its hook on the bathroom door and pulled it on as she hurried to the door. The buzzer sounded again. "All right, Kurt," she shouted. She'd give him a piece of her mind he'd never forget. She slipped the chain lock, unlatched the door and yanked it open.

She got a glimpse of a tall, dark man in a heavy overcoat, his hat pulled low; then something hard slammed into her face, driving her backward into the apartment.

Something horrible had happened to her right ankle; she could only stumble for balance.

The man closed the door behind him, his hat falling off, and even in her daze Joan thought he looked familiar. She tried to open her mouth to cry out, but she was choking.

Somehow she managed to throw up her left arm as the man struck again, but she could not defend herself. She knew she was going to die.

The force of the second blow broke her shoulder, knocking her down, her head bouncing on the carpeted floor, black spots swimming in front of her eyes.

She was helpless. It was happening so fast. He was so strong.

The killer stood over her, an awful smile on his face.

She could hardly move. Her legs seemed to be miles from her body, and she could hardly lift her arms. This could not be happening.

The killer was on his knees beside her now, his eyes locked onto hers.

"Why?" she wanted to cry, but she could only whimper.

The killer pulled open her robe and looked at her breasts. He touched her nipples with a gloved hand.

Joan tried to push herself away. The murderer punched her, first in the left breast, then in the right, pummeling her into excruciating pain.

"Oh God," she screamed in her brain.

The killer pulled back, opened his coat, unzipped his trousers and roughly spread her legs. He entered her, thrusting brutally, as if more than anything else he wanted to hurt her.

"Whore," he growled in her ear.

Almost immediately his body shuddered and he pulled away and scrambled to his feet. His penis glistened, already flaccid. The killer turned away to rearrange his clothing, then turned back, calmly smiling.

Joan could do nothing now.

The murderer's lips were moving but no sounds came out. He backed away.

Would he leave her? A tiny flicker of hope rose within her. But then the killer stepped close.

"No," Joan screamed silently.

30

THE KILLER looked down at the woman's body. She was like the other one, too easy. She had not fought back. She had not even cried for mercy.

He raised his right foot, the heavy-soled shoe directly above her face, and stomped down with all his might, crushing her cheekbone, nose and forehead. He stomped again, blood splattering outward. The third time, Joan's skull caved in with a sickening crunch.

For a long time the killer looked down at the ruined remains of the woman, listening to the vagrant sounds of the building, the wind at the windows.

He did not feel good, not how he'd thought he would feel, but a great clarity came to his mind and eyes.

Everything was suddenly larger and more sharply defined.

He went into the bathroom and shut off the water running in the tub. With a large bath towel, he cleaned the blood from his shoe.

At the front door he did not bother looking back as he quietly let himself out.

Then the building and the night were quiet.

31

THE APARTMENT was cold and quiet. The radio station had gone off the air sometime in the night as Roemer slept in his clothes on the couch. Only a soft hissing came from the speakers as he lay awake watching the first uncertain light of a Monday dawn graying his windows.

He was a failure. He didn't know what had gone wrong, or when, but he no longer had control over his life. A failed marriage, now a failed relationship with Gretchen (she had not returned from Berlin), a dying father, a stagnating murder investigation. And Leila Kahled, for whom his feelings were confused.

For a moment at the hospital her eyes had become transparent to her soul. She was human, after all. She hurt, she was alone. They were kindred spirits in some eerie way.

Roemer's head was splitting. He lit a cigarette, the smoke burning his throat. It had been a nightmare moving his father from the hospital back to the Interlaken house. He'd driven through the night, fearful of being followed, but even more fearful that his father would die in the car.

Max Rilke, his father's sergeant, himself in his early seventies, had readied the master bedroom, and with his wife's help they had managed to give the old man at least a modicum of comfort. A discreet private nurse would be hired, and a dialysis machine would be secretly purchased.

"They will find out about this place sooner or later," Roemer told them.

"He should never have been moved to the hospital," the tough old sergeant said. "But the bastards will never get him. Not alive."

Roemer had driven up to Munich that morning. He was in need of company, any company, but his ex-wife, Kata, had not been at home. He had considered going up to Berlin to confront Gretchen and her new lover. In the end he drove back to Bonn, where he lay on the couch listening to music and getting stinking drunk.

He stubbed out his cigarette, pushed himself off the couch and stood for an unsteady moment until the room stopped moving.

He put water on for coffee, then took a shower, shaved and dressed.

This morning he would present his evidence to Colonel Legler. Then either he would be pulled off the case (which he hoped) or Legler would give him the go-ahead.

Legler was a political animal, but he had been one of the clean Germans, his past untainted by the Nazis, so he would not be afraid of making waves. He had the clout to deal with Whalpol as well, or at least to insulate Roemer from the BND long enough for him to complete his investigation.

The telephone rang. It was Manning. "Roemer? You'd better get over here, we have another murder."

The cobwebs cleared. "Where are you?"

Manning gave him an address in Putzchen, which was

on this side of the river and very near. "There is a connection between this one and the other."

"I'll be there in a few minutes."

Manning couldn't know about Whalpol, so what connection was he talking about?

32

THE WIND had died and it wasn't as cold as it had been over the past couple of days, though the sky was overcast and it would probably snow again soon. What traffic there was flowed the opposite way, into the city, people on their way to work, and within five minutes Roemer pulled up in front of the ten-story apartment building. There were a lot of police cars, the Criminal Investigation van, the coroner's car and hearse, as well as a crowd of newspeople.

Flashing his badge, Roemer crossed the police lines and entered the building. He took the elevator up to the tenth floor. Manning, his tie loose, hair mussed, a cigarette dangling from his mouth, left the evidence tray and came to the doorway. He looked mean.

Beyond him a body was laid out on the floor beneath a sheet. Blood spread around it on the carpet.

"You said you would have something for me on Friday," Manning grumbled. "It's Monday and we've got another murder."

"Who?"

"Joan Waldmann. An investigative reporter with Television One. She was working on a KwU story."

"How do you know that?"

"Notebook in her purse. It's all there." Manning

looked at the body. "Same as before. Crushed her skull. Fucking pervert."

"Let me have a look and then we'll talk."

"You're goddamned right we're going to talk. You may be a federal investigator, but this is my city." Manning stepped aside.

"I'll want to see the notebook."

Manning nodded. "Let's call it a trade."

Roemer thought about the file Whalpol had pulled from behind the *Schrank* in Sarah Razmarah's apartment, about the bloody footprints and about Pavli's diary. He also thought about Leila. "All right," he said.

As at the last murder scene, Manning's people were prowling the apartment. There was an almost casual disregard for the body beneath the sheet, except that the coroner, Dr. Sternig, and the forensics man, Stanos Lotz, were in discussion over it.

"Good morning, Investigator," Sternig said.

"What can you tell me?"

"She died sometime last night. Possibly as long as eight hours ago. The same as Sarah Razmarah." Sternig knelt and gently eased back the sheet.

Roemer took a deep breath. The young woman's face was destroyed, as Sarah's had been. "Was she raped?"

"I think so. I'll let you know later this morning as soon as we do an autopsy."

"Not very pretty," Stanos Lotz said.

"No."

Lotz looked down at the body. "Did you notice the other similarity, Roemer? Curious, isn't it? Both women were young, attractive, dark-haired."

Sternig reached down and gently lifted an eyelid. "Black eyes," he said softly.

Roemer had his suspect. It all pointed to Major Whalpol.

But pretty dark-haired young women with black eyes? Was it an Arab, after all? Some Islamic fundamentalist who believed women should cover their faces and obey the ancient social rules?

"I made the connection right off," Lotz said. "But I didn't tell anyone."

"Don't. I'll talk to Manning."

Sternig was troubled. "Investigator, if you're implying what I think you are, we have a homicidal maniac on our hands. In that case we have a certain responsibility."

"Our responsibility is catching this killer. I'll tell you what, telephone Chief Prosecutor Schaller. Do you know him?"

"Of course."

"Talk it over with him before you do anything."

Roemer went out to Manning in the corridor.

"Not a pretty picture, is she?" Manning said.

"Sternig thinks she was raped."

"I know." He looked into Roemer's eyes. "I tried to get you over the weekend. There was no answer. Where'd you go?"

"Out of town."

"Anything to do with this?"

"No."

Manning was quietly simmering. "I waited for your call Friday."

"It would not have prevented this."

"Are you sure?"

Roemer wasn't. Especially not now. "You mentioned a notebook."

"In her purse," Manning said. "She knew or suspected that KwU was selling a nuclear reactor somewhere outside the country."

"Is that all? Had she any idea who was getting the reactor?"

"Not that her notes showed," Manning said. "But you and I know."

"Who did she talk to at KwU?"

"No one important. But she did put at least half the story together."

"You think the Iraqis killed her to keep her quiet?"

"Goddamned right."

"What about Sarah Razmarah? Why would they want to stop her?"

"Come off it, Roemer, you saw the impression in her palm."

"Which means nothing if the killer wanted to throw off the investigation."

A new look came into Manning's eyes. "What have you got, Investigator? What little secrets? It's time for our trade now."

Roemer glanced into the apartment. No one was paying them any attention. "I was recruited on Sarah Razmarah's murder by Chief Prosecutor Schaller . . . at the request of the BND."

"Why . . . good Christ, she was a spy!"

"For us."

"So the Iraqis killed her."

"Sarah Razmarah was a good spy, but she had a big heart. She fell in love with her target."

"Ahmed Pavli, the Iraqi who killed himself."

"None other."

"And Leila Kahled, the Iraqi cop. Is she a spy too?"

Roemer nodded.

Manning pondered a moment. "If Sarah Razmarah's spying on the Iraqis went sour because she'd fallen in love, there'd be no reason for the Arabs to kill her."

"Something like that."

"But whoever killed her wanted it to appear as if an Arab had done it."

"That's right."

"But it was probably the same one who killed Joan Waldmann last night. The connection is still the KwU."

Roemer remained silent, letting the KP lieutenant finish his theory.

"If it wasn't an Iraqi, who then? The only other party with a vested interest is . . . the BND." Manning took a deep breath.

From the elevator two morgue attendants emerged pushing a trolley stretcher. Manning and Roemer stepped aside to let them into the apartment.

Manning lowered his voice. "Christ, Roemer."

"It's my intention to turn this over to my chief this morning. He can bounce it back down to Pullach."

"Bullshit. They won't let either of us off the hook and you know it. Who was it from the BND who recruited you?"

"Don't get yourself involved, Manning. You're a good cop. Find the killer through normal channels."

Something else dawned on Manning. "The *Schrank* in Sarah Razmarah's bedroom had been pushed away from the wall. She'd hidden something back there. Notes. Whoever killed her knew where they were hidden. The other man who visited her often. Not Pavli, the tall, thin man. Her BND control officer. And you know who he is."

Roemer turned away.

"Goddammit, Roemer, who is he? Arrest the bastard!"

He had tried, but Schaller had laughed in his face. And rightly so. There wasn't enough hard evidence. He was kidding himself by believing he could go up against the BND.

"It's more complicated than that," Roemer said softly.

"We could work together, Roemer. We could nail this bastard."

"It's possible I'm wrong."

"Don't bullshit me, Investigator."

The ambulance attendants loaded Joan Waldmann's covered body on the cart and went to the elevator, Sternig and Lotz right behind them.

Roemer looked at Manning. "We'll need to search his house, put a tap on his telephone and place him under round-the-clock surveillance. All without the Chief Prosecutor knowing about it, which means we'll have to go through our usual routines as well. Nothing out of the ordinary."

Manning was finally smiling.

33

LEILA KAHLED came down to breakfast at seven-thirty, after a difficult night. Her father and his chief of staff, Lieutenant Colonel Habash, were already at the table deep in discussion.

Habash jumped up. "Good morning, Leila."

"Morning," she mumbled. She went around to her father and kissed him on the cheek. He looked worn out. His color was bad.

"Good morning, kitten," he said.

"Did you sleep well, Father?"

He shook his head as she took her place across the table from him. "It was a tiring weekend. And dinner last night with that fool Schaller didn't help."

"We were just discussing it," Habash said, his piggish eyes on Leila.

"Just coffee," she told the maid.

The maid poured the coffee and left.

"Is there anything to what the man says?" the general asked. He was a tall man with a heavily lined face, fierce glistening black eyes and thick black hair.

"I don't know," Leila said. "But I think Roemer is sincere."

"You know this investigator?" Habash asked sharply.

"He was at Pavli's apartment. It was in my report."

Habash looked at the general. The breakfast room was chilly. Leila lit a cigarette. It tasted horrible.

"I stopped by to see the young man's parents in Baghdad," the general said softly. "They are good people. I felt sorrow for them." He sighed. "I don't know where it all leads, you see. It is very confusing. Two years ago when this all came up I argued against it. But that bunch with Hussein on the Revolutionary Command Council wouldn't listen. We cannot deal with the Germans, I told them. Not so soon. But they are blind. They have nuclear stars in their eyes."

"To me it sounds plausible," Habash said. "And I think it was decent of Chief Prosecutor Schaller to warn us."

"Nonsense," the general snapped. "We know that the BND did not kill that girl." He turned to his daughter. "It was Pavli. He killed her and then committed suicide."

Leila remembered how Pavli had sounded and looked. "I don't think so."

The general leaned forward. "I do." He shook his finger sternly. "If it is proved that an Iraqi killed a woman, the entire project will be jeopardized. Iraq will be made to suffer once again."

Her father's face was flushed. Leila was frightened for him, what this assignment was doing to him. Like so many other PLO soldiers, he had lost much at the hands of Westerners. His parents, two brothers and three sisters had been killed in raids on their squatter camps. His survival of the nightmare was something he seldom talked about.

"You say you have met this chief investigator . . . on more than one occasion?" Habash asked.

Leila looked at him. He was cunning. She had not wanted this to come up, but when Roemer's name had been mentioned last night, it had become inevitable. Her father, she feared, would take this badly.

"I went to his apartment."

"You what?" her father asked, his eyes narrowing.

"He took something from Pavli's apartment. A diary."

"Allah in heaven," the general said. "He knows about you, then."

Leila nodded.

"I'll speak with Schaller again. This morning. This is impossible."

"The diary is not important, I think," Habash interjected. "It's Roemer we must worry about. He is a Nazi. Germany for Germans. I telephoned an acquaintance last night in Vienna who worked for Simon Wiesenthal."

Leila was torn by something she had seen in Roemer's eyes. There was danger everywhere.

"Our chief investigator's father was Lotti Roemer," Habash said.

The general shrugged. "So?"

"SS Major Roemer," Habash said. "The Butcher of Dachau."

The general turned to his daughter. "What does this mean?"

"They have control over him. The fact that his father is still alive is supposed to be secret. They're going to use him against us."

"Probably to extort even more money from us," Habash said.

"Hussein will never agree to it."

"He may have no choice, General," Habash said. "It's possible the Germans staged this murder and will use Roemer to blame us." Habash turned his gaze to Leila. "You were gone Friday night. Where did you go?"

Leila flared. "My movements have never been, nor shall they ever be, any of your concern, Colonel!"

"Leila," her father warned.

"I'm sorry, Father, but this is a Mukhabarat operation. We are no longer in the Dark Ages."

"I am chief of this mission," the general retorted. "Need I remind you?"

"My guess is that she went to Switzerland," Habash said.

"Switzerland?"

"I suspect that she followed the chief investigator," Habash went on. "Perhaps Pavli's diary is important after all. There could be things in it that would be injurious to Iraq."

"But why Switzerland?"

"There is a sanatorium outside of Bern," Leila said in a small voice.

"You actually saw him?" Habash asked, his eyes bright.

"No. But he was there. I confronted the investigator."

"I expect he moved his father someplace else."

"Did you follow him?"

"No, I came back here."

"Did you report this to Colonel Mikadi in Baghdad?"

Leila lowered her eyes. "Not yet. Roemer's father is dying. He has only a few weeks to live."

"All the more reason for us to hurry," Habash said. "He must be killed before the Germans make use of him."

"Leila will find him," the general said.

"There is more to it, General," Habash said. "My contact in Vienna told me that Major Roemer smuggled gold into Switzerland." He looked directly into Leila's eyes. "We could use it to pay the Germans. It would be fitting."

Leila shuddered. After her confrontation with Roemer, she'd driven back to Bonn hurt and confused. She felt like a traitor.

"You are detached from project security as of this moment," her father said. "You will spend your time now finding out where Roemer has hidden his father."

She knew what was coming. "I won't be able to get close to him. He knows what I am after."

"You will have some help," Habash said smoothly.

"What are you talking about?"

"Dr. Azziza is on his way to Geneva at this moment."

Even the general was surprised, but he grunted his approval. "Azziza is a hard man, but very good."

"The best."

"He is a killer," Leila snapped. Khodr Azziza was probably the most cold-blooded man in Saddam Hussein's Presidential Guardians. He was the last resort for dealing with the enemies of the state, expert at what he did. Leila had met him several years before at Mukhabarat headquarters in Baghdad. He had the eyes of a panther: totally devoid of human warmth. If Azziza was on his way to Switzerland, Roemer's father was a dead man.

"Yes, he is a killer," Habash was saying.

"Between the two of you I expect results," the general said.

"If I refuse, Father?"

The general's eyes widened. He pushed his coffee cup aside and got slowly to his feet. His nostrils flared, his face flushed. "Do you know what you're saying to me?"

"Dr. Azziza will find him," Leila said.

"Have you any idea what we could lose at his hands?"

Leila could feel tears welling up. "I'll do it, Father."

Habash was smug. She knew he had engineered this confrontation to make points for himself. "I'll find him," she said. She left the breakfast table.

Upstairs in her bathroom, she looked at her red-rimmed eyes in the mirror and splashed cold water on her flushed cheeks. Her heart was racing. Something would have to be done about her father. The bastard Habash had maneuvered him into this, had practically turned her father against her.

34

THE EMBASSY of Iraq in Bonn–Bad Godesberg was in a baroque three-story residence that had once belonged to a wealthy shipbuilder's wife. The green copper roof was gabled, and iron-railed mock balconies fronted each of the second- and third-story windows. Some embassies had moved to Berlin, but the majority of countries still maintained the foreign missions in the old capital.

Leila's office was at the rear of the second floor. But she preferred spending most of her time either at the KwU facility, where she could keep an eye on things, or visiting with team members off-duty—a task she had neglected for the past few days since Sarah Razmarah had been killed.

It was early when she let herself into her Spartan office. Even before she took off her coat, she picked up the telephone, dialed the communications center in the basement and asked for a secure line to Mukhabarat Headquarters in Baghdad.

While she waited for her call to go through, she phoned upstairs to Bassam abu Zwaiter's office. Zwaiter was the embassy's cultural affairs officer. In actuality he was Bonn Station chief for the Mukhabarat. His secretary agreed to have him stop down when he came in.

Her Baghdad call came through ten minutes later.

"Uncle Bashir," she said. The connection wasn't very good, made only slightly better by the encryption. It was just eleven in the morning there.

"Leila. We're becoming very concerned. What's going on out there?"

"It's Father. I want him pulled home. Talk to the president. We must do something before it kills him."

"We need him there, at least until these murders are cleared up," Bashir Kahair said.

"Murders?"

"Yes, Leila. Don't you know? There has been another killing there in Bonn. Last night. It was on my wire this morning. A German television reporter who was working on a KwU story. It must have been on your overnight Interpol wire."

She hadn't bothered to look this morning.

"She must have talked with people at the facility," Uncle Bashir said. "Didn't you hear anything?"

She had, but she had dismissed it. "She didn't talk with any of our people, Uncle Bashir. I didn't think she was important."

"Someone certainly did. Not more than an hour ago we received a call from Helmut Kohl himself, worried that this could have a devastating effect on our project."

Leila sat forward, pressing the telephone to her ear. "Uncle Bashir, there are more complications."

She quickly explained what Chief Prosecutor Schaller had told her father last night at dinner, that Roemer was making noises about the BND being behind the murder of Sarah Razmarah. The German government didn't believe it, of course.

"Impossible!" Kahair exploded. "They would not jeopardize this project any more than we would. I'm sure it was Ahmed Pavli. You were right when you called for his removal."

"But not now, with a second murder."

"They may not be connected," Kahair said. "In any event it is not the BND. I know that for a fact, Leila."

Leila closed her eyes. She understood why Roemer had been picked for the investigation. Habash was correct. "It's even more complicated than that," she said. "Dr. Azziza is on his way to Geneva. The German investigator working on the American girl's murder is the son of Lotti Roemer, the Butcher of Dachau. He's still alive in Switzerland."

There was a long silence on the line.

"My father has taken me off my security duties. He wants me to find Roemer's father and turn Dr. Azziza after him. Uncle Bashir?"

"What are you not telling me, Leila? What is it you are holding back?"

Leila's heart sank. "I followed Roemer to Switzerland over the weekend, to a hospital outside Bern where his father is dying."

"And you did nothing about it, Leila? You made no report? Why didn't you call me? You know what the Germans might make of this."

"I don't know," she said softly.

"For once I agree with Habash. I want you to go after Lotti Roemer. His son could be Iraq's most dangerous enemy."

35

THE INVESTIGATION of the two murders was ostensibly proceeding on course along two different routes: Manning's for the City of Bonn, and Roemer's for the BKA at Chief Prosecutor Schaller's behest. Lab reports were being generated in a blizzard of paperwork, a second autopsy was being performed, and Rudi Gehrman continued to watch the comings and goings of the Iraqis through passport control.

Unofficially, however, Manning had arranged to place taps on the telephones in Whalpol's Bad Godesberg house. It would be up to Roemer to lure the BND major from Munich back to Bonn.

In the meantime, Roemer wanted to make one final check before he faced Colonel Legler with his perfidy.

The German National Television Network's Bonn studio was downtown in an ultramodern stainless-steel-and-glass building.

Kurt Bruckner's secretary had been crying. "Herr Bruckner, he is here," she said into the intercom.

The door opened and the station manager, his jacket off, his tie loose, beckoned Roemer. "Please come in."

Along one wall of the large office was a bank of television monitors and other electronic equipment.

"This has been a very difficult morning for us, as I am

sure you can understand, Herr Roemer. The police were here not more than ten minutes ago."

"There's just one question I'd like to ask you, Herr Bruckner. Did Fräulein Waldmann ever mention the name of Ludwig Whalpol in connection with her story?"

Bruckner couldn't hide his knowledge. The mention of Whalpol's name had an almost physical impact on him.

"I see," Roemer said. "I must know if they actually met face to face."

"I think I should call my attorney."

"You are not under investigation," Roemer said sharply.

"Still, I think it's best."

Roemer looked around the office. "He was here, wasn't he?" he said, taking a stab in the dark.

Bruckner reacted as if he had been shot.

"When?" Roemer demanded.

"Gott in Himmel, what is going on? He was here, all right. Last night. Late. She'd made a tape to be aired this morning. Major Whalpol showed up and insisted that we hold off."

Schaller had lied about Whalpol's being in Munich. Why?

"Joan was upset. She stormed out of here and went home."

"I would like to see that tape, and any notes she may have made on her story."

"Major Whalpol took them. He took everything."

"I see. Herr Bruckner," Roemer said gruffly, "keep your newspeople off this story. When it is over I personally will give you an exclusive."

"Just find Joan's killer, Investigator."

"You can count on it."

36

RUDI GEHRMAN carried a bundle of computer printouts into Roemer's office. "The colonel has been asking for you."

"What have you got?"

"Passport control." Gehrman handed him the printouts. "There has been a lot of coming and going."

Roemer spread the sheets out on his desk.

"This covers only the commercial carriers, unfortunately," Gehrman was saying. "If they crossed our border by car we have no way of knowing."

Roemer scanned the arrivals and departures on the dates just before and after Sarah Razmarah's murder. A lot of traveling had been done by Leila Kahled's father, the general, as well as his chief of staff and other high-ranking members of the team.

Roemer shook his head. "It was worth a try." He was simply going through the motions now. The killer was almost certainly Whalpol. It would only be a matter of time before the man made a mistake, and he and Manning would nail him.

"What about your friend, Major Whalpol?" Gehrman asked, lowering his voice.

"Rudi, forget about Whalpol. Forget what I said to you, forget that you ever pulled his national security file. Erase it from your mind, and no matter who asks about it, deny everything."

Gehrman's eyes narrowed. "What's going on, Walther?"

"Stay out of it."

"I'm a big boy—"

"Stay out of it, Rudi, goddammit!"

Gehrman stepped back. "All right, old friend. All right." He went to the door. "You listen to me, Walther. Don't get yourself in trouble over this. They play very rough down in Pullach."

"Right."

"I mean it. They know more about you than you do about them. About your past."

37

COLONEL HANS LEGLER, the BKA's Chief District Investigator for the region, was an old army man, a brilliant administrator, and had risen spectacularly within the German Criminal Investigation system. He was a tall man, strong, with steel-gray hair, dark blue eyes and an erect, Prussian bearing.

Roemer presented himself, coming to attention and saluting. Bonn was the only BKA district in which such military formalities were required.

"At ease, Walther. Have a seat."

"Sorry I missed you on Friday, sir."

"No matter; in fact I was having dinner with Ernst Schaller. We spoke about you and this KwU business."

"Yes, sir."

The colonel hunched forward. "Afterwards we spoke with Helmut Kohl, who wants a resolution in short order."

"I understand."

Legler studied Roemer, as if coming to a decision. "Ernst and I go way back together, Walther. We are the best of friends. We talk frequently."

Roemer held his silence.

"No one is above the law. But in gathering information, one must take care not to damage the fabric of our society. Do not become a zealot. In the collective German spirit, we are past all of that now."

"Yes, sir." Roemer could just imagine what Schaller had told Legler.

"Do you understand? Perfectly?"

"Perfectly."

"Then there will be no need to have this sort of conversation again."

"No, sir."

Legler nodded. "Very well, then. Is there anything I should know about your investigation at this point? Anything I can help you with?"

"Not yet. But I expect to have a break in the case very soon."

"Do you know who killed the young woman?"

"I have a suspect."

"Do you have the evidence to satisfy the Chief District Prosecutor?"

"Not yet."

"I suggest you get to it."

"Yes, sir," Roemer said.

"There was another murder last night. A television personality."

"Yes."

"I understand you were at the scene this morning."

Roemer nodded.

"Do you believe there is a connection between the two?"

"It is very likely both women were killed by the same person."

Legler sighed and turned in his chair to look out the window at the Chancellor's ornate residence. But he didn't say anything more, and after a second or two, Roemer let himself out.

38

JOAN WALDMANN'S body lay on the autopsy table. Dr. Sternig was there with Stanos Lotz. A strong overhead light illuminated the body, which had been cut open from sternum to pubic bone. Dr. Sternig spoke into an overhead microphone as he worked.

Roemer stood just within the doorway. He had no desire to come nearer. The place stank of formaldehyde.

Stanos Lotz looked up. "I expected you to be along sooner or later, Roemer."

"What have you got for me?"

Dr. Sternig reached up and covered the microphone with his hand. "She was raped, just as we suspected."

Roemer waited.

"From the sperm samples, which show the man had O positive blood, I'd say that whoever did this may have also killed and raped Sharazad Razmarah."

Lotz pushed his glasses back up on his nose with the back of his hand. "Ahmed Pavli was blessed with A negative blood, if that's any help."

Whalpol had the motive in each case. The worn heel of his shoe matched the bloody footprints at Sarah Razmarah's apartment. And now the blood type. Whalpol's was O positive.

"Was she pregnant?"

"No," Dr. Sternig said.

"Good," Roemer replied. Sarah Razmarah's pregnancy by Ahmed Pavli was just a coincidence. "Thanks."

39

ROEMER SPENT the remainder of the morning pulling together the files on Sarah Razmarah, Major Whalpol and Joan Waldmann. He wrote a brief synopsis of what he'd done to date, including his initial conversation with Schaller and Whalpol.

Lieutenant Manning telephoned for lunch, and they met at a small, crowded *Bierstube* around the corner from the town hall.

Roemer passed on the autopsy information.

"Both O positive from the sperm samples," Manning said, drinking his beer. "So what? We knew it was the same killer."

"Whalpol's is O positive. He was at the television station last night."

"Christ."

Quickly Roemer told him what he had learned from Bruckner, the station manager.

Manning thumped his beer glass down on the table. "The bastard followed her home and killed her. Just like that."

"What about the phone tap?" Roemer asked.

"Tonight. My people will be over there around midnight. Will you be there?"

"I wouldn't miss it for the world."

40

TWO FINAL nagging doubts lingered at the back of Roemer's mind. The first was Stanos Lotz's observation at Joan Waldmann's apartment this morning. Both women had been young, dark, pretty and black-eyed.

The second was that the evidence was circumstantial, and had come too easily. Whatever demons lived inside Whalpol's head, he was a highly trained German Secret Service operative. Would he have made such obvious mistakes? Could it be put down simply to arrogance, and insanity?

Roemer drove back to his apartment in the Oberkassel in time to bump into Gretchen. The apartment door stood wide open. She had a load of clothes on hangers in her arms, and was evidently on her way down to her car.

"Moving out?" Roemer didn't think he cared. The business with his father and Leila Kahled had him off balance.

"Yes," Gretchen said defiantly.

"Can't we talk about it?"

"I've tried, Walther. But you're so pigheaded . . . so goddamned . . ."

"German?"

"*Verdammt.* What are you doing at home at this hour anyway?"

"I thought I'd get some sleep. It's been a long weekend."

"Well, why don't you come back later?"

Roemer glanced toward the open apartment door, suddenly understanding that she had brought along Kai Bauer, her new lover, to help her move out.

"Don't start a scene," Gretchen said.

He went into the apartment. Things lay in disarray everywhere. The furniture had been shoved aside and the carpeting, which belonged to Gretchen, had been rolled up ready to go.

"We were coming back this afternoon to straighten the place out, Walther. We wouldn't leave it like this for you."

Roemer went to the bedroom door in time to see Kai Bauer, a trim man with thick blond hair, look up from Roemer's family photo album.

"*Scheiss,*" the man said.

Roemer was across the room in three long strides, and he hit the man in the jaw, sending him crashing against the wall.

"You bastard!" Gretchen screamed in the doorway.

"I'll be back in a few hours. See that this place is clean."

41

THE GOVERNMENT of Iraq had established liaisons with the government of Germany on many levels. Through trade agreements, exchange students, technical services and Interpol, information was passed back and forth between Bonn and Baghdad, with a stop at the Iraqi Embassy. And it was with these records that Leila began her investigation of Walther Roemer, searching for his flaw, the weakness that could be exploited to find his father.

She spent the morning with the records in the basement of the embassy.

She learned that Roemer's salary was something over forty thousand marks per year, around twenty-seven thousand U.S. dollars. Old newspaper clippings showed that in college at Westphalia he had been an outstanding soccer player. He had been married (no children), and his former wife, Kata Zimmer, lived in Munich. And twice in the past two years he had turned down promotions that would have involved substantial raises but would have stuck him behind a desk. Roemer was definitely a man of action. A field man.

Roemer knew Iraqi homicide detective Jacob Wadud. They had worked together on two different occasions: the first when Wadud had come to Germany chasing a man and a woman suspected of strangling an eighty-year-old woman in Diyala, and the second when a German gang smuggling hashish to Iraq had had a falling-out and killed one another on the docks in Bremerhaven.

It was likely that Roemer and Wadud had spent more time together one year ago, in Paris, during an Interpol-sponsored gathering of police detectives from three dozen countries.

In her office, she directed the embassy operator to place a call to Wadud in Baghdad.

While she was waiting, the embassy Mukhabarat station chief, Bassam abu Zwaiter, came in. He was a short, intense little man, brilliant and easygoing. He and Leila got along well.

"Sounds as if you have your hands full," he said, perching on the seat above the radiator by the window.

"Did you talk to Uncle Bashir?"

Zwaiter nodded. "Is it true that Lotti Roemer is still alive somewhere in Switzerland?"

"Apparently."

"But you'd just as soon not get yourself involved with Dr. Azziza," Zwaiter said.

"I don't have a choice, Bassam. But what about Joan Waldmann?"

"It was on the morning wire. I guess your friend Walther Roemer was there at the scene."

Leila sighed. Uncle Bashir had evidently told him the entire story. But it rankled. Everyone knew her business. "He's not a friend. But I'm going to have to use him in order to get to his father."

"And that bothers you as well?"

"Yes it does."

The telephone rang. Jacob Wadud was on the line from Baghdad. "What can I do for you, Ilehnisa Kahled?" The detective's voice was raspy.

"I understand you know a German homicide investigator in Bonn. Walther Roemer."

"A good man. We've worked on a couple of cases. And last year, just to show there were no hard feelings over the Gulf War, we spent a week raising hell in Paris."

"He's an infidel," Leila said sharply.

"I'm sorry, Ilehnisa Kahled, I wasn't aware that you had those feelings about nonbelievers. Is there something I can tell you about Roemer?"

"I'm trying to find his father."

"For what reason?"

"The man is wanted by the German government for war crimes."

"Do you think Walther is a Nazi?" Wadud laughed. "What do you want with his father?"

"Investigator Roemer and I are working on a delicate case. It's my belief that his government will use its knowledge of his father to . . . influence what he shares with us."

"So you're looking for the old man. What will you do when you find him? Bring him here out of harm's way?"

"It's possible," she lied.

"What would you do, Ilehnisa Kahled, if it were your father?"

Leila started to answer, but Wadud went on.

"I'll be happy to supply information. But you're going to have to go through channels. Happy hunting, and I sincerely mean it." Wadud hung up.

For a long moment Leila held the telephone to her ear. Wadud's attitude was curious. Her father would have him fired if he became aware of it.

"Jacob Wadud is a good man, Leila," Zwaiter said. "I hope you don't intend to make trouble for him."

"I'm not going to make trouble for him." Leila felt terrible. "He said Walther Roemer was a peach of a fellow."

Zwaiter smiled. He looked out the window. The air was cold and clear. "It's only been a few years, and yet here we are on the outside again. A lot of Westerners still think we're trying to blow up the world."

"What are we doing here, Bassam? Where's the rationale?"

"Someone has to hold the Zionists in check." He shrugged. "And the president is on a *jihad.* All we can do is follow him." He got to his feet. "What do I need to know about this KwU business?"

"The Germans are paranoid. Major Whalpol is running the show for the BND. He's a tough one, but when this is over I'm going home. I've had it here."

"What about your father?"

He has Colonel Habash, she wanted to say. "He'll be all right, Bassam, better off with me out of his hair."

Zwaiter went to the door. "If you need any help, Leila, or perhaps just a shoulder to lean on, give me a call."

"I might just take you up on it."

Leila was glad to be rid of the project, and yet another part of her balked at walking away from something not finished. She'd never done that before.

She returned to the problem of Walther Roemer and his father. After their confrontation, two burly sanatorium aides had escorted her out to her car. They had followed her for twenty miles.

She should have returned. There was a great probability that Roemer had been moving his father out that very night. They would have been vulnerable. It would have been relatively simple to kidnap the old man, whisk him out of the country and get him back to Baghdad out of the German government's reach.

But she had not. There had been something in Roemer's eyes, in the anguish in his voice, that had stayed her.

42

IT WAS after four in the afternoon when she placed a call to the Simon Wiesenthal Institute in Vienna.

"We're very excited here, Fräulein Kahled, about Lotti Roemer and the possibility of his arrest," a young man told her. "There has been a lot of uncertainty about your interest in helping us, but we're grateful."

"What about his wife and children?"

"Unimportant," the aide replied. "His wife died some years after the war. There was a son, Walther, who is, as a matter of fact, a German federal investigator right there in Bonn."

"I know," Leila said. "The son was never followed? Never watched?"

"For a time, naturally. But the son had suffered the most from his father."

It sounded slipshod to Leila, knowing what she knew now. Roemer had apparently been aware of his father's whereabouts all along. But then not every relative of every Nazi whom the Wiesenthal people were hunting could be watched twenty-four hours a day. It was simply impossible. Choices were made. Some of them wrong.

She could hear the shuffling of papers at the other end. Then the aide was back on the line.

"As a matter of fact, from what I'm reading, the son is a friend of Iraq. He has cooperated on a number of occasions with Detective Jacob Wadud. Perhaps if you telephoned him. But I'm curious, Fräulein Kahled. Do you suspect there is a connection now between the father and son?"

"I don't know," Leila said and wondered why she lied. "I'm exploring all possibilities here."

"I see," the aide said. "Well, we are wishing you the very best. There are a lot of people who would like to see the man put on trial finally."

"I'll keep you informed."

"Please do."

Without dwelling on what she had learned so far (she was somewhat fearful of the directions her thoughts were already taking her), she gave the embassy operator Kata Zimmer's name and asked that a number be found and a call put through. It took the embassy operator nearly a half hour to find the woman in Munich, where she worked as a classifications aide at the Bavarian National Museum. Leila had given a lot of thought to the way she would approach Roemer's ex-wife.

When the woman came on the line, Leila turned away from the phone. "I have her on the line now," she said as if she were talking to someone else. Then, "Frau Zimmer?"

"Yes?"

"I'm so sorry to bother you, but we are trying to locate Investigator Roemer. He left the city over the weekend and has not returned."

"Who is this?" Kata Zimmer demanded.

"I am sorry, this is his office calling. Bonn."

"Why have you called me? I have no idea where he might be. Try his girlfriend, Gretchen Krause. She may be at work, at the Federal Parliament. I believe she is a translator."

"Thank you, Frau Zimmer. Apparently Investigator Roemer is out of the country. You would not know where he would be?"

"No," Kata Zimmer said curtly, and hung up.

The operator had Gretchen Krause on the line within two minutes.

"Fräulein Krause, this is Investigator Roemer's office calling."

"What do you want?" Gretchen snapped.

"We are trying to locate him. Apparently he's gone out of town."

"He's here in Bonn, all right. I just saw the bastard."

"Fräulein?"

"I've moved out, you hear? We'll probably file assault charges. The sonofabitch is never home. He's never there when you want him. He's off chasing some murder mystery somewhere or he's running off to Bern."

"We understand he was in Bern over the weekend. Could you possibly give us a name there where we could reach him?"

"There or Interlaken . . ." Gretchen said, but she cut herself off. "Who is this?"

"His office."

"Let me talk to Rudi."

Rudi who? Leila wondered. "I am sorry, Fräulein Krause, but Rudi is not here at the moment."

"Who are you?"

"Perhaps we could meet . . ." The line went dead.

Interlaken. Another sanatorium, perhaps?

It was late when Leila finally left the embassy. She drove across the river to the house she and her father occupied, but at the last moment, before entering through the gate, she turned around and went back to the Oberkassel.

Roemer's car was parked in front of his apartment building. She parked behind it, shut off the headlights and lit a cigarette.

For half an hour she sat there, smoking, listening to the radio and staring up at his apartment, all the while wondering just what she was doing here. Her opinion of him had undergone a curious change, one over which she had no control.

What would she say to him if she went up? *You're all right, but I want your father so that you can be insulated.*

Finally she turned on the headlights and drove off. The confrontation between them would come, but not just yet. In the meantime, at the back of her mind was the thought of Dr. Azziza lying in wait in Switzerland. What in the name of Allah could she do?

43

ROEMER SPENT a restless evening alone in his nearly bare apartment, made more unsettling by Leila Kahled's appearance on the street below. He had watched her car for twenty minutes, until she pulled away. She was the most dangerous person in Germany to his father's safety.

Manning telephoned near midnight to say that he and his team were on their way out to Whalpol's house in Bad Godesberg. They agreed to meet behind the ornate town hall before moving in.

Before he left, Roemer checked his gun to make sure that the ejector slide moved freely. Whalpol was a dangerous man.

Traffic was light as Roemer drove down from the Oberkassel, crossed the river on the Konrad Adenauer Bridge and worked his way back up to the Bad Godesberg town hall. Manning's Cortina was parked behind a black windowless van in a rear courtyard where town hall officials normally parked during the day.

Roemer pulled up behind the Cortina and doused his lights. Manning and another man got out of the car and came back just as Roemer was climbing out. He recognized the second man as Sergeant Jacobs, Manning's pinched-faced assistant.

They all shook hands.

"We can pick up his line from the junction box," Manning said. "There's one in a tunnel a half-block away."

"How many in the van?" Roemer asked Manning.

"I drew a couple of techies from Division. Mundt and Achmann. I want to keep this to a minimum."

"We're going to have to move fast. If he goes to ground before we get anything concrete, we'll never stop him."

"We're going to get the bastard, no doubt of it."

"But I want to know why he killed those women. I want to know what he thought he could accomplish."

"The bastard is crazy," Manning said.

"Probably." But Roemer wondered. Whalpol seemed ruthless, cynical, but not unbalanced.

"It will take my people fifteen minutes to identify Whalpol's line and place the tap," Manning said. "They'll rig a small, narrow-beam transmitter that will bring the signals back to the van."

"Good," Roemer said. "Sergeant Jacobs can stay with the van once they're set, while you and I go over to the house for a quick look. Let's go."

They drove the half dozen blocks to the telephone junction box, located in a tunnel beneath a manhole cover in the sidewalk just off the Hinterholerstrasse. Whalpol's house was around the corner, out of sight.

Sergeant Jacobs and the two technicians from the van hurried across the street, pried open the manhole cover and disappeared into the tunnel.

Manning offered Roemer a cigarette and then lit one for himself. "All this is for money, isn't it?" the KP lieutenant said.

"It would appear so." Roemer hunched up his coat collar against the chill. The residential street was very quiet.

Manning's face was pale in the light from the street lamp at the corner. "What if Whalpol isn't working alone? Have you considered that?"

"He has his own people. He answers to Pullach."

"But what happens if the killings were part of a government operation? A cover-up to make sure their little project out at KwU remains safe?"

The thought had crossed Roemer's mind. "I don't know, Manning, I simply don't know."

Manning looked away. "Do you ever get the feeling that we're in the wrong business?"

We're a nation of laws, Colonel Legler had said. But the legacy of fifty years ago was still too close to the surface, with the recent anti-foreigner riots, and it was frightening that something similar could be starting again.

"No," Roemer answered.

"Why don't you just call Pullach? Talk to the head of the BND? Make him see?"

"Without proof it would be worse than useless, Manning."

Sergeant Jacobs crawled up out of the tunnel and came across the street. His eyes sparkled. "We've got his line. He's definitely home, talking on the phone right now."

"With whom?" Manning asked.

"Don't know yet. But it sounded as if he's mounting a surveillance operation. Mundt is monitoring it, but we won't have the recorders set for another few minutes."

They followed Jacobs back to the manhole.

Mundt, a headset pressed against one ear, motioned for silence. "He just hung up. Sounded as if he was talking to a mobile number. Something about a safe house."

"Where?" Roemer asked.

"Sorry, sir, but they didn't say. Apparently they both understood the location. But it sounded as if the mobile number was on his way there now."

Mundt again held up his hand for silence. "He's dialing," the technician said. "Two."

Roemer pulled out a notebook and pen and wrote down the numbers.

"Three. Seven. Zero. One. Two."

Roemer recognized the number: Chief Prosecutor Schaller's. He stuffed the notebook in his pocket, hurriedly climbed down into the close confines of the tunnel and took the headset from Mundt. The number was ringing.

Schaller answered. "Yes?"

"It's Ludwig."

"Where are you calling from?" Schaller sounded upset.

"I'm in town. Did you talk to Hans?"

"This afternoon. Roemer is convinced that you murdered both of those women. He was at your house."

"I know. The monitors were on. He took one of my shoes."

"They were your footprints, evidently, in the apartment."

"It was a silly mistake on my part. But it will probably work out for the best in the end."

"What in God's name are you talking about? Do you realize what kind of trouble this could bring? Helmut Kohl is damned upset, he calls here four times a day."

"In two months it will be all over, so don't worry."

"Two months!" Schaller exploded. "What if there is another killing?"

"There won't be, I can guarantee it."

There was a long silence on the line. When Schaller came back his voice sounded strained. "Legler seems to think you have the motive."

Whalpol laughed, the sound harsh in the headset. "Don't be an ass."

"If Roemer brings him proof, any kind of proof, he'll get all the backing he needs."

"Roemer can't possibly come up with proof of something that isn't so, Ernst. But I don't want him diverted. Don't interfere with him. He's keeping that Mukhabarat bitch out of my hair."

"What are you talking about now?"

"Roemer went down to see his father at the sanatorium. She followed him. If Roemer is smart he's already moved the old man."

"Where?"

"God only knows, Ernst. But the two of them will keep each other busy. Busier once Roemer gets wind of the fact she's got help."

Roemer's grip tightened on the headset.

"Khodr Azziza, Hussein's top hit man, went to ground in Baghdad more than twenty-four hours ago. Word is, he's out of the country. My guess would be Switzerland. He's one bad bastard. Frankly I didn't think Leila played that rough. But once she finds Roemer's father she'll call Azziza in like a guided missile."

Again there was a silence on the line. Roemer glanced up. Manning and Jacobs were staring down at him. Roemer held up his hand for silence. His heart was aching. No matter what happened now, it seemed that time had finally run out for his father. He must not be dragged back to Baghdad. A bullet in his head would be better for everyone concerned.

"Do you know who killed those girls?" Schaller asked.

"I think so."

"Who is it?"

"It will not happen again. I will see to it. In any event you don't want to know."

"Will he be brought to justice?"

"That would be impossible, Ernst."

"One of the Iraqis, then?"

"I must go now, but keep me informed about our friend Roemer."

"I did what you wished, Ludwig, I told Sherif that Roemer was on the case, and that he suspected the BND."

"Good," Whalpol said.

"Roemer should be told."

"Absolutely not. I forbid it."

"Sarah Razmarah's murder can be blamed on that Iraqi who shot himself. But the newswoman. Television One will never let it rest."

"We'll find a scapegoat. It won't be too difficult," Whalpol said.

"Just like that? I sincerely thought we had risen above such things."

"No government can rise above such unfortunate happenings. It is not pleasant, Ernst, but such things at times become necessary."

Schaller started to say something, but the connection was broken.

Roemer continued holding the headset against his ear. If not Whalpol, then who? One of the Iraqis, after all? Or was Whalpol merely continuing to cover his own tracks?

"He is off the line now, sir," Achmann said.

Roemer handed him the headset. "Rig up your transmitter. I want every call recorded."

He climbed out of the tunnel and stood facing Manning, angry. Even if Whalpol had not murdered those women, he knew who did and planned to protect the killer. He had manipulated Sarah Razmarah into coming to Germany, to her death. He had sidetracked Joan Waldmann. And he had, in effect, engineered the coming confrontation between Leila and Roemer's father.

"Who was he talking with?" Manning asked.

"I'll tell you on the way," Roemer said. "We'll take my car; leave yours for Jacobs."

"Watch yourself," Manning said to Jacobs, and then he and Roemer went across the street, climbed into Roemer's car and took off.

"What happened?" Manning demanded.

Roemer didn't answer until they pulled around the corner and parked, the headlights off. At the far end of the block stood Whalpol's house. Lights shone in the upstairs windows. Whalpol's Mercedes was parked in front.

"He was talking with Chief Prosecutor Schaller. He knows who killed the girls."

"It's a cover-up. He's lying."

"He told Schaller there would be no more killings."

"Who else would have the motive?"

"I don't know," Roemer said.

The lights in Whalpol's house went out. A couple of minutes later the front door opened and a man emerged, passed through the gate, crossed in front of the parked car and opened the driver's door. For a brief moment he was illuminated by the dome light. It was Whalpol.

"Call the van. Tell them we're on the move," Roemer said.

Whalpol's car pulled away from the curb. Roemer waited until it disappeared around the corner, then followed. Whalpol turned onto the Hinterholerstrasse and sped up.

Traffic was light, but there was enough to conceal them behind Whalpol.

They reached the Kölnerstrasse, paralleling the river.

"Where the hell is he going at this hour?" Manning growled.

"He's evidently set up a surveillance team to watch whoever he suspects is the killer."

"Could we have been so wrong, Roemer?"

Roemer shrugged. He felt numb. A lot of bad memories coursed through his head.

They crossed the Konrad Adenauer Bridge and Roemer had to fall back farther. On the other side, Whalpol turned east on the Königswinterstrasse and sped up again in the general direction of the Köln-Bonn Autobahn.

Roemer thought Whalpol was heading out to the KwU research facility beyond the airport, but when he crossed the interchange and headed up toward Siegburg itself, a chill passed through Roemer.

He knew where Whalpol was heading. Suddenly he could see the entire thing all laid out for him like a nearly solved crossword puzzle. It was stunning.

They came around the corner onto the Bonnerstrasse, and Manning suddenly sat forward.

"God in heaven," he said. "The Klauber estate."

"Yes."

Whalpol's car turned up a driveway that led to a small house behind and above the estate. Roemer shut off his headlights and parked just below.

"General Sherif," Manning said.

"Or one of his staff."

44

IT WAS cold in the car. Roemer could see his breath. From where they were parked they had a clear line of sight to both houses. A few lights shone on the first floor of the Klauber estate, but Whalpol's surveillance house was dark. The BND team would probably have a lot of sophisticated equipment up there. Certainly a telephone monitor, probably an infrared telescope and camera, possibly a long-range sound-detection dish and amplifier. They'd be picking the Klauber house apart electronically.

Whalpol was guilty of nothing more than an awesome German cynicism. Roemer could see it now. The man had probably had some fatherly feeling for Sarah Razmarah. When she was murdered he had called on Schaller to hire a BKA homicide investigator—but one who could be controlled if the situation got out of hand. It was likely that Whalpol had had his suspicions about someone on the Iraqi team, but no proof. Perhaps with the second killing, Whalpol had discovered something that led him to the general's staff.

Whalpol would be working under tremendous pressure; the project must be kept safe at all costs. In a couple of months, if they could all hold out that long, the project would be completed, the Iraqis would have their reactor and their team would go home, and the Germans would have their money. The murders would eventually be buried as unsolved, or with any luck they'd come across a known sex offender dead, the "scapegoat."

Manning was now confused, torn between his duties. "What the hell do we do?"

"Find the killer and arrest him," Roemer said.

Manning shook his head. "Do you think Whalpol and his crowd would allow that? We're playing with fire here."

"You should have a clear conscience that there wasn't a conspiracy after all."

A hard look came into Manning's eyes. "I don't know which disgusts me more. A conspiracy, or a cover-up. I don't understand it, Roemer."

"Understand this. I'm going to find out who the killer is, arrest him and see that he stands trial. I don't give a damn who it is, or what Whalpol and his people do about it."

45

SERGEANT JACOBS relieved them a few minutes after two. Roemer dropped Manning off downtown and went over to his own office. He got a cup of coffee and a roll from the canteen and took the elevator up. The only people on duty were the switchboard girl and the night officer. Neither noticed Roemer's arrival.

He took off his coat and opened the six-inch-thick sheath of files he had amassed on this case. He thought once again about Leila Kahled. She was a trained Mukhabarat operative, and she lived under the same roof as the murderer. Did she know who it was? Did she have suspicions? Or had she become so blinded by pursuing old Nazis that she had seen or heard nothing? *Frankly I didn't think Leila played that rough.* Whalpol's words. Yet Roemer suspected that Khodr Azziza had come to Switzerland at Leila's behest to kill or kidnap Roemer's father. It would take them a little time, so he had some breathing room. Time enough, he hoped, to identify and arrest the murderer. Afterward he would go to Interlaken to take up the vigil with Sergeant Rilke.

From the original files that Whalpol had supplied, Roemer began digging into the backgrounds of General Sherif and his entourage at the Klauber mansion.

In addition to the general and his daughter, there were thirteen others. The general's chief of staff, Lieutenant Colonel Mahmud Habash, and twelve men and officers from the Iraqi Department of Security. For each, Whalpol's files provided a few scant paragraphs of information.

Habash had been with the general the longest, but the others had served in the army with the man at one time or another. All had been detached to the Security commandos. Specialist soldiers. Several had training in demolitions or communications, but not one of them was a nuclear technician.

A curious staff, Roemer mused, for a deputy minister of defense to bring with him on such a project. They were more like a bodyguard or an elite strike force. Perhaps the general felt unsafe here in Germany.

Seven of the men were married, but none had brought a wife or children.

Whalpol's notes yielded no indication of what the men had been doing over the months they had been here. Certainly there would be little for them to do at the KwU research or assembly plants. They would have to be like caged animals by now.

Perhaps he was dealing with nothing more than a bored soldier who had escaped his prisonlike existence to take his revenge on two young women.

But that would not explain how he had come to kill the two who had strong ties to the KwU project. Ties inimical to project security.

Roemer sat back and lit a cigarette. Stanos Lotz's observation that both Sarah Razmarah and Joan Waldmann were dark, black-eyed, pretty career women kept going through his mind.

He was looking for an Iraqi soldier who lived in the Klauber estate and was familiar enough with the project to understand the threat both women presented; further, it had to be a man with an intense hatred for young career women. Perhaps an Islamic fundamentalist who thought women should know their place and remain in the background. Someone strong. Someone who had come at last to Whalpol's attention. Someone, therefore, important.

Who fit such a description? Roemer looked at the files spread out on his desk. Someone who had suffered for the cause, who had gone to Mecca on the hajj, who professed his faith five times each day. *There is no God but God, and Muhammad is His Prophet.*

All the general's troops were under the age of thirty-five. If they had suffered, it had not been for long. Only Colonel Habash and General Sherif himself even came close to fitting the picture, if the information in Whalpol's dossiers was correct.

Roemer's cigarette stopped in midair, another piece of the puzzle dropping into place. Leila was the chief of Mukhabarat activities for the KwU project, Whalpol's counterpart. She knew that Sarah's relationship with Ahmed Pavli had gone sour. She would have known about Joan Waldmann's threatening to expose the KwU project on television. And she had been raised to be anti-West in the PLO by her widowed father.

The father knew what the daughter knew.

Roemer opened the general's file. Several photographs showed him coming out of the Council of Ministers building in Baghdad, one with Saddam Hussein, and another showed him inside at a conference table with the Revolutionary Command Council—Iraq's governing body.

Josef Assad Sherif, born June 15, 1940, in Jerusalem to a father who was an attorney and a mother who was a medical doctor. His parents were killed in an Israeli Irgun raid in 1957, the day before his seventeenth birthday. The file was vague about the next part, but whoever had written the dossier speculated that the murders of several prominent Israeli citizens in Tel Aviv over the next few months might have been committed by Sherif.

That fall, he turned up at the Arab University at Beirut for double master's degrees in international law and political science. It was there that he met Hanna Kanafani, who was also studying law. They were married in 1962, and their only daughter, Leila, was born the next year.

There were few details about the general's life over the next ten years except that he was very active in the PLO, especially Yasir Arafat's al-Fatah. He was also one of the *fedayeen,* a freedom fighter, helping to defend the Tall al-Za'tar PLO camp, where in 1957 the civil war in Lebanon really began.

Sherif's wife was killed at this camp in 1976, a few months before it finally fell, and he and his daughter disappeared, turning up at Saddam Hussein's side in 1979 when the Tikritis took over the RCC, and therefore the actual leadership of Iraq.

Sherif's had been a tough life, but nothing in his dossier suggested that he could be a rapist and a murderer of young women, or that he was an Islamic fundamentalist. If anything, Sherif (Hussein had promoted him to general in the Special Security Forces in 1984) was an opportunist, albeit a very mysterious man.

Roemer wondered if he was following another dead-end hunch. To imagine that General Sherif was the killer was even more difficult than to believe that Whalpol had committed the crimes on orders from Pullach. Sherif was a highly respected soldier turned diplomat. It was hard to believe that he would risk a project of such importance to his adopted country for the murders of two women.

And where was the motivation? Locked somewhere in his experiences in war-torn Lebanon? In the horrors of Tall al-Za'tar?

Roemer turned next to the computer printouts that Gehrman had supplied him from passport control. The general and his chief of staff, Colonel Habash, were often out of the country. Perhaps they had been gone during one or both of the murders—the perfect alibi.

Sarah Razmarah had been murdered sometime late on the evening of Wednesday, November nineteenth. Roemer spread out the passport printouts. The general and his COS had left for Baghdad the very next morning. He himself had watched them leave the house together shortly before Leila had raced off to Pavli's apartment. They had taken a direct flight from Bonn to Baghdad. Anxiously, Roemer flipped through the printouts, to Saturday. General Sherif and Colonel Habash had returned late that day. A full twenty-four hours before Joan Waldmann was murdered.

There was the triple-star imprint on Sarah Razmarah's palm. And Whalpol warned that Schaller would not want to know who had killed the two women.

Roemer lit another cigarette and went to the window, which looked out over the city. It was nearly five o'clock. Soon traffic would begin and Bonn would awaken. He was weary. No matter what the outcome, his life would never be the same. How badly he had misjudged people was just coming into focus for him. Gretchen, Leila, Whalpol and now the general. He felt alone and cold in the predawn darkness.

The telephone on his desk rang. Manning was on the line.

"Whalpol returned to his house about an hour ago."

"Alone?"

"Yes."

"Have there been any more phone calls?"

"None. But listen, Jacobs just called me. Leila left a few minutes ago."

Roemer snapped out of his introspective mood. "Did Whalpol's people follow her?"

"No. There's been absolutely no activity up there. No lights, nothing."

She would be going to Bern, now that the assassin was presumably in Switzerland to pick up his father's trail from the sanatorium. She would find him.

"Where is she going, Roemer, have you any idea?"

"I don't know."

"Is she part of this?"

"I don't think so, at least not directly."

Manning hesitated. "You know who killed the two girls?"

Roemer sighed. "I think so."

"Who?"

"You're not going to like it. No one will."

"Who?"

"I think General Sherif is the murderer."

"God in heaven! Why?"

"I don't know. But we're going to have to go very slowly now, Manning. Whalpol is watching the general. If it comes to a confrontation, Whalpol will protect the man."

"What do we do?"

"I'm going to try for a search warrant later today."

"From Schaller? He's in bed with Whalpol. He'll never give it to you."

"We'll see," Roemer said. "But keep yourself available. If it happens we'll have to move quickly."

"What about Jacobs?"

"Keep the tap on Whalpol's phone. If anything happens he'll be the first to know. But pull Jacobs away from the Klauber estate before dawn. I don't want him spotted."

Again Manning hesitated. "How sure are you about this?"

"Not very."

Now it would begin, Roemer thought. And no one would be happy with the outcome. He telephoned Rudi Gehrman. His friend answered the phone on the second ring.

"I think you'd better get down here as soon as possible," Roemer said without preamble.

"What's happened?"

"I'm going to need some fast information. There were some assassinations in Tel Aviv in 1957."

"Of Jews?"

"Yes."

"I don't suspect the Israelis will cooperate with us," Gehrman said. "We'll have to go to Washington, the Central Intelligence Agency. We might be able to get access through the FBI."

"Do you know anyone over there?"

"I have just the man," Gehrman said. "But it's still the middle of the night in Washington."

"Get him out of bed."

"Who is it, Walther? Do you know who killed those girls? An Iraqi?"

"I'll fill you in when you get here."

Roemer dialed the Interlaken number. It took a long time before the telephone was answered by Sergeant Rilke.

"Max, this is Walther. Is everything all right down there?"

"The major had a very bad night," the sergeant grumbled. "He only got to sleep an hour ago. I do not think he will last much longer. His mind is going."

Kill him, Roemer wanted to say.

"There is big trouble coming your way, Max."

"Who is it this time?"

"A man by the name of Khodr Azziza will find you sooner or later."

"I don't know this name."

"He works for Saddam Hussein."

The sergeant laughed, short and sharp. "We don't have a quarrel with them. But let him come. I've not had a decent fight in years. The diversion will be interesting."

"Max, he might want to take my father alive. They want to use him as a hostage in Baghdad. No matter what happens, Max, my father must not leave Interlaken alive."

"Neither of us will, Walther. You have my word on it."

46

IT WAS early morning in Bonn, midnight in Washington, D.C., when Rudi Gehrman called his friend who worked for the FBI. Roemer listened on an extension in his office.

They spoke English.

"Tom Karsten, Rudi Gehrman here in Germany."

"Rudi, how the hell are you? Have you any idea what time it is here?"

"Sorry, Tom, but I need your help. Unofficially but fast."

Karsten, an agent attached to the Bureau's Special Investigative Division, had worked with Gehrman a number of times over the past couple of years. Karsten's specialty was running down Nazis who had hidden in the United States after the war.

"It's a two-way street, my friend. What do you need?"

"I want you to get out to Langley. The CIA."

"I know where it is," Karsten said dryly.

Gehrman glanced at his notes. "I want you to look up some records from the late fifties. Israeli criminal records on a series of assassinations in Tel Aviv."

"Just a sec," Karsten said. A moment later he was back. "Go ahead." He'd probably switched on a recorder.

"In June of that year the parents of a man named Josef

Assad Sherif were killed in Jerusalem by the Irgun. In August, September and October, eight prominent Israeli citizens—four men who were attorneys and four women who were doctors—were assassinated. Sherif's father was an attorney, and his mother was a doctor."

There was a pause.

"Let me ask you something, Rudi," Karsten said. "This man wouldn't be any relation to Iraq's deputy minister of defense?"

"One and the same, Tom. But this has to be kept very unofficial, very quiet."

"What does your office have to do with an Iraqi general, can you tell me?"

"No. You're going to have to trust me on this one."

Again there was a pause.

"All right," Karsten said cautiously. "I can run this first thing in the morning."

"No. Right now. I need this as soon as possible."

"I can't get in there at this hour."

"Pick the lock, Tom. Really, this is extremely important."

"I'll see what I can do, but I can't promise anything. What specifically do you need to know?"

"Anything you can get. I want to know if an arrest was made, and if not, who the Israelis pegged as their top suspect."

"You think it was General Sherif?"

"It's possible."

"Will you be at your office?"

"Yes," Gehrman said. "And one other thing. We have an incomplete dossier on the general. Find out whatever you can about him."

"For instance?"

"Has he ever been considered a murder suspect, outside of those assassinations in Tel Aviv?"

"What the hell have you got going there, Rudi? Christ, do you know what kind of noises my government would make if they found out you people were conducting an investigation of an important Iraqi officer without sharing it with us?"

"I'm sharing it with you, Tom."

"No you're not. In fact, you're putting my ass on the line. I'm going to want an explanation."

"Call me as soon as you have anything."

"Right," Karsten said, and the connection was broken.

Gehrman shook his head. "Are you sure about this, Walther?"

"I've never been less sure of anything in my life."

"What about our BND friend?"

"It looks as if he's protecting the general."

"Frankly, I'm a little more comfortable with that notion," Gehrman said, getting to his feet. "What's your next move?"

"I'm going to force the issue."

"Whalpol will run you over."

"He'll try," Roemer said. "But he's backed himself into a corner now."

Roemer drove to his Oberkassel apartment. The place was practically empty. He realized that he lived a mostly barren existence. Except for a few photographs of his mother, and his record albums, he had nothing. The personal touches in the apartment had been Gretchen's. Before that, Kata's, and long ago, his mother's. He himself had never collected any of the baggage that most people accumulate: the souvenirs, the knickknacks, the paintings and plants.

He fixed himself a couple of scrambled eggs with spinach, some bread and butter and a cool beer, then took a long hot shower. He shaved and dressed in his best gray suit and tie.

He looked a lot better than he felt. His wound hurt and he was dead tired. In the six days since he had been called out to investigate Sarah Razmarah's murder, he had gotten little sleep. It seemed as if the week had merged into one long, cold, gray evening.

At eight-thirty he drove back to his office, picked up his files on the murders and his investigation report and walked next door to the Chief District Prosecutor's office, presenting himself to Schaller's secretary at the stroke of 9:00 A.M.

Schaller's large office was thickly carpeted, richly paneled and adorned with dozens of photographs, certificates and awards, all looking down on a huge cherry desk.

The Chief District Prosecutor's eyes flitted from Roemer's suit to the thick bundle of files. He seemed harried.

"What are you doing here?" he asked irritably.

"I've come for a search warrant."

Schaller sighed theatrically. "You're chasing after shadows, Walther. But if you insist on this, I'll do it for you. I'm sure Major Whalpol will have no objections."

Roemer laid the files on the large desk calendar. "Major Whalpol did not kill those two women. I was mistaken, and for that I intend apologizing to him in person."

Schaller eyed the thick stack of files. "You have another suspect?"

"Yes."

"Whose home you wish to search."

"Yes."

Schaller lifted his eyes. "Who?"

"The Klauber estate. I believe General Josef Sherif murdered Sharazad Razmarah and Joan Waldmann. Later this morning I expect to have further information.

But a search of the general's living quarters would be helpful."

Schaller was stunned. "Do you realize what you're saying, Walther?"

"Last night, with the help of Bonn Kriminalpolizei technicians, I placed a monitor on Ludwig Whalpol's telephone. We intercepted two telephone calls, one partial, one complete. The first one was from Whalpol to what we presume was a BND surveillance unit onsite. The second call was to you yourself, and you know what he said."

Schaller's mouth was half open, his eyes wide. A blood vessel throbbed at his right temple. But he said nothing.

"Directly after the call to you, I followed Major Whalpol to a small house above and behind the Klauber estate. I believe the BND surveillance unit is located in that house to watch the Klauber estate, to monitor someone's movements."

"The general has a large staff up there," Schaller said, finding his voice.

"I have considered that." Roemer stepped forward, opened the top folder in the bundle, extracted the report he had typed out this morning and handed it to Schaller.

"Impossible." Schaller laid the report on his desk without looking at it.

"A copy of that report will be filed with my department this morning, along with a request for the results of the BND's investigation and surveillance of General Sherif."

Schaller slammed his fist on the desk and sprang to his feet. "God in heaven, Roemer, do you realize what you are doing?"

"Investigating a double murder."

"You are jeopardizing the entire project!"

"Will you sign the search warrant?"

"When you came to me some days ago with the request

that Whalpol be arrested for these murders, you told me you had the proof. Something about one of his shoes, and about his motives. I denied your request. Now you have come up with another suspect. You must continue your investigation until you have *proof!* And then you will find me cooperative, no matter who it turns out to be."

"That evidence will be found in General Sherif's quarters, and in the BND surveillance records. I want both."

Schaller shook his head. He was calmer now. "I simply cannot do such a thing. But I will arrange a meeting between you and Major Whalpol."

"It is also my intention, Chief Prosecutor, to formally charge Major Whalpol with obstruction of justice. We are a nation of laws."

"Indeed." Schaller's eyes narrowed. "Criminals shall be punished for their criminal acts. I couldn't agree with you more. Murder has no statute of limitations. Not ten years, not fifty."

Roemer knew exactly what Schaller was getting at. "My father won't live much longer."

Schaller's eyebrows rose. "Obstruction of justice, I believe you were saying. You are an officer of the law. You have known the whereabouts of your father for years."

"So have you."

Schaller said nothing.

"Will you sign the search warrant?"

"No."

Roemer turned and went to the door.

"Your files," Schaller called after him.

"Those are merely copies. I have the originals in safekeeping."

Schaller picked up the telephone.

47

ROEMER WALKED back across the courtyard, but instead of going up to his office, he got his car. In forcing the issue, the first step had been his formal request for a search warrant. The second had been accomplished with Schaller's telephone call. Roemer had no doubt that the Chief District Prosecutor had called Whalpol. Now that Schaller knew there was a tap on Whalpol's telephone, he would be arranging a meeting with the BND major. Roemer wished he could be present at that tête-à-tête, a little bird in the corner. They would talk about how to stop Roemer before any real damage was done. Schaller was running scared. But Whalpol was the real danger.

Roemer crossed the Kennedy Bridge, the traffic quite heavy this morning, the riverbanks lined with dirty snow.

Murder was a crime relatively simple to solve. In ninety percent of the cases, the killer and victim were related either by blood, marriage or some close emotional tie.

When the killer was smart and the motive obscure, however, the only way he could be caught was if he made a mistake. Mistakes were made under stress, natural or contrived.

Roemer turned up the Siegburgerstrasse and then the

Bonnerstrasse before he halted near the driveway to the Klauber estate. He lit a cigarette to calm his nerves.

Up behind the estate, Roemer could make out the roofline of the small house from which Whalpol's surveillance team was watching. Undoubtedly they had spotted Roemer on the Bonnerstrasse. Coming on the heels of Schaller's disturbing call, Roemer's showing up here would enrage Whalpol.

Roemer was running out of time. His focus was beginning to shift to Switzerland. No matter how the situation with his father turned out, it would not be satisfactory. He did not want the murderer to slip through his fingers as well. General Sherif had only to get on a plane and fly back to Baghdad, where he would be safe.

Roemer cranked down his window, flipped his cigarette away and drove up the driveway to the front of the three-story house, which looked big enough to hold a medieval army.

He got out of the car, straightened his tie and went to the front door. He was about to knock when the door swung open.

One of the German house staff faced him. *"Guten Morgen."*

Roemer showed his BKA identification. "I would like to speak with General Sherif."

"Of course."

Roemer followed the servant to a large room beyond the main stairhall, a book-lined study with a wide leather-topped desk and a huge fireplace. French doors led to a veranda at the side of the house.

"If you will just wait here, Investigator, I will announce you to the general." The servant left.

Roemer started across the room. He stopped in midstride. The desk was a mess. Papers were scattered, an ashtray overflowing, a ring of keys next to a wooden tray containing two gold objects. His eyes locked on the tray. It was unbelievable. The man's arrogance was even greater than Whalpol's.

An angry voice rose in the hall. Roemer grabbed the two gold cuff links from the wooden tray. They were heavy and square, with three stars in bas-relief. Roemer pocketed them and stepped away from the desk as General Sherif barged in, an imperious, angry scowl on his face. He was dressed in a thick wool sweater over a casual shirt.

"What are you doing here?" he demanded in English.

"I'm Investigator Walther Roemer from the—"

"I know who you are."

A heavyset man appeared at the doorway behind the general. Colonel Habash, Roemer assumed.

"I've come to ask a few questions, General."

"Concerning what?"

"The murders of two young women the past week."

General Sherif's left eyebrow rose. "Have you a search warrant to enter my home?"

"No, sir. I'd hoped you would cooperate with me in my investigation, so I took the liberty—"

"Leave immediately, Investigator." The general stepped away from the door.

"Just one or two questions, about Jerusalem and the Irgun. I understand that—"

"Colonel Habash," the general said, without taking his eyes off Roemer.

"Sir?"

"Telephone Helmut Kohl, and tell him that I would like a word with him."

"Yes, sir." Colonel Habash walked past Roemer and picked up the desk telephone.

"That won't be necessary," Roemer said. "I'll leave. For now." Habash stared at him coldly as he went.

Roemer got into his car and headed down the driveway. General Sherif stood at the open French doors watching him.

48

LEILA THOUGHT a lot about Walther Roemer on the long drive to Switzerland. By the time she crossed the border at Basel she'd come to no firm conclusion other than the simple one that she was confused. Jacob Wadud's gibe—*What if it were your own father?*—kept drumming through her mind.

She had hoped that by the sheer act of movement her resolve would solidify. That by doing her duty, driving to Interlaken, finding Roemer's father and reporting the location to Azziza, she would rid herself of her troubles. She would not stick around for the outcome. Despite what Lotti Roemer was, she wouldn't have the stomach for a murder or kidnapping. She would return to Bonn, pack her things and leave immediately for Baghdad. There was a place for her at Al Kumait on the Tigris, where she would bury herself for a few weeks or months —whatever it took to put everything in perspective. By then the KwU project would be completed, her father would return home and she would get back to work.

Worst of all was that she knew Roemer would despise her for what she was doing. He would understand why she was doing it, but at the sanatorium she had seen anguish on his face. Lotti Roemer, the Butcher of Dachau, was all he had.

Interlaken, a lovely town of about five thousand people, lay in the valley between the lakes of Thun and Brienz, amid vast, wild mountain scenery.

Leila arrived at noon and got a room with a magnificent view on the fifteenth floor of the Hotel Metropole. Among the few things in her overnight bag were her files and notes on Walther Roemer and his father, including the incident at the sanatorium.

She taped the files to the underside of a bureau drawer and went up to the hotel's top-floor bar and restaurant, where she ordered a glass of wine, French onion soup and a croissant.

This lovely place was so different from what Baghdad had become. Beautiful. Peaceful. Open. There seemed no room here for violence. Yet it was coming.

After her lunch she dawdled over a cigarette and coffee. She was being a fool. Lotti Roemer had killed thousands of people, even if they were Jews. Jews, not Zionists. The man's death would free the son from his influence. For Iraq's safety, it was as simple and as necessary as that.

Leila took the elevator down to the lobby and got directions to the town hall, just off Interlaken's main, tree-lined boulevard, the Höheweg.

It was just three blocks from the hotel, in a splendid, ornate old mountain chalet.

The clerk of property records was alone behind his counter on the second floor. He was an old man with thick glasses and thinning white hair.

"Good afternoon, Fräulein," he said in heavily accented Swiss-German.

Herr Walkmann, the nurse in the sanatorium had shouted at Roemer. For just a moment her resolve weakened. "I've just come from Bonn, on behalf of Walther Walkmann."

"Yes?"

"I've been sent to pay the taxes on the Walkmann property here in Interlaken."

The clerk squinted. "Walther Walkmann? I don't know . . ."

"Perhaps the property is in his father's name. I'm not sure."

"You must mean Lotti Walkmann."

Leila stayed calm. She nodded.

"But the taxes have been paid. Max Rilke was here . . . perhaps eight weeks ago. Nine. They are paid, Fräulein."

Leila acted confused. "That cannot be. I have personally driven all this way at Herr Walkmann's . . . the son's instructions. He was quite concerned."

"I am quite certain."

"Please, if you could just check your records. It has been a terribly long drive."

"Of course." He shuffled into a back room.

The outer office was small. Behind a narrow wooden counter were two desks and a couple of ancient file cabinets. The place smelled musty.

The clerk came back with a large ledger, which he opened on the counter.

"See for yourself, Fräulein. The taxes on the Walkmann property have been paid. In full and on time, as usual."

Leila ran her finger down the columns as if she were checking amounts and dates, but she was staring at the top of the page, the address. The property was listed under the name of Lotti Bernard Walkmann, a Swiss citizen. The land and house had been purchased in 1941. The address given was Jungfraujochstrasse, No. 15, Interlaken.

She looked up. "I'm sorry, but it seems as if my trip all the way down here was for nothing."

"You say Bonn, Fräulein?"

"Yes."

"Perhaps you would like me to call Herr Walkmann."

"That won't be necessary. I had planned on stopping out there to pay my regards anyway."

"I see," the old man said. He had become suspicious. The Swiss had a penchant for order. Leila's story had not been neat.

"Thank you very much for your kind help," Leila said, smiling warmly. "I'm sorry to have been such a bother."

"Of course," the clerk said coolly.

Leila left the office and started downstairs, but she stopped. The building was very quiet. She could hear someone talking on the telephone. She hurried back up the stairs.

The clerk, his back to the door, was speaking on the telephone, and although she could not make out what he was saying, she could hear the urgency in his tone.

Lotti Roemer had come here with a lot of money, for which the Swiss would treat him as a favored citizen. He was apparently being warned about her presence.

Leila turned, hurried back downstairs and left the town hall. She had two choices, now that she had located Lotti Roemer. She could go out to the house and confront the old man tonight. There would be a fight, but she could handle herself against the sick old man and his sergeant. Or she could call Khodr Azziza at the Geneva number she had been given by Colonel Habash, and return to Bonn. In that event she would be clear of the issue. She would not have to be present when the end came for Walther Roemer's father.

49

BY THE time she had arrived back at the hotel, Leila had decided to telephone Dr. Azziza in Geneva. The moment she opened her door she knew something was wrong. She was fumbling in her purse for her gun when Khodr Azziza appeared from the corner by the window. She froze.

Azziza was a wiry man with jet-black hair, thick eyebrows and black, piercing eyes. His lips were thin, his nose sharp. He was smiling, but there was no warmth to his smile.

"If you're going to shoot me, Leila, get it over with. Otherwise come in and shut the door. We should talk."

"What are you doing here?" She closed the door behind her.

He had searched the room. The bureau was open, her files spread out on the bed. "Have you found Herr Walkmann . . . the elder, that is?"

"I thought you were in Geneva."

"Habash telephoned me. Told me you got information from Gretchen Krause."

They had a monitor on her telephone at the embassy. That meant Zwaiter was in on it, a sickening realization. Yet she could hardly blame them. The Butcher of Dachau was quite a prize for them just now, and it was evident to those around her that she wasn't thinking straight.

"Are you here to kill him?" she asked.

Azziza's back was to the window. He was silhouetted in the strong sunlight. "I understand the man may be too old and sick to be moved. A termination would probably be for the best. I don't relish the idea of carting a dead body back to Baghdad."

Azziza radiated a chill. He was of the Hasson al-Sabbath, the ancient assassins. She shivered.

"I see," Azziza said, evidently reading her expression. He languidly lit a cigarette. He was dressed in dark trousers, a light shirt, dark leather jacket and soft leather boots.

"He's dying," Leila said. "He probably hasn't got a month to live."

"Tell that to the men, women and children he killed."

"What do you care? They were Jews!"

His eyes flashed. "I do not kill innocent people. You're young, you have no conception of what I am."

He moved out of the direct light. Leila tried to put an age on him, but he could have been anywhere from thirty to fifty.

"He wasn't one of the worst ones, but we do know he personally tortured and killed at least a hundred men and women with his own hands. And undoubtedly he signed the orders for several thousand more to die in the gas chambers."

"Killing him won't do anything for us."

"No." Azziza smiled sadly. "Killing him will simply deny him another month or so of life."

"If he is dying, maybe it would be better to let him suffer."

"You don't know a thing, little girl, so prim and pretty. Life isn't given up so easily. We fight for our last breath.

Believe me, I know." He laughed. "I've been called a soldier."

"You enjoy it."

Azziza's face tensed. For a moment Leila feared for her own life.

Then he relaxed. "It was a good piece of work you did, following the son to Bern, picking up the Walkmann name. And I can understand why you didn't pursue it then and there, though Colonel Habash is at a loss."

"What are you talking about?"

"You are in love with him," Azziza said casually.

Leila felt as if she had been punched in the gut.

"It was also a nice bit of work tracking down Interlaken from his girlfriend. I must say, he has terrible luck with women. But then, all the good ones do." Azziza smiled. "Don't look so surprised. I happen to agree with Jacob Wadud. Walther Roemer is one of the good ones."

"Someone on our KwU team has probably murdered two young women," Leila blurted.

Azziza nodded. "You may be right, little girl. But that is not my assignment. Walther Roemer will find the killer. His father is my concern. You can make it easy or difficult. Where did you fly this morning, little bird? Who did you talk with?"

"His sergeant is with him."

"Max Rilke. A tough old bastard."

"Will you kill him too?"

"I expect he will get in the way."

"And the house staff? There may be nurses."

"Who did you talk with this morning, Leila?" Azziza stopped within an arm's length of her. He smelled faintly of cloves. His aura seemed to produce an electric current that paralyzed her.

"Who are you protecting, Leila? The son?"

"Jungfraujochstrasse," Leila said softly.

"Number?"

"Fifteen."

"And this information came from whom?"

"The clerk of property records. I asked about taxes on the place."

Azziza nodded. Gently, he touched her cheek with his cool fingertips. The gesture shocked her. She reared back, bumping her head on the door.

Azziza took her arm and led her away from the door. "Get in your car now, little girl, and drive away. Don't look back."

He stepped to the ashtray by the window, picked out his two cigarette butts and pocketed them. He put on a pair of thin leather gloves, then went to the door.

"What if his son comes down here?"

Azziza turned back, a distant look in his eyes. "Pray he doesn't, little girl. He is one I have no desire to kill."

He left. For a long time Leila stared at the door, numb. Then she roused herself enough to gather her things and repack her overnight bag.

The Butcher of Dachau was as good as dead. Azziza would wait until tonight and go in under cover of darkness. The property clerk's call would put them on their guard. They would not run, however. The dying old man was too sick to be moved so soon after the trip from the sanatorium. His sergeant would be on the lookout tonight. Azziza had called him a tough old bastard. But it wasn't likely he'd be able to stop the assassin.

Leila went down to the desk, where she paid her bill, assuring the curious clerk that nothing was wrong with her room or the service; urgent business had come up.

She drove out of the city. The cold sky was crystal clear, the sun bright at this altitude. Her involvement with Lotti Roemer was over. It was time to go home. To forget.

On the superhighway toward Bern, she let her mind

drift to the warmth of the Tigris Valley. There was work for her there. A million years ago, she had been trained as a nurse. Whenever she went back to her adopted home she opened the tiny clinic, and all the sturdy Bedouins, who for most of the year were as healthy as pack animals, suddenly came down with everything from sprained ankles to mysterious backaches and migraine headaches. She didn't mind. She enjoyed the busywork. The camaraderie of the clinic. But it was also lonely. Uncle Bashir visited from time to time, but always came with an assignment for her. Something for her special talents.

She pounded the steering wheel. It wasn't fair. Where was the love? Where were the bells and the golden path that led out to some garden of togetherness?

Against her will, Walther Roemer's strong, good face swam before her mind's eye. Impossible, she told herself. Utterly impossible.

"What if his son comes down here?" Her own words.

"Pray he doesn't, little girl. He is one I have no desire to kill."

The property clerk had probably called Sergeant Rilke. Would Rilke, fearing the worst, have called Walther Roemer?

50

STANOS LOTZ looked up from his microscope, his weak eyes wide and watery until he put on his thick glasses. He plucked the heavy cuff link from the instrument's stage and turned it over in his hands.

"No blood, unfortunately," he said.

"Is it the same one?" Roemer asked. He had come directly from the Klauber estate to Lotz's laboratory.

"If you mean to ask could this cuff link have caused the pattern on Sarah Razmarah's palm, the answer is yes. But was the impression caused specifically by this cuff link? I don't know."

Roemer had hoped Lotz could pull some trick out of his instruments and chemicals.

Lotz picked up a large magnifying glass and studied the back of the cuff link, on which the Roman initials JAS were engraved. "These were probably handmade," he said. "There is a maker's mark just below the S in the initials." He looked up. "Find the maker."

"It's the best you can do?"

Lotz shrugged. "I'm a scientist, not a wizard. Who's JAS?"

"You don't want to know."

* * *

Roemer parked on a side street near his office and walked to a *Bierstube* a block away. It was a few minutes past noon and the bar was crowded with secretaries, clerks and low-level government employees.

He ordered a beer and telephoned Gehrman's office.

"Where are you? The colonel has been raising hell trying to find you."

"I'll be in soon," Roemer said. "Has Karsten called back?"

"About half an hour ago. Do you want the good news or the bad news first?"

"The good."

"He found Sherif's file with no problem at all. It was on microfilm, and what there was of it was well indexed. His medical records were there. His blood type is O positive."

It was no surprise to Roemer, but it represented nothing more than another piece of circumstantial evidence. O positive was common.

"Now the bad, or at least the surprising," Gehrman said. "Sherif may have been suspected of the 1957 Tel Aviv assassinations, but if he committed those murders, then he and the international terrorist Michael are one and the same man."

"That's fantastic."

"Don't get your hopes up, Walther. The Israelis looked into the possibility, and even queried Langley in sixty-two and again in seventy-nine, shortly after Sherif and his daughter showed up in Baghdad by way of Beirut. It's the reason the CIA had a file on him. But they and the Mossad dropped that line of investigation for lack of evidence."

"Sherif was a fighter."

"No doubt about it. But the way the CIA sees it, he was first a soldier for the PLO in Lebanon, and when that became a stinking quagmire, he bundled up his daughter and emigrated to Iraq, where he became a professional soldier. From what Karsten was able to dig up, he was one of the few Iraqi officers in the Gulf War Schwarzkopf had any respect for."

Roemer thought about it for a moment. "So now he comes to Germany to kill young women—" He cut himself off. "What about his wife? Anything in the file about her?"

"Brace yourself," Gehrman said. "She had long dark hair and black eyes and she was arguing for Arab women's rights when husbands could still legally cut off their wives' noses and subject them to clitoridectomies."

"A career woman."

"Just like his mother. Same description too."

"Just like Sarah Razmarah and Joan Waldmann. I'm going to ask Colonel Legler for an arrest warrant. Sherif knows that I suspect him, and I think he'll try to leave the country."

"He has diplomatic immunity, Walther. You won't be able to touch him."

"We'll see."

Roemer found himself thinking about Leila. She too fit the description. The news that her father was a murderer would hit her at the very moment she was going after his father. Was there any justice in it? He didn't think so.

He telephoned Manning's office.

"Did you get the search warrant?" the KP lieutenant asked.

"No."

"I didn't think you would. But that's not our only problem. We had to pull the tap on Whalpol's phone. My boss received a very specific call from Pullach. He was told in no uncertain terms that we were to back off. None of the fervor was lost when he passed the message along to me."

"That doesn't matter now," Roemer said. "I went out to the Klauber estate."

"Oh?"

"I got inside the general's study."

"You live dangerously," Manning said. "Find anything?"

"Cuff links." Roemer explained what had happened, including Lotz's assessment.

Manning whistled. "Whalpol will know that you were there. He'll probably have you shot. But it's still nothing more than circumstantial evidence, and doesn't give us a motive."

"There's more." Roemer told Manning about the call to the FBI in Washington and the results of Karsten's records search.

Manning didn't reply immediately. "He'll skip, and once he gets back to Baghdad there won't be a thing we can do about it. Even if you show them your evidence, no one will believe you."

"I'm going to arrest him this afternoon," Roemer said. "Do you want to come along?"

"He's got a goddamned army out there."

"We won't be going alone."

Again Manning hesitated. "There isn't a lot I can do without authorization. I'm going to need orders."

"I'll clear it with Legler. In the meantime, can you station someone at the airport?"

"Sure," Manning said. "But I don't know how much good it will do. If he and his people insist, I won't be able to stop them."

"It might slow him down," Roemer said. "But stay available. When I get the go-ahead, we'll have to move fast."

Schaller and Whalpol weren't having much luck controlling Roemer directly, so they'd go to Legler. But he was not easily cowed.

Roemer slipped into the Justice Building the back way and took the stairs two at a time to his office. He telephoned across to Gehrman's office.

"I'm back. Bring the files over."

"Colonel Legler picked them up not two minutes ago. But Walther, he has company, Chief Prosecutor Schaller and Major Whalpol. They're waiting for you."

It was happening faster than he'd thought it would. "Don't say anything to anyone, Rudi. I need a few minutes."

"Whatever you say."

"Get Jacob Wadud on the telephone. Transfer the call to me."

"It would be stupid of me to ask you what the hell you're trying to do, so I won't."

While he waited, Roemer lit a cigarette and stared out the window. How far was he going to push this? Until justice was done? Until the guilty party was punished? He kept telling himself that, but in the back of his mind he knew there was more. Roemer had his own guilt. The sins of the fathers, after all, were visited upon the sons.

The telephone rang, and Roemer went back to his desk. It was Jacob Wadud, the Iraqi detective.

"I'm not glad you called, Walther. I don't think there's a thing I can—or even should—do for you."

"What are you talking about?"

"The past is the past, I told her. But I cannot help you, Walther. I'm sorry."

Leila had evidently called him for information. She was on the hunt. And now she was probably in Switzerland. Doing what? Sniffing around the sanatorium? Even if she broke in and stole the records on his father, they wouldn't tell her much. It would give her a name that would lead back here to Bonn. But there was no connection between the sanatorium and Interlaken. He had made sure of that when his father had been admitted.

"It's not that at all, Jacob. But it'll be even less pleasant for you."

"I don't like the sound of that."

"I have two murders on my hands, here in Bonn."

"I've heard."

"I think one of your people killed those women. As a matter of fact, I'm going for an arrest warrant as soon as I'm done talking with you."

Wadud hesitated a moment. "I have to ask you, Walther, if this has anything to do with your father."

"No."

"But it is delicate for you at this moment."

"It's worse than that."

"Do you have any evidence?"

"Yes."

"Then arrest him. Murder is murder, Walther. Doesn't matter the national boundaries. We've gone over that before."

"The suspect has diplomatic immunity and is a very important person. His arrest could be . . . explosive."

"What can I do?"

"A lot of pressure is on me to drop or delay my investigation. They want me to forget about it."

"I don't care who he is. Do you want me to come over?"

"There's a possibility I'll be too late. He may be getting ready to skip."

"Back here?"

"I think so."

"I'll arrest him. Send me the evidence, and your people can begin extradition procedures."

Roemer ran a hand over his eyes. "It's General Sherif."

Wadud did not reply.

Roemer could hear the hiss of the long-distance line. "Jacob?"

The line went dead. Wadud had hung up. Roemer put down the telephone. General Sherif was a personal friend of Saddam Hussein. The Iraqi detective would come under immense pressure as soon as he passed along his information.

Roemer straightened his tie, put on his jacket and went upstairs. Colonel Legler was just putting down the telephone.

"Investigator Roemer reporting, sir."

Whalpol and Schaller sat in front of the desk. A third chair was empty.

Legler motioned to the chair. The room was tense.

"Have you any idea what you've done?" the BND major snapped.

"I'll have none of that in this office," Legler said wearily.

Roemer sat down. "General Sherif is a murderer. I want a warrant for his arrest today, before he has a chance to leave the country."

"Good God, Walther, you don't have the proof," Schaller said. "I promised that when you did, I would cooperate."

"I am happy to hear that, Chief Prosecutor, because I now have the proof, and the motive."

Even Whalpol was startled. "Sherif admitted it?"

"No."

The case files were spread open on Legler's desk. The colonel glanced at them. "There is nothing concrete here."

"Three other pieces of evidence have come to light since I wrote those reports." Roemer turned to Whalpol. "But first I would like to ask Major Whalpol how he came to suspect General Sherif."

"Come off it, Roemer," Whalpol said. "The murders are going to stop, but the project cannot be put at risk. If you can't understand that simple fact of life, then I will personally put you under arrest under the National Secrets Act and have you locked up until we are finished."

Roemer looked at him. "I wouldn't advise it, Major. If need be I'll go to the newspapers with this thing. The foreign press."

"Enough!" Colonel Legler roared, thumping his meaty fist on the desk.

"I went out to the Klauber estate this morning," Roemer said.

"Major Whalpol informed me."

"I found a pair of gold cuff links on the general's desk. They were stamped with the initials JAS. I brought them to Stanos Lotz, who told me they matched the impression found on Sarah Razmarah's palm."

"Anyone could have been wearing those cuff links," Schaller said.

"Overnight I had the American FBI conduct a records search at the Central Intelligence Agency in Virginia."

The color drained from Schaller's face. He looked at Whalpol, who was holding himself rigidly erect.

"I told them nothing," Roemer said. "I merely requested anything they might have on Sherif. Among other things, he was suspected of murdering eight Israelis in Tel Aviv in 1957. The killings may have been in retaliation for the deaths of his parents in Jerusalem."

"Interesting, but it proves nothing, Walther," Legler said.

"Whoever carried out the Tel Aviv assassinations was

believed to be the international terrorist named Michael."

Whalpol cut in. "The Israelis dropped their investigation of Sherif."

Roemer nodded. The BND major had seen the same files. "His wife was killed in a raid on a PLO camp in Lebanon in 1976. She was a businesswoman, same description. Like Sherif's mother, she did not fit the Arab mold of a dutiful wife."

"He's unhinged, is that what you're telling us?" Legler asked.

"I think it's possible."

"What made you suspect him, of all people?"

"My question for Major Whalpol."

Whalpol cleared his throat. "Fräulein Waldmann was putting together a story on the project. I told her that we could not allow it. She stormed off. I felt it might be wise to go to her apartment and try to reason with her. When I got to her apartment, I saw General Sherif driving away, and she was dead."

"Sherif's blood type is O positive," Roemer said, "which has already been established as the killer's blood type."

"What do we do now?" Schaller asked softly. He looked at Roemer reproachfully. "We can't arrest the man, Walther. It would blow the entire project."

"Sherif might simply return to Baghdad and be out of our hair," Whalpol said. "No one will ever know."

"The Iraqis know," Roemer said.

Whalpol snorted. "You incredible fool. You called them. You told someone."

"An Iraqi homicide detective in Baghdad. I told him everything."

51

IT WAS one in the afternoon when the black Mercedes-Benz limousine bearing BKA colonel Hans Legler, Chief District Prosecutor Ernst Schaller, BND major Ludwig Whalpol, and BKA investigator Walther Roemer pulled up in the circular driveway at the German Federal Chancellor's residence on the Adenauerallee.

Two army guards in crisp uniforms opened the car doors on both sides, and the four men were ushered inside the ornate building and upstairs to a second-floor conference room.

Roemer had all his files and notes, as well as the pair of cuff links he had taken from General Sherif's study. He had telephoned Manning to tell him to stand by, that something might be happening this afternoon.

On the drive over, Colonel Legler had been stern. "A decision will be made this afternoon, and whatever it is, the matter will be put to rest. Is that understood?"

Roemer nodded. Now that all the pieces had been fit together, he really didn't care what happened. His thoughts had already turned back to his father, and Leila with her hired gun somewhere in Switzerland.

"It is possible you will be asked some very difficult personal questions."

Roemer looked up out of his thoughts. "The man is guilty, there can be no doubt about it."

"But the Iraqis are almost certainly going to ask about your past."

An eye for an eye. A friend of Saddam Hussein was being destroyed by the Germans. Hussein would certainly want retribution. His father was going to have to die before the Iraqis got to him.

Helmut Kohl, along with Minister of Defense Bernard Mahler and special adviser to the Chancellor Rolf Länger, entered the sunlit room and took their places at the head of the long table. A fire was burning in the fireplace that dominated one end of the room.

For twenty minutes Roemer detailed every step of his and Lieutenant Manning's investigation, including their early suspicion that Whalpol was the killer. Once or twice Kohl interrupted to ask a question, but through most of it he had no visible reaction.

Roemer finished and sat down.

"Extraordinary," Kohl said.

Defense Minister Mahler sat forward. "You say Sherif has troops up there?"

"Yes, sir. A dozen."

"Your contact at the FBI in Washington had no idea why you wanted this information on Sherif?" Länger asked. He was an elderly man with thick white hair.

"No, sir," Roemer said. "He promised to keep our request confidential. We have worked with him in the past."

"What would you recommend, Investigator Roemer?" the Chancellor asked.

"General Sherif is a murderer. He should be arrested and stand trial here in Germany for his crimes."

"What would you say to his government concerning his diplomatic immunity?"

"Under the circumstances, we should request that they waive those rights."

Kohl thought about it for a moment, then shook his head. "You are aware of the important project under way at the present time?"

"Yes, sir."

"In the face of that, you would still seek Sherif's arrest and trial?"

"Yes, sir."

"I see," the Chancellor said slowly. "What is his present status? Where is he at this moment?"

"At the Klauber estate," Whalpol said. "We have him under surveillance."

"What is your feeling in this, Major?"

"It was our preference to isolate him so that he caused no further harm until the project was completed. Then we would have been willing to turn our case files over to the government of Iraq for action. It's possible they would have prosecuted."

"Of course it is too late for that now," Kohl said. He turned to Roemer. "Do you also understand, Investigator, that the government of Iraq will almost certainly insist that you be interrogated as to the present whereabouts of your father?"

"Yes, sir."

"In the face of that you would want us to proceed?"

"Yes, sir."

Again Länger spoke up. "In light of Investigator Roemer's contact with this Iraqi homicide detective, our options are limited. We will have to make a statement this afternoon."

"I'll see their ambassador at three. At the very least, General Sherif will have to be removed from the project. Immediately."

"Of course."

"But I tend to agree with Investigator Roemer. If the man is indeed guilty of murdering those two young women, he should stand trial, with proper psychiatric examination, of course."

The Chancellor got heavily to his feet. Everyone else stood as well.

"We are a nation of laws, Investigator," he said to Roemer. "But we are also a nation responsible for our past and our future. This puts us in a very difficult position."

Roemer held his silence. The victory gave him no pleasure.

"Major Whalpol will keep General Sherif isolated for the time being. Without force," the Chancellor said.

"Yes, sir," Whalpol said.

"A very disturbing situation from which no one will emerge unscathed," the Chancellor said. He looked at Roemer. "It might be wise if you removed yourself from this business, at least for now. Perhaps I can sidetrack any unpleasantness."

"Thank you, sir," Roemer said.

"I'll have my office prepare the legal briefs," Schaller said. "Though there will be no precedents."

52

ROEMER RODE up in the elevator with Colonel Legler. They'd driven back in silence, each with his own thoughts.

Roemer got off, and Legler held the door for a moment.

"I can't say that you handled this in the best way possible, Walther. Although you did find the murderer."

"I wonder if the project is worth it."

"It's not for us to say, you know. We're policemen, and nothing more."

"Yes, sir."

"Take the next few days off. Straighten out your personal life. Get some rest."

Roemer went back to his office, where he stood staring out the window.

Gehrman came in. "Well?"

Roemer turned around. "I'm taking the next couple of days off. The politicians have it now. We're finished."

"They believed you?"

"What choice did they have?" Roemer said. "Call Manning for me this afternoon. Thank him. I'm going to go home and get quietly drunk."

Roemer drove back to his apartment. The Iraqis would increase their efforts to find his father, which meant there wasn't much time left. Max Rilke would fight, but he was an old man, and Azziza was a pro. It would be like General Sherif's case: People would get hurt, and there would be no satisfactory solution.

Roemer fixed himself a sandwich but didn't want it. He took a beer into the living room and sat down by the window. There wasn't much traffic now, only an occasional delivery truck. It was quite cold and the sun was already low in the west.

He had been a cop all of his adult life. Even in the Luftwaffe, under NATO command, he had been attached to the Military Police. He had never made a conscious decision to make law enforcement his career. He suspected that it had something to do with his need for a sense of belonging. He had felt the camaraderie of shared purpose in the military, and it had seemed natural.

Now, however, it was ruined for him. Compromise was something he didn't accept. Yet the political system demanded it. Men such as Whalpol, who were adept at juggling several mutually exclusive principles, belonged in this system.

Roemer looked around his nearly bare apartment. Perhaps he was at heart a loner. Perhaps he did not belong in the BKA.

Yet his only talents were in unraveling mysteries: catching the bad guys.

The telephone rang and he started to get up to answer it, but then slumped back. He did not care any longer. He'd found the killer for them, unraveled the mystery. Only one thing remained for him to do. In the morning he would drive to Interlaken to take care of it. Afterward . . . He let the thought trail off. The phone stopped on the tenth ring, leaving a thick silence.

Roemer held the cool bottle of beer against his forehead. When Interlaken was taken care of, he would return home and resign from the BKA. Whalpol would demand it. Schaller would be relieved. And Colonel Legler would believe it was in the best interest of the Bureau.

He closed his eyes. Once, when he was a young boy, he woke in the middle of the night and heard his mother crying. Their apartment was very small; his bed was a couch in the tiny living room. He crept to his mother's room. She was crying in her sleep. *Lotti, why have you done this to me?* He could remember his confusion and fear. Had she cried because her husband was a mass murderer, or because he had deserted her?

A couple of hours later Roemer woke, stiff and cold, to the sound of someone pounding on his door. The beer had spilled and when he got up he stepped in the puddle. He went to the door and opened it.

"Rudi told me you were here, but you didn't answer your phone," Gretchen said.

Roemer came fully awake. She surprised him. "Did Kai Bauer kick you out already?"

"May I come in? I have to talk to you."

"Why not?" Roemer went into the kitchen, got a towel and wiped up the spilled beer.

Gretchen came in but stood by the half-open door as if she needed an escape route.

"What is it, Gretchen? Are you in trouble?"

"No. But I think you might be."

Roemer smiled wearily. "Bauer is going to press the assault charges? Is that what you've come to warn me about?"

"He deserved it," she grumbled. "This has to do with Leila Kahled."

A sinking feeling came over Roemer. "What about her?"

"She telephoned me yesterday afternoon. Or at least

Rudi thinks it was her. He told me I'd better tell you right away."

"What are you talking about?"

"This woman called me at work. Said she was from your office, and was trying to locate you. When I asked to speak to Rudi, she told me he wasn't there. But she had no idea who he was. I could hear it in her voice. When I told Rudi what had happened, he said it was probably Leila Kahled. He said she is with the Iraqi Secret Service or something." Gretchen shook her head. "Christ, Walther, I had no idea. I'm so goddamned sorry."

"What did she ask you, Gretchen?"

"She said that you had gone out of town, that you were in Bern over the weekend. She wanted to know where she could reach you."

"Go on." Over a year and a half ago he had confided in Gretchen about his father. She'd never mentioned it since. "What did you tell her?"

"I didn't mean it, Walther. Honest to God."

"Interlaken? Did you mention Interlaken?"

"She knew about Bern. I was so mad at you for what you did to Kai. It just slipped out."

The telephone rang. "Yes?" he shouted into the receiver.

It was Rudi Gehrman. "Did Gretchen get in touch with you?"

"She's here now." Roemer was breathing hard.

"Listen, Walther, don't do anything foolish. I'll call the Swiss police. I have a friend down there—"

"Don't you do it!"

"Goddammit, you're not thinking right!"

"I'll take care of it myself."

"If you go charging down there, they'll probably kill you. If it's a Mukhabarat operation they won't fool around."

"Have you told Colonel Legler?" Roemer made an effort to bring his voice back to normal.

Gehrman hesitated. "No."

"Don't." Roemer hung up. Gretchen was gone. It was just as well. He didn't know what he might have done to her.

He dialed his father's chalet outside Interlaken. The telephone rang a half dozen times before Max Rilke answered it.

"Max, this is Walther. There is trouble coming your way much sooner than I thought."

"We've been getting ready. Peter called from Town Hall, told me a woman was asking about taxes on the place."

It was Leila. "She'll be calling Azziza."

"If it's just him and the girl, they'll be in for a nasty surprise," Rilke said.

"I'm coming down. I'll take a plane to Bern and then rent a car."

"That's not a great idea, kid. If all hell breaks loose you'll have a lot of questions to answer. The Swiss police aren't exactly our friends."

"I'll be there. But meanwhile if it gets too rough, you know what to do."

"I do, Walther."

There was a Swissair flight at five-thirty for Bern, with a fifteen-minute layover in Zurich. Roemer threw a few things into his overnight bag and stuffed his gun deep inside. With luck it would not be found by Swiss customs, but his BKA identification would help. From Bern he would rent a car and get down to Interlaken in about an hour.

He looked around his apartment as if seeing it for the last time. There was nothing here for him any longer.

53

BY LATE afternoon, Leila had decided to turn back to Interlaken. She'd had enough killing. Lotti Roemer would have to be brought to Baghdad and kept out of harm's way for the duration of the project.

The old man would be dead soon in any event, and his son would finally be free.

Azziza's ominous accusation that she was in love with Walther Roemer still clung. Back home, it would eventually be used against her. No matter her father's influence with the RCC, she could be charged with treason. Uncle Bashir was disappointed in her. Even the friendly Bassam Zwaiter had apparently arranged to bug her office telephone. If only she could have found the killer of the two women. It was probably someone from the team. Crazed with a holy rage against the infidels. How could she have failed to recognize the signs, unless she had been too preoccupied with her own life?

She sifted options. She could telephone Zwaiter, explain the entire situation, make him see that it was best not to assassinate the old man. But Zwaiter did not have the authority to stop Azziza even if he wanted to. Uncle Bashir had the authority, but what could he do from Baghdad? She could tip off the Swiss police that someone was on the way to murder Lotti Roemer. The old man's sergeant would cooperate with her or stand alone against Azziza.

She shuddered, thinking about Azziza, and her grip tightened on the steering wheel. He would know she was there, in the house. But that wouldn't slow him down. All this for what? To give an old monster the chance he never gave thousands of innocent people?

54

THERE HAD been a lot of activity all through the early afternoon at the Klauber estate. From their vantage point in the surveillance house, they had watched through powerful binoculars and listened to the telephone conversations over a monitor.

Major Whalpol dialed the Chancellor's office. An aide answered.

"Any news yet?" Whalpol asked.

"The Ambassador from Iraq is here. They are in conference, Major. Any change at your end?"

"Plenty." Whalpol was getting nervous. It looked as if General Sherif was about to make a move, but when and to where were unclear. "Six technicians from the plant arrived twenty minutes ago. Apparently they're moving something back to the KwU. Possibly a computer."

"Anything else?"

Whalpol leaned forward to look through the binoculars set on a tripod. Three panel trucks had pulled up on the driveway leading to the garage and other service buildings behind the main house. The technicians and four of Sherif's men were loading crates marked with the IBM logo into the vans. They were in a hurry. More disturbing was the fact that Sherif's troops, dressed in battle fatigues, carried Kalashnikov automatic rifles.

"It looks like a military operation. Sherif's people are all heavily armed."

There was a hesitation on the line. "Do nothing to aggravate the situation, Major Whalpol, is that perfectly clear?"

"There isn't much I could do. If Sherif did decide to make a move and I tried to stop him, there would be a lot of bloodshed."

"Avoid that at all costs. As soon as a decision is made here, you will be informed. Their ambassador will have to cable Baghdad for instructions. In the meantime just observe the general's movements."

"I understand."

Whalpol poured a cup of coffee and lit a cigarette, then went back to the binoculars. He had eight people on this project. Three were asleep in the next room, two were here watching the monitoring equipment and the other three were in an unmarked car just around the corner from the estate driveway at the bottom of the hill. They were armed only with handguns. In a firefight with the Iraqis they wouldn't last sixty seconds.

It was curious to be thinking in such terms, but in fact he and Roemer had discovered that General Sherif was insane. If indeed the man was the terrorist Michael, the situation was doubly dangerous. Carlos had been an amateur compared to Michael, who'd been implicated in everything from the massacre of the Israeli team at the Munich Olympics to the murders of the entire cabinet of South Yemen's President 'Ali Nasir Muhammad in 1986, and more than a dozen spectacularly successful airliner hijackings.

With such a man commanding a dozen heavily armed

troops, this would turn to bloodshed unless the Iraqi Ambassador could talk Sherif down.

One thing Whalpol was certain of was that General Sherif would never stand trial in Germany.

55

THEY WERE late. It was dark when the small commuter airplane touched down at Bern's tiny airport and taxied to the terminal. The handful of passengers who had flown with Roemer were grumbling.

On the short, bumpy flight from Bonn and then over from Zurich, Roemer had kept coming back to the way Leila Kahled would take the news that her father was a murderer. He could understand what she would have to endure; he had lived with just such a burden all his life.

Roemer brought his nylon overnight bag to the customs table. He handed the officer his BKA identification.

"Is your visit to Switzerland official, sir?"

"No."

The officer returned the ID. "You may pass."

He took the airport bus into town to the Europcar/National office, where he rented a small Fiat. He was on the road to Interlaken ten minutes later, pushing the car to its limit, hoping he wasn't already too late.

He unzipped the bag on the seat next to him, fumbled inside until he found his gun, pulled it out and stuffed it into his belt.

He wished his father were dead. It would have been so much easier had he died on the move from the sanatorium. He could have been buried in the small Interlaken graveyard, and that entire hidden portion of Roemer's life could have been over.

"Die," he mumbled. "Get it done with, for God's sake."

56

JACOB WADUD raced through the night as fast as he dared drive from the Second Armored Division Headquarters at Al-Falluja to Baghdad, a highway distance of forty miles.

He was a big, meaty man with a barrel chest and thick, weathered features. He had been raised on the wrong side of Kirkuk in the north, where he fought his way through school and onto the police force. Twelve years ago, after his young wife's death from cancer, he had moved to Baghdad, where he had done a two-year stint in the army and then had become a federal homicide detective.

He had been in riots and wars, and yet tonight he was frightened. General Sherif was a national hero. They called him the Lion of Baghdad. His photograph still hung in the orderly room of the Second Armored, which he had commanded during the wars with Iran and Kuwait until his elevation to this government post. He was the soldiers' general, still, in a nation of soldiers. Hardly an Arab in Baghdad (including Wadud himself, who had served under Sherif) didn't know and love him. But he was a murderer, and almost certainly he planned some private war against the West.

Wadud entered the city from the southwest forty-three minutes after leaving Al-Falluja. Downtown, he parked his battered old Chevrolet around the corner from the Central Telegraph Office.

He hurried the final block on foot, turning down a narrow alley that opened into a well-tended courtyard bordered by tiny shops and a narrow brick building marked MINISTRY OF FINANCE—ANNEXE. The Annexe was a front for the Mukhabarat operational headquarters. Iraqi Federal Police often worked hand in hand with the Secret Service.

He rang the bell; the door buzzed and he went in. He showed his identification and turned in his handgun to the civilian guard in the small anteroom.

"Go right up, Inspector. *Is-say-yid* Kahair is expecting you."

Wadud took the elevator up to the third floor, where Bashir Kahair was waiting. They had agreed this afternoon, after Roemer's stunning telephone call, that Wadud should go to the general's old command to find out about the twelve troops he had taken with him to Germany. All of them had been drawn from the Second Armored, which was still fiercely loyal to the general.

"Well?" Kahair asked without preamble.

"You're not going to like it," Wadud said.

They went down the corridor into Kahair's office, closing the door behind them. They didn't bother sitting.

"Give it to me straight, Jacob," Kahair said sharply.

"All twelve he has with him are trigger-happy crazies."

Kahair's eyebrows rose.

"High combat time for every last one of them in Iran and Kuwait. Hand-to-hand, infiltration, weapons, strategy. The worst part is that every damned one of them is a demolitions expert."

"What can he be thinking?"

"I paid a call to an old friend working munitions," Wadud said. "He wouldn't tell me in so many words, but he seems to believe that the general took along enough explosives—plastique, he thinks—to blow half of Germany off the map."

Kahair was staggered by the news. "The German Chancellor called our ambassador for a meeting late this afternoon. Told him that the general probably murdered the two women, and that the German government requested a release of his diplomatic status. They want to arrest him."

Wadud shook his head. "We'll bring him back here."

"That's the least of my worries, Jacob."

Wadud knew what the Mukhabarat deputy meant. If the Germans tried to arrest General Sherif, he would resist them with force. The fanatics he had with him would love a firefight. According to the sergeant in munitions, they called themselves the Basra Brigade.

"I'll arrange transportation for you," Kahair said. "Can you be ready to leave within the hour?"

"Yes, sir," Wadud said. "I'll bring the general home."

57

THE CHALET at Jungfraujochstrasse, No. 15, was a modest structure built into the side of a hill. The dark, hulking mountains rose all around it.

Leila passed the entrance and parked her Mercedes a half mile farther up the road. She headed back on foot, stopping at the side of the road fifty yards from the driveway. She could see a few lights from the chalet through the trees ahead, and she could smell wood smoke from the chimney.

A chill wind rustled in the trees. It was cold and lonely here.

She'd seen no other car parked along the road. Dr. Azziza was not here yet. Perhaps he would wait until after midnight, when the household would be bedded down.

If the property clerk had telephoned Sergeant Rilke, they'd be waiting for her to sneak up on them. They would have an alarm system. Dogs. Possibly even armed security guards.

She wondered, though. All these years the old man had lived here, or at the sanatorium, without making any fuss that would call attention to him. Elaborate security precautions would in themselves create a stir.

At the very least, however, Sergeant Rilke would be

armed and ready to open fire on someone sneaking up to the house.

But if a woman were to walk openly up the driveway, knock on the front door and ask for help, it might throw them off long enough for her to get inside.

Was she doing this because of a sense of justice? Because she hated Khodr Azziza and his kind? Or because . . . she had fallen in love with Walther Roemer?

Leila transferred her automatic from her purse to her coat pocket and continued down the road, turning in at the driveway and trudging up the steep slope to the house.

The lights she had seen from the road were all outside. Not one window was lit from within. The doors and windows were all in shadow.

Leila stepped onto a broad parking area between the garage and the front door. She was exposed here under the bright lights; one shot would be plenty. She would not have a chance.

A voice came out of the darkness somewhere ahead. "That's far enough, Fräulein."

Leila stopped. "I cannot see you, Herr . . . ?"

"Turn around and leave, and I may not shoot you."

"I have come to help."

"With your killer, Khodr Azziza?"

Leila was stunned. How had the man known? It wasn't possible.

"Macht schnell! Go away. Leave before I kill you."

"You must believe me, Sergeant Rilke. I have come here to help. Dr. Azziza will be here soon, and then you will have no chance."

Rilke laughed. "You have a sense of humor. Leave before I lose mine."

A bullet ricocheted off the driveway inches from her left foot, spraying her legs with stone chips. The muzzle flash had come from the left of the door. Probably an open window.

Rilke fired a second shot, this one whining off the stones to Leila's right.

Then three shots were fired in rapid succession from behind and above Leila.

"Don't move, Leila," Dr. Azziza called. "I don't want to kill you."

Azziza had been waiting in the darkness. He had pinpointed the muzzle flash from Rilke's gun and had targeted it. Azziza had known she would be coming here. She was his bait.

Behind her a branch snapped. Azziza had been waiting in a tree.

She turned slowly as she put her right hand in her coat pocket, her fingers around the grip of her Beretta .380.

58

THE NIGHT had turned transparent. Here in the mountains the air was thin, hard to breathe. Leila's heart hammered.

Azziza, dressed in black, a high-powered rifle with a night scope held loosely in one hand, came out of the darkness.

"You took a big chance coming back," he said. "Rilke could have shot you."

"I'm not going to let you murder the old man."

Azziza stood ten feet away, near enough for Leila to see his strong face. "Your love is misplaced, wouldn't you agree?"

"Don't be a fool. I returned to make sure that Lotti Roemer is brought back to Baghdad to be used as a hostage."

"He wouldn't survive the trip."

"If he died in transit, at least we would not have killed him."

Rilke was surely dead. Azziza would not have exposed himself unless he was sure. But there was still the house staff. Perhaps they had telephoned the Swiss police when the shooting began. Perhaps if she could only delay him long enough . . .

"I cut the telephone lines to the house," Azziza said,

"and Rilke sent the German staff away more than an hour ago, so don't be concerned about innocent people getting hurt." He moved forward, and Leila's grip tightened on the automatic. "Long before you could get that little gun out of your pocket, I would shoot you. Don't make me do that."

Leila was paralyzed. She had killed before, but she was not a seasoned, cold-blooded expert like Azziza. She operated with courage, brains and sometimes her good looks. This was new.

"Take the gun out and very slowly lay it on the ground, and then step away," Azziza said.

She eased her grip on the Beretta and slowly withdrew her hand from her pocket, holding it well away from her side so that Azziza could see she was unarmed.

"The gun, Leila."

"No." She turned and walked up to the house. Behind her she heard the snick of the rifle bolt, and she expected the shot to come. But it did not.

A window to the left of the front door was open. Leila stepped up and looked inside. Sergeant Rilke's body was jammed up against a large chair. Most of his forehead was gone, and a large dark stain had spread from a hole in his chest.

She stepped back—into Azziza's arms.

"Not a pretty sight, is it?"

Leila spun around and raked his face with her fingernails, trying for his eyes. He reared back, hissing.

"Bitch!" Blood streamed down his cheek.

Leila came at him again, but this time he was expecting it. His fist caught her high in the stomach just below her breasts. Her lungs emptied, nausea rose and she fell back on the step, her head banging against the door frame.

She fumbled in her coat pocket for her gun, but she

couldn't make her fingers work. She bent over and vomited.

Azziza stepped around her, opened the door and went inside. She began to shake violently, tears filling her eyes. Al Kumait had never seemed so far away.

She had lost. Azziza had won. After tonight there would be nothing left for her. Trying to save a dying mass murderer, she had destroyed herself as surely as if she had put her gun to her own head.

As a true Palestinian, born in Jerusalem, she had nowhere to go. Her father would never understand; he had lost too much in the war and now was incapable of change. All the lost souls of relatives who had died in the PLO camps talked to him in the night.

Headlights flashed in the trees, and a small car screamed up the driveway, sliding sideways to a halt, spewing gravel.

Leila propped herself up as Walther Roemer leaped out, gun in hand, and raced toward her. "No," she tried to cry out.

"You!"

Leila raised her right hand, as if to fend off a blow. Roemer dove to the ground, snapping off two shots toward a spot behind her.

Azziza's high-powered rifle cracked from inside the house, the bullet chinking a tree. Roemer fired again.

"I didn't kill your father," Azziza shouted from inside.

Roemer was fifteen feet from Leila, his gun trained on the open doorway behind her.

"I tried to stop him," Leila called too weakly for him to hear.

"I have no quarrel with you, Investigator. But I swear to you that your father was already dead. There was a pillow over his face. I think Rilke killed him rather than let him be taken."

Roemer's eyes were wild. Leila wanted to tell him to back down and Azziza would leave. Otherwise, Azziza would almost certainly kill him.

"Come out of there, Azziza. Or I'll shoot your partner."

The assassin laughed, his voice closer now. He was just within the doorway. "She came here to stop me. She's in love with you. Didn't you know it?"

Even from a distance Leila could see that Roemer was suddenly confused, uncertain—exactly what Azziza wanted.

She heard a soft scuffling inside; Azziza was going around to the open window for a clear shot at Roemer. She reached into her coat pocket, pulled out her gun, thumbed the safety off and lurched to her feet. Roemer shouted something, then fired a shot, the bullet smacking into the door frame.

She reached to the edge of the window, bringing the Beretta up as Azziza appeared. She pulled the trigger. The automatic bucked in her hand and surprise spread across Azziza's dark features. She fired a second time, the shot hitting the killer in the chest near the first shot, and he crashed backward on top of Rilke's body, the rifle clattering to the floor.

For several long seconds there was no sound. Azziza was looking at her, his lips parted in a grimace, or perhaps a smile, his eyes wide. Then his head drooped forward on his chest.

Leila turned slowly. Roemer was on his feet. His gun was pointing at her.

She let her hand go slack at her side and the Beretta dropped to the ground.

"Why?" Roemer asked.

"I came to take your father to Baghdad. I'm not a murderer."

Roemer winced. "But you called him."

She shook her head. She still felt weak. "They had a bug on my telephone. They knew I was coming here."

Roemer stared at her. He wanted to say something. He sighed deeply, then came up the walk, passing her without a word, and went into the house. She followed him.

In an upstairs bedroom, Lotti Roemer's frail, wasted body lay on a bed. His lips and face were blue, his eyes open and bulging. Leila stood by the door. Roemer looked down at his father's body.

The room was filled with photographs and old certificates in gilded frames, mementos of Lotti Roemer's career in the SS. Photographs of Hitler and Himmler and other Nazi leaders, of Dachau and its administrators, of some nightclub where, in his uniform, he sat at a booth with his arms around two women. Finally it was over. She could return to Baghdad. At least it was home. They could do whatever they wanted with her. Maybe the Jews would thank her. Who could know?

Tears streamed down Roemer's cheeks, but he looked as if a tremendous burden had been lifted from his shoulders.

59

THE LONG black limousine glided up the Bonnerstrasse and turned into the driveway of the Klauber estate. It was dark. Whalpol watched the big car through the infrared spotter scope his technicians had brought up earlier in the day.

The images in the lens were clear, but ethereal, washed of color.

He was alone in the house with Robert Neuenfeld, his communications specialist. An hour ago, four of Sherif's uniformed troops had gone with the three vanloads of IBM-marked crates. Thalberg and Adler, two BND fieldmen from Munich, had followed them out to the KwU facility while Whalpol's other men took up their positions below the driveway so that they could watch the approach roads. Sherif's staff had off-loaded the crates into the main research and development building. Whalpol had expected them to return here, but they had not; they had so far remained in the R&D building. A half hour ago the plant's day shift had been released, and Whalpol's men reported that the gigantic facility seemed nearly deserted.

The limousine pulled up at the front door of the main house. The chauffeur jumped out and opened the rear door for a tall, gray-haired man in a dark overcoat.

Whalpol immediately recognized him as the Iraqi Ambassador.

"Get me Chancellor Kohl's office," Whalpol told his communications man without looking away from the scope.

The Iraqi Ambassador came up the walk as the front door opened. General Sherif stepped outside. Amazingly, he was dressed like his troops, in camouflage battle fatigues, a sidearm strapped at his hip. He and the Ambassador shook hands and disappeared into the house.

Whalpol straightened up. Sherif was expecting trouble. But did he believe he was going to have to run some sort of military operation to save his skin?

"I have Herr Lessing on the telephone," Neuenfeld said.

Whalpol took the telephone. "The Ambassador just arrived."

"Good. We were expecting it. From what we understand, he is going to ask the general to stand down and return with him tonight to Baghdad. Under the circumstances we feel it is for the best. The government of Iraq has given us assurances that the man will undergo immediate psychiatric evaluation."

Whalpol agreed. He was glad that Roemer wasn't here to cause trouble with his inflexibility.

"They're bringing in an Iraqi Air Force jet transport to fetch him back. Should be showing up in an hour or so."

"What about his troops?"

The aide hesitated. "That may be a problem, Major. We're sending you some people. But it may take an hour for them to arrive."

"People? What people?"

"Military. From Wiesbaden."

Whalpol went cold. "What are you telling me now?"

"Sherif's staff are heavily armed and combat-trained."

"I know that. We've seen their Kalashnikovs."

"You and our people must stay out of sight if at all possible. We don't want to start anything. Sherif's people all are demolitions experts. They've brought a large quantity of high explosives."

"God in heaven," Whalpol breathed. "The R&D facility at KwU. Four of Sherif's troops are there now. They took along a lot of heavy crates."

"Do you know what that building contains?"

"Not in any detail."

"A fuel rod reprocessing facility. If Sherif's people should detonate a charge, they'd spread radioactive material over half of Bonn."

Everything fell into place for Whalpol. "Divert the soldiers to the plant."

"It'll probably be too late."

"For now, General Sherif doesn't matter. He's only got four of his people at the facility. I'm taking most of my men with me. We'll see what we can do."

"They have to be stopped."

Whalpol slammed down the telephone and jumped up. If Sherif wanted to force the issue, he would have no problem fighting his way from here to the KwU plant if he did it before the army unit showed up. The general had evidently planned for this, even before he came to Germany. Whalpol didn't think the Ambassador was going to do much good.

Sherif's daughter, however, could be the key if the situation got out of hand. He turned to Neuenfeld.

"It is essential that we get the general's daughter up here as soon as possible. She is somewhere in Switzerland. Call Investigator Roemer. He'll know where she might be. Or talk to Rudi Gehrman. He'll know. Get a chopper out of Pullach to fetch her once she's located."

"Yes, sir." Neuenfeld was young but he knew his business. "What if the general and his troops head out?"

"Radio me immediately. I don't want him sneaking through my back door with all that firepower." Whalpol headed for the door. "Listen, kid, there is a good chance we've been spotted. If any of General Sherif's men head up here, get the hell out."

Whalpol hurried out to his car and headed down to the Bonnerstrasse.

He stopped and quickly explained the situation to his lookouts parked at the bottom of the hill, and they followed him down to the Köln-Bonn Autobahn.

The sonofabitch Roemer had started the entire mess by shoving his way into Sherif's study and snatching the cuff links. Whalpol growled in frustration. He figured there wasn't much of a chance of stopping them. The four had been in the R&D facility for about an hour now. Within the first ten or fifteen minutes they had probably rigged their explosive charges.

They'd be waiting for their general and the others to show up, though. They did not have enough people to cover the entire facility. They were as vulnerable now as they'd ever be. It was possible to get in and disarm them.

Whalpol had a fair idea why Sherif was doing this, but was he going to hold the entire city for ransom? What could he possibly want?

From two miles away, Whalpol spotted the flames in the KwU parking lot, and he pushed his car even harder, a cold weight pressing his chest. Several cars had pulled over onto the side of the road, the drivers getting out to look.

He raced up the hill to the main parking lot to see a car furiously burning a hundred yards behind the back gate to the R&D facility. He hoped his two people had gotten out.

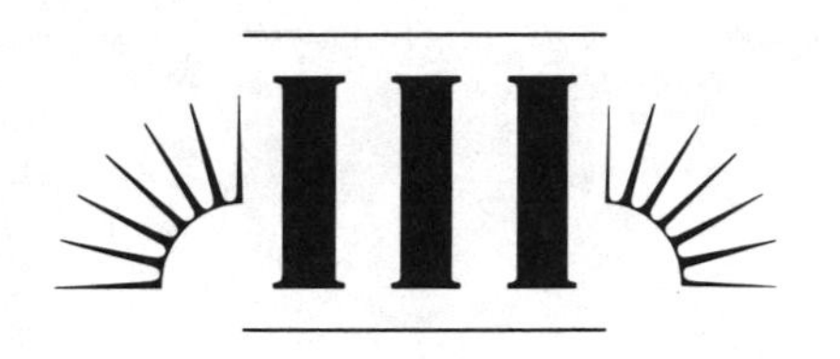

60

AT TWENTY-FIVE, Robert Neuenfeld was the youngest member of the BND's Special Operations Team out of Pullach, near Munich, but he was highly respected. He expected one day to be director of the entire Secret Service.

There was no answer at Investigator Roemer's apartment. Neuenfeld let it ring fifteen times. The office number was answered on the second ring.

"Bureau of Investigation."

"I'd like to speak with Investigator Walther Roemer."

"I'm sorry, sir, the investigator is not here at the moment. Is this an emergency?"

Most definitely, Neuenfeld said to himself. "Do you know where he might be reached?"

"No, sir."

"Is Rudi Gehrman there? I am calling for Major Whalpol."

"One moment, sir."

The Ambassador had been inside for nearly a half hour now. There had been no further activity, but Neuenfeld was nervous with all the firepower they had seen. Major Whalpol was normally unflappable, but Neuenfeld had caught the fear in his eyes.

"What can I do for you?" Rudi Gehrman asked.

"We're trying to reach Investigator Roemer. He doesn't answer his home telephone. Major Whalpol said you might be able to help."

"Does this concern the situation with General Sherif? Can you tell me that?"

"Yes, sir, it does. We're actually trying to reach the general's daughter. Major Whalpol felt that Investigator Roemer might be able to locate her for us."

Gehrman hesitated. "Let me talk with Whalpol."

"I'm sorry, sir, but he's not here at the moment. He asked me to track down Fräulein Kahled and get her up here as soon as possible. We have a helicopter standing by at Pullach, in the event she might be in Switzerland."

"What's going on up there? You're at the surveillance house above the Klauber estate?"

Neuenfeld wasn't surprised that the BKA knew about this operation. Major Whalpol had been having a lot of trouble with them over this business. It seemed strange to be discussing BND business so openly. But it was an emergency.

"Yes, sir. This situation is becoming critical."

"Can you be more specific?"

"I'm sorry, sir, no."

"She's in or near the town of Interlaken."

"Would she be at a hotel or perhaps a private home?"

"Goddammit," Gehrman said. "Is there any way you can get me in contact with Major Whalpol? This is a hell of a lot more complicated than you can guess."

Neuenfeld stiffened. He leaned forward and looked through the spotter scope. The Ambassador had come out of the house. He didn't have his hat.

"Please, Mr. Gehrman, this situation could get out of hand very soon."

Colonel Habash, the general's chief of staff, dressed in

battle fatigues, came out behind the Ambassador. They seemed to be arguing, both waving their hands around.

"Jungfraujochstrasse, Number Fifteen," Gehrman said. "It's a chalet in the mountains north of town, under the name of Lotti Walkmann, Roemer's father. Investigator Roemer should be there now, along with Leila Kahled. But listen to me, there could be some trouble . . ."

"Thank you, sir," Neuenfeld cut in. "If it's possible, I'd like you to contact Investigator Roemer for me. Tell him we will be sending a helicopter to pick them up. It should be across the border to them within the hour."

Neuenfeld broke the connection and immediately dialed the Pullach Operations Center. He continued to look through the scope.

The Ambassador was getting into his car; Colonel Habash went back into the house. The big limousine headed down the driveway.

"Operations."

"Neuenfeld. I have that location." He gave the address. "Roemer will be there. It is his father's house."

"Has she called Azziza?"

"I don't know, but you'd better pick them both up. All hell is about to break loose up here."

"Where do you want them?"

"I don't know yet. I'll let you know on the run."

"We'll be in the air in five minutes. We'll have it cleared with the Swiss authorities before we cross the border."

"Right." Neuenfeld hung up.

Below, the garage doors opened behind the main house. A Mercedes 600 limousine pulled out and stopped. A half dozen troops trotted out of the house, followed by Colonel Habash and General Sherif. They all carried automatic weapons.

Neuenfeld pulled out his SigSauer automatic, laid the gun on the desk and keyed the microphone for the mobile transmitter that would connect him with Major Whalpol, code-named Abel One.

The door crashed open behind him. He spun around, grabbing for his gun, as two Iraqi soldiers in battle fatigues brought up their Kalashnikovs and fired.

61

A BURST OF machine-gun fire from the R&D reactor building slammed into the car behind which Whalpol and his men were crouched. They'd come within one hundred meters of the open gate in the tall chain-link fence when the shooting began, forcing them to pull up short and leap out.

Thalberg and Adler, who'd followed Sherif's troops out here, had been gunned down. Their car was still burning. They'd been trapped in it.

It was quiet for a time. Whalpol eased himself up to look over the hood.

The R&D facility was contained in a three-story blockhouse enclosed behind two perimeter fences, both electrified. Twenty meters of open area between the inner and outer fences was a no-man's-land bathed in harsh lights. A single access road pierced the two fences through tall gates, both of which stood open. Behind the facility was a railroad spur line, tracks passing through two larger gates directly to the back of the blockhouse. Those gates were locked.

Evidently, Sherif's troops had set themselves up on the third floor or possibly the roof so that they could command all approaches with a line of fire.

It would be no use trying to rush them now. They had

the upper hand with their superior position and firepower. Whalpol's main concern was General Sherif and the rest of his troops.

Keeping low, he opened the driver's door and reached inside for the mobile radio microphone.

They were going to have to get help, and then Neuenfeld would have to get out of the surveillance house.

Whalpol keyed the microphone. "Abel Two, this is Abel One."

There was no answer.

"Abel Two, this is Abel One, copy?"

"They may have hit our radio," one of the technicians said. Suddenly the radio blared: "Abel One, this is Basra Brigade." The transmission was coming from the blockhouse, so loud as to be distorted. What the hell was Basra Brigade?

"This is Abel One, I copy you," Whalpol said. He rose so that he could see the blockhouse.

"Listen to me very carefully, Major Whalpol, because I will not repeat myself." The speaker's German was heavily accented. "The person you identify as Abel Two and his position have been neutralized. Within the next five minutes our commander and reinforcements will be coming through the main gate from the Autobahn. They will drive directly to the gate of the research and development building in front of you. We are giving you two choices for the moment. Either remove yourself from KwU property, or move as far away as possible from the gate-to-gate direct line. Do this immediately, and we will not open fire. You have thirty seconds."

"You bastards," Whalpol said.

"We're counting."

They had probably hit Neuenfeld from behind. He wouldn't have had a chance. Whalpol felt sick about it.

He keyed the microphone. "What do you want? Why are you doing this?"

"Twenty seconds," the speaker boomed.

Whalpol stood up to be in plain view and looked across at the blockhouse. A figure appeared briefly, moving along the roofline.

"We're going to have to withdraw." He turned to Jim Heffernan, one of his Pullach field officers. "Get down to the BKA office and set up our comms relay. Call the Chancellor's office and let them know what's happening out here. I don't know if Robert had a chance to find the general's daughter. Call Pullach first and see if they've dispatched the chopper. If they haven't, you might have to locate Roemer, and through him the girl. I want them both here as soon as possible."

"Fifteen seconds," the speaker blared.

Whalpol keyed the microphone. "We're getting out of the way. We won't interfere. But can you tell me what you hope to gain by all this?"

"Thirteen seconds."

"Get the hell out of here," Whalpol ordered. Heffernan hurried back to the Mercedes. BND special operations officers Ebert and Kleiner climbed into Whalpol's car and drove with him over to the west side of the big parking lot, near the administration building, a kilometer from the R&D blockhouse.

There were a few cars in the lot, but most of the people in administration probably had no idea yet what was happening. The security people at the R&D building would have been the only ones directly involved.

Whalpol picked up the mike. "Basra Brigade, this is Abel One. Can you tell me what is happening to the technicians and security people in the R&D building?"

"If you do not interfere until this situation stabilizes, they may be released unharmed."

It was something. The first minutes of any hostage situation were always the most dangerous. Nerves were at a raw edge, tempers high. It wouldn't take much to snap them.

General Sherif and his people would come from the Bonnerstrasse and then out the Autobahn. They'd be moving fast. Whalpol just hoped that some fool didn't try to stop them.

62

LIEUTENANT MANNING happened to be in the KP operations center downtown talking with Sergeant Jacobs when the call came in: A woman reported gunfire in the vicinity of the Klauber estate.

At Roemer's behest, Rudi Gehrman had called earlier and explained the situation. It was to be hands off while the diplomats worked it out.

But someone had evidently gotten in the way up there. If General Sherif and his troops were on the move, the city would have to be protected, diplomats or not.

"Sherif?" Jacobs asked.

"Sounds like it," Manning said. They hurried downstairs to the dispatcher's desk. Jacobs went to get the shotguns out of the trunk of their car.

Sherif had a dozen crack troops with him. Manning could field ten times that many. But he had a bad feeling that a lot of people were going to get hurt. Sherif was a crazy. No telling what he might do. The dispatcher, a young woman with wide eyes, looked up.

"I want every available city unit, code one, out to the Klauber estate in full riot gear. Then call the Köln KP, tell them we're going to need help on the double. Call Klein at the airport, tell him that General Sherif and his gang may be heading his way. I want the terminal cleared. Call the BKA and find out if Roemer is there. Advise them of the situation. Then start the call-up list for all off-duty personnel. Have you got that?"

"Yes, sir," the girl said. She had been through riot management training. "I'll set you up on the Tactical One frequency."

Manning hurried out the back door as Jacobs was coming around with the car. He climbed in and they took off, tires squealing, lights flashing, siren blaring.

The two riot guns were in the rack between them. As they screamed up the Adenauerallee, traffic parting for them, Manning loaded both weapons.

The radio crackled with instructions, calling units from all over the city. One by one they responded, then switched to the tactical frequency used for special operations.

They roared past the University am Hofgarten on their left and the modern Bonn Municipal Theater on their right, and over the Kennedy Bridge. Two units with lights flashing came down from Königswinter across the river, and others were coming from the city proper.

Manning got on the radio. "Listen up, people. We have a dozen or more heavily armed combat troops at or near the Klauber estate. Gunfire has already been reported, but we don't know yet exactly what is happening. These people will be hostile and extremely dangerous. They may be trying to move out to the airport. I want the Siegburg entrance to the Autobahn blocked to all traffic. Watch yourselves."

They screamed up toward the Bonnerstrasse beyond the Konrad Adenauer Platz, the traffic here much heavier. Manning had a vision of General Sherif's troops coming down the Autobahn, guns blazing, leaving in their wake a trail of destruction. If it was true that the general had killed those two women, he would not be beyond such senseless violence. Manning could still see the ruined bodies of Sarah Razmarah and Joan Waldmann in his mind's eye. A madman had done that.

A bright fireball lit up the night sky near the Autobahn entrance. The radio came alive with a dozen voices shouting frantic orders and questions. A few seconds later the sound of an explosion rumbled over the noise of their siren.

"Gott in Himmel," Jacobs said.

"What happened? What happened?" Manning shouted into the microphone.

"It was Otto," the radio blared. "A bazooka or a rocket or something! He didn't have a chance!"

They came over the TEE railroad tracks and could see the burning, tangled wreckage of a car in the drainage ditch beside the entrance to the Autobahn. Cars were pulled over everywhere. Police units were screaming in from every direction.

Manning spotted the limousine shooting from the entrance ramp and speeding toward the airport. Pinpricks of light flashed from the car windows, muzzle flashes from automatic weapons.

"It's the black Mercedes heading north on the Autobahn," Manning radioed.

"We have him spotted," one of his units came back. Jacobs expertly wheeled the car up the ramp, passing the burning wreckage.

"Dispatch, this is Manning."

"I have you," the dispatcher radioed. He could hear the strain in her voice. Behind him three more police units came up the ramp.

"We're in pursuit of a black Mercedes limousine, license unknown, heading north at a high rate of speed on the Köln-Bonn Autobahn. They may be heading for the airport. Have the Köln police block off the exits, but with extreme caution."

"They may be heading to the KwU facility, Lieutenant. We just received a report of automatic weapons fire from there."

Manning was nonplussed. KwU? What the hell could be happening out there? But then it struck him, and he went cold. They built nuclear reactors.

63

ROEMER HAD not told Leila about her father. They sat across from each other in the living room of the Interlaken house. Swiss police came and went with their usual efficiency, photographing and cataloging the crime scene. Two men dead in a shootout on the first floor, one dead upstairs in the bedroom. The coroner was upstairs.

A police lieutenant from Bern leaned against the grand piano watching them through hooded eyes.

"You brought weapons illegally into Switzerland. For that alone you will spend a long time in prison," the sour-faced cop said.

Roemer looked up tiredly. "When your ballistics people finish, it will be clear what happened here."

"I don't need you to tell me my business," the cop snapped.

The first police had shown up within five minutes. Someone had reported the shooting.

"I would like to telephone my embassy, if I may," Leila said politely.

"I'll let you know when you can call someone. I want to know why you were here chasing Nazis. And I want to know who the dead men are in the study."

"One was Khodr Azziza," Roemer said. "The other was Max Rilke."

"We know about Rilke." The cop turned to the piano and opened a passport. "The other one was Lawrence Behm. Austrian citizen."

"He was an Iraqi. Worked for Military Intelligence, from what I understand."

"You know this one? You knew he was coming here? Any idea why?"

"I had a fair idea," Roemer said.

"How did you come by that information, Investigator?"

Roemer glanced at Leila. She turned away. Her eyes were closed. She was shivering.

"A BND officer, Major Whalpol, told me that Azziza was probably somewhere in Switzerland." Roemer no longer cared who was implicated now.

The Swiss cop tossed the passport down on the piano. "What was this Azziza doing here? What is your relationship with the old man upstairs?"

"He was my father."

"You found out Azziza was coming here so you intercepted him."

"I killed Azziza," Leila said.

"I figured the Beretta we found outside might be yours," the cop said. He opened Leila's passport. "May I ask what you are doing with a diplomatic passport?"

"You may not."

The cop's jaw tightened. "You say that you killed Azziza, whom Investigator Roemer claims was your fellow countryman. I don't understand, Fräulein Kahled."

"Azziza wanted to kill the man upstairs. I wanted to bring him to Baghdad for . . . questioning."

"You and Azziza were working together?"

"No."

The cop shook his head. "Iraqis and Nazis and German Federal Investigators. This will make for some juicy headlines, let me tell you."

The coroner, an older man with thick white hair and gold wire-rimmed glasses, came down the stairs. "We can move the body now, Arndt."

"He was murdered?" the cop asked.

"Smothered to death, several hours ago, I'd guess." The doctor shrugged. "He would not have lived much longer in any event. I'd guess he had heart problems, at least, and probably a liver or kidney dysfunction."

"Cancer," Roemer said.

The doctor looked over at him. "He was recently in a hospital? There are intravenous needle marks in his arms."

"A sanatorium outside of Bern."

"Did you kill your father?" the cop asked, the first hint of compassion in his voice.

"Max Rilke, his sergeant, did, I think. He knew someone would be coming here. We agreed on the phone that my father would never be taken alive."

"So you ordered him to kill the old man?"

"We agreed to it as a measure of last resort. I was too late getting here."

"I arrived first," Leila said. "Azziza killed Sergeant Rilke, and then tried to kill me."

"It will be months before this is straightened out."

One of the uniformed cops came in. "Pardon me, Lieutenant, but there is a radio message for you outside. It's Captain Frick."

"Watch these two," the lieutenant said, and he went out. The coroner left too.

"I didn't want it to work out this way," Leila said.

"There will be no talking," the young police officer barked.

Roemer ignored him. "You didn't call Azziza?"

"No. He just showed up at my hotel in town."

"Stop this . . ."

Roemer glared at the cop, whose voice trailed off. Roemer turned again to Leila. "How did he find this house?"

"I told him."

"Then why did you come back?"

"Azziza meant to kill him."

She seemed fragile and frightened. Sooner or later he was going to have to tell her that her father was a murderer. Now, though, she would probably believe that he was striking back at her for leading Azziza here. Azziza's taunt hammered in his head. *She came here to stop me. She's in love with you. Didn't you know it?*

Roemer no longer knew what was solid or real. Going back was impossible for him. But going forward didn't seem to hold any promise either.

Lieutenant Arndt returned five minutes later, his cheeks red. He went directly to the piano, where he had laid the passports with Roemer's BKA identification card and shield and the weapons. He gazed at the things, the young cop behind him fidgeting. It was obvious that the lieutenant had just received some disturbing news. Something that he could not accommodate.

He turned finally and looked at Leila and Roemer. "You mentioned a Major Whalpol. Do you also know a Rudi Gehrman?"

"He's Operations Chief for the BKA Bonn District," Roemer answered.

The lieutenant looked at Leila. "You are not what you present yourself to be. It says in your identification that you are an Iraqi Federal Police officer. On the contrary, you are a case officer for the Mukhabarat. Your father is Deputy Minister of Defense."

Leila sat forward, her eyes alert.

The cop gathered up their passports and IDs and weapons and laid them on the heavy oak table in front of them.

"A helicopter will be here in a few minutes to return you to Bonn. My people will take care of everything here, including your automobiles."

"My God, what has happened?" Leila demanded.

The lieutenant went on as if he hadn't heard her. "We have an agreement with your Chancellor's office that you will return to answer questions. There will be a hearing."

Roemer had a fair idea what might be happening. Apparently they had tried to arrest General Sherif and a firefight had erupted. It wasn't so much him they wanted back in Bonn, it was Leila, who was needed to help calm her father.

"She does not know?" the lieutenant asked.

"No," Roemer said.

"What are you talking about?" Leila asked fearfully.

"I feel sorry for you, Fräulein Kahled," the lieutenant said. "Truly."

64

WHALPOL STOOD beside his car, listening to dozens of sirens converging from the north and south. They would be Bonn and Köln police. Newspeople would be swarming in response to the sirens. This place would be crawling with people, every damned one of them in the direct line of fire from the blockhouse, vulnerable to the explosion should Sherif's troops get nervous and touch off their charges.

He'd sent Ebert and Kleiner into the administration building minutes ago to make sure the KwU security people did not get into the fray. They were also looking for any plant personnel who might be able to provide them with engineering plans of the R&D building. It was a safe bet Sherif's troops weren't going to be smoked out with a frontal attack. They would either have to be convinced to stand down voluntarily (Leila Kahled was their single hope on that score), or somehow they would have to be ambushed. Whalpol didn't think they'd have much chance with the latter.

Whalpol reached inside for the microphone as the black Mercedes limousine sped through the main gate and raced directly across to the gates of the blockhouse.

"Basra Brigade, this is Abel One. General Sherif has arrived. We will not interfere."

"There are many police units in pursuit," the radio blared. "Stop them."

The Mercedes screeched to a halt just within the inner fence, and two soldiers leaped out and closed both gates. The car moved to the front of the building. A moment later, General Sherif, striding tall, along with his chief of staff, Colonel Habash, and the rest of the troops, went inside.

A green and white Bonn police cruiser screamed up from the main gate and angled across the parking lot. Whalpol flashed his headlights until the squad car came around in a wide arc and headed toward him.

Three other squad cars followed. Whalpol pulled out his BND identification, held it high over his head and stepped away from his car.

The first squad car slammed to a halt and two Bonn police officers, guns drawn, leaped out, crouching behind their open doors.

"Whalpol! BND!"

Still more police units entered the vast parking lot. One brought Lieutenant Manning.

"Manning, it's Ludwig Whalpol! BND!"

"General Sherif and his men made a break for it!" Manning shouted.

"They're in the blockhouse," Whalpol said. "You're going to have to keep everyone away. They've taken hostages."

Manning had a hard look. "They've already killed two of my people. They've got a bazooka or a rocket launcher."

"It's likely that they have set explosives around the nuclear stockpile. Get your people settled down. Block off the main approach to the gate and get someone behind the R&D building along the railroad line."

"Tell them not to get nervous. First thing is to get the hostages out of there."

"An army unit is coming up from Wiesbaden," Whalpol said.

"We have to coordinate communications."

"What about Roemer?"

"We're trying to find him and Sherif's daughter. She might be able to defuse the situation."

More sirens were coming in from the distance.

Whalpol picked up his microphone. "Basra Brigade, this is Abel One."

"We read you."

"It's going to take a few minutes to get everybody calmed down. I don't want anyone trigger-happy."

There was no answer for several long seconds. One by one the police sirens were being switched off, creating an eerie silence.

"Basra Brigade, are you there?" he radioed.

"We copy, Abel One, stand by."

Manning came back from his car. "My dispatcher tells me that our switchboard is flooded with calls—every second one a journalist."

"Abel One, this is Basra Brigade," the radio blared.

Whalpol lifted the mike. "I'm here."

"We have four initial demands for you. When they are met we will release our hostages and make our final demand. From this point on we will communicate only with you. Do you understand?"

"I copy."

"Number one: We want a one-hundred-meter fire zone immediately established around the entire perimeter of this building. If there is any movement within that zone, we will detonate the high explosives we have placed at the fuel rod pool. Two: We demand that you immediately turn over to us BKA investigator Walther Roemer. Three: We demand that Roemer's father, Lotti Roemer, who is known in Switzerland as Lotti Walkmann, be turned over to us. If he is already dead, we want his body. Four: Once these three conditions have been met, we demand to be put in radio contact with Chancellor Helmut Kohl."

"We copy that. May I speak with General Sherif?"

"Request denied."

"This will take time. Roemer and his father are both in Switzerland."

"We understand that, Major Whalpol. But time is the enemy. Sooner or later a mistake will be made—by one of your people, or one of ours."

"May I speak to one of the hostages?"

"Request denied."

"How do I know they are alive and unharmed?"

There was no answer.

"Basra Brigade, this is Abel One, do you copy?"

"Stand by for a demonstration."

Seconds later a tremendous explosion shattered the scene, an orange ball rising from the rear corner of the R&D building, debris flying hundreds of feet into the air.

"We are prepared in here, Major. Don't try our patience."

65

THE SPRAWLING KwU parking lot had become the staging area for a military operation. Army trucks formed a semicircle in the middle of the lot opposite the blockhouse. A big communications truck with a dish antenna had been set up and army troops in combat gear formed a perimeter guard, blocking anyone from coming within a hundred meters of the R&D building.

Dozens of police cars and vans blocked the main gate, behind which scores of journalists from newspapers, wire services and television stations had set up their equipment.

Whalpol, Manning, Colonel Thomas Faulkner, who commanded the two companies of soldiers from the base at Wiesbaden, and Albert Trautman, who was the KwU chief engineer and plant supervisor, stood on the roof of the administration building. They had an unobstructed view of the blockhouse a kilometer to the east. A large section of its roof had been destroyed in the explosion.

Colonel Faulkner, a tall man with ramrod bearing, put down his field glasses. "We could drop a dozen of my people right on top of them with a chopper."

"That would be suicide," Whalpol snapped. They had gone over this a dozen times since the army had shown up. It took a call to Helmut Kohl's staff to convince the colonel that Whalpol was in charge of this operation.

"Then what the hell do you suggest, Major?"

"We'll play along with whatever they want for now. General Sherif's daughter should be here within the next few minutes."

"You're not actually going to turn Roemer over to them, are you?" Manning asked.

"That's up to Roemer. But for the moment we can stall."

They spread out engineering drawings behind one of the big air-conditioning units. Trautman, a scholarly looking man, studied the plans. "There's one possibility, but it would be dangerous."

Whalpol hunched over the plans with the engineer. The long page was marked VENTING and showed the substructure beneath the blockhouse.

"There are six one-hundred-fifty-centimeter water lines in and out of there," Trautman said. He tapped the plans with his pencil. "Three are intake lines, all the way up from the pumping station."

"Cooling water for the storage pool?"

"Exactly," Trautman said. "No way of accessing them. However, there are three outflows, only two of which are used under normal conditions. The third is used for an emergency standby."

"Where do they lead?"

"They end up in our holding ponds down the hill across the tracks, just this side of the Autobahn. We could get to the outflow from a pond by lowering the water level. Shouldn't take more than half an hour to expose the pipe opening."

"What about on the other end, inside the building?"

"They come up beneath the holding pool, into a pump room. Each line has a cleanout plate. Twenty-four bolts.

The plate could be cut open with a torch. Tight quarters, but it could be done. So we could get a man in there."

Trautman nodded. "There's only one problem, Major. Your people would have to wear radiation suits. Once they got out of the pipe and into the pump room, they'd have to go into the emergency decontamination stalls."

"The pipe is radioactive?"

"Nothing serious if they can get in and out in a half hour. Providing they don't tear their suits. And they must get to the decontamination station before they trigger the in-plant radiation alarm system."

Whalpol sat back on his haunches and studied the plans. "Where are the controls for the pipelines?"

"Everything is operated from the main control room above the reactor. The outflow pipes are reasonably dry now because the reactor is in standby mode. Only one of the outflows is circulating any water. But if those people in there find out what you're up to, they could easily divert pool water through the pipes. Your men wouldn't stand a chance."

"Once they're in and decontaminated, we'll need a demolitions team to find and disarm whatever charges they may have placed."

"If General Sherif's men are any good," the engineer said, "I can tell you where they probably placed the explosives for maximum effectiveness. From there, the only way up to the control room unseen would be through the false ceiling from the floor above. It's a big space, with walkways and cable runs."

"I have the demolitions people," Colonel Faulkner said.

"What about exposure suits?" Whalpol asked.

"We have plenty in Engineering."

Colonel Faulkner's walkie-talkie beeped. "Foxtrot One."

Faulkner answered: "Here."

"Major Whalpol is needed in the comms van on the double."

Whalpol nodded.

"He's on his way," the colonel said. They were on a different frequency from the one the Iraqis monitored.

Whalpol rubbed his chin. "If you start draining water from one holding pond into another so that the outflow pipe is exposed, will it show on gauges up in the control room?"

"We can short out the sensing unit in the pond."

"Then do it," Whalpol said. "If we need that route as a last resort, we'll have it ready."

"I'll get my people on it immediately," the colonel said.

Down from the roof, Manning walked with Whalpol to the communications van.

"What about the news media?" Manning asked. "What do you want me to tell them?"

"Not a damned thing. But certainly nothing about General Sherif, or the reactor."

"What's left?"

"Have them pick two pool reporters, one from print and one from television. Tell them that an unknown terrorist group is holding hostages in the R&D facility. So far they have not made their demands known."

"What about the explosion?"

"An accident. A steam pipe not associated with the nuclear processing system burst when struck by a stray bullet."

"What if they've been monitoring the radio transmissions with General Sherif's side?"

"Isolate them immediately."

66

BASSAM ABU ZWAITER, chief of Mukhabarat activities from the Iraqi Embassy in Bonn, was waiting in front of the communications truck.

"Hello, Bassam," Whalpol said. They shook hands.

"I'd like to speak with General Sherif, but your people won't let me use your communications facility."

"I suppose it would be futile to ask if you knew of the weapons and explosives he brought with him, or the nature of his troops," Whalpol said.

"Of course not! This project means more to us than to you."

"Well, the cat is out of the bag, as they say."

The blockhouse was bathed in spotlights. The sounds of portable generators were mixed with the babble of voices and the crackle of communications radios.

"Have you any idea what they want?" Zwaiter looked frazzled; his voice was ragged. "Walther Roemer seems to think the general killed two women here in Bonn."

"He did. And there's more. Roemer dug up records from the Mossad and the CIA. We know your general has been the suspect in a number of murders, and possibly some hijackings. It was thought at one time he might be the terrorist Michael."

Zwaiter shook his head slowly. "You Germans have

always had a fantastic imagination. His name has been cleared."

Whalpol shrugged. "Do you know that he is threatening to blow up the reactor in there? Terrorism, if you ask me. And they've made their first demand. They want Walther Roemer and his father. Dead or alive. They won't let me speak with Sherif directly. But we have Roemer and Fräulein Kahled on the way up here now."

Zwaiter's eyes narrowed.

"We know the entire story, Bassam. We know about Dr. Azziza. But don't look so surprised, this is my backyard."

Zwaiter studied the blockhouse. "I don't understand. He has everything going for him. The entire country loves him. He is a national hero. President Hussein treats him like a brother."

"Azziza is dead. So is Roemer's father."

"So, the doctor was successful."

"No," Whalpol said. "The old man's sergeant killed him. Your assassin killed the sergeant. Leila got Azziza."

"Incredible!" Zwaiter closed his eyes.

"General Sherif is unhinged, of course. We hope his daughter can talk him out of there."

"Roemer telephoned one of our homicide investigators, Jacob Wadud. He served with the general. He's on his way here. Maybe he can help. But now let me try to talk to General Sherif."

They climbed up into the communications truck. A technician handed Whalpol the microphone.

"Basra Brigade, this is Abel One."

"Have Roemer and his father arrived yet?" the voice came from the speaker.

"No, but they'll be coming by helicopter, so don't get nervous when it approaches. Someone here would like to speak with you."

Whalpol handed the microphone to Zwaiter. "Habash, this is Bassam Zwaiter. I would like to speak with the general."

There was no answer.

"I recognize your voice, Mahmud. I know that you recognize mine."

"I'm sorry, Bassam. Perhaps later."

"By the grace of Allah, this is crazy! You've got half of Germany out here ready to pounce on you."

"We are willing to die for our general, Bassam, to right the wrong done to him."

"What are you talking about?"

The technician looked up.

"Mahmud?"

Nothing.

Zwaiter handed back the microphone. He glanced at his watch. Jacob Wadud should be touching down at the airport. "Before you let Leila speak with her father, I would like to talk to her and Wadud and you. I hope we can figure out what Colonel Habash meant just now."

"You want to get the general out of there and take him home?"

"Yes. He's a sick man."

"He's raped and murdered. His fanatics have killed three of my men and two police officers. No guarantees, Bassam."

A telephone softly burred from one of the monitors. An automatic tape recorder started. The technician at that console looked over. "It's an incoming telephone call to the reactor-control room, sir."

The telephone rang a half dozen times before it was answered. "Yes?" Colonel Habash's voice came from the speaker. The caller spoke in Arabic.

Zwaiter stiffened. "Bashir Kahair. He demands to speak to the general."

The line was silent for several seconds, and then Whalpol recognized the voice of General Sherif.

"Speak in German, Bashir. This call is being monitored, no doubt."

"Josef, for the love of our Prophet, stand down. I can guarantee your safe passage home."

"We need a few more hours, Bashir."

"What do you hope to accomplish? Have you spoken with Leila?"

"Old friend, I must go now."

"Josef!"

Sherif said something softly in Arabic; then the line went dead.

Zwaiter rubbed his eyes. "He asked Kahair not to be terribly disappointed in him when he found out."

67

LEILA, STRAPPED in her seat across the helicopter's passenger bay from Roemer, stared out the window at the lights below as they churned steadily north toward Bonn.

She had taken the news exactly as Roemer had thought she would. First disbelief, then anger and finally quiet resignation. They hadn't spoken since they'd lifted off from the Munich airport after refueling.

Roemer closed his eyes. His father was finally dead, but the relief he had hoped for had not come. Where there had been guilt, now was emptiness. He had hoped to go away when this was over, but he'd merely be running away from himself, which he had been trying in vain to do all his life. Alone, he was incomplete. With Kata he'd looked for respectability. With Gretchen, warmth. Neither had been able to fill his void, but he knew now that the trouble had been in his own closed lonesomeness.

He opened his eyes. Leila was looking at him. She had been crying. Roemer wanted to go to her, hold her, but it was impossible. The entire thing was impossible. Dr. Azziza had merely been taunting him, trying to throw him off his guard.

"Why won't they let us use the radio?" she asked, her

voice barely audible over the roar of the big transport helicopter's engine.

"I don't know."

Even in his weary eyes, she was beautiful. He moved closer to her, sitting on the floor so that they could hear each other.

"I think they mean to return your father to Baghdad. Chancellor Kohl was going to speak to your ambassador."

"He'll never go back like that. It's just the kind of fight a Palestinian loves. He'll be fighting the *jihad* all over again. A hero of Iraq can't return in defeat."

They didn't speak for several minutes. "What was he like in the old days?"

"Gone most of the time. There was always a lot of fighting to do. But when he came home he always brought presents."

"And later?"

She managed a slight smile. "He was proud of me when I finished school with my degree, but he didn't say much when I went to work for the Mukhabarat. I think he was disappointed. When I graduated from college he told me that it was good to have a woman in the family who'd taken off the veil. He said it balanced the equation."

Roemer wondered why he was interested in the human side of her father. Sherif was a murderer; he had always been a murderer.

"I hate you," Leila said. "I'll always hate you even though you were just doing your job."

And he loved her. With a sudden, strange clarity, he could point to the exact moment it had happened: when he looked into her eyes at the sanatorium outside Bern. He had seen her soul. He had been drawn in against his will.

Roemer's already confused world had been turned upside down, made unreal.

Leila stared out the window. "Oh . . . my God!"

The helicopter's rotors changed pitch as they began to descend. At first all he could make out below was a confused jumble of lights, moving vehicles and a large building bathed in spotlights.

Suddenly he saw that they were landing on the KwU parking lot.

Whalpol awaited them when the helicopter's side door clanked open. He helped Leila down. Roemer jumped down behind her.

Amid the noise of the helicopter's engine, Whalpol motioned for them to follow him into the administration building.

The sudden quiet in the broad lobby made their voices loud.

Leila avoided looking at Roemer. "What is going on here, Major?" she demanded of Whalpol.

"I'll give it to you straight, Fräulein Kahled. Your father, his chief of staff and twelve combat troops have barricaded themselves in the research and development building. They have seven hostages in there, and they have placed explosives around the nuclear reactor."

"Get all those people away from here and he'll leave," Leila insisted. "He wants only to return to Baghdad, where he might get a fair trial."

"He's been offered that. He wants you, Walther. And your father, dead or alive."

Roemer wasn't surprised. "What else?"

"Then he wants to speak with Chancellor Kohl."

"Any hints what he's up to?"

"None."

"Let me talk to him." Leila was more subdued now.

"Understand that I'm not simply going to allow Walther to walk over there. Your father will kill him."

Leila was struggling with her composure. "I'll talk to him."

"First, Zwaiter would like a word with you. He's here with your ambassador and several others from the embassy—all of them Mukhabarat. Explain to them that interference will not help in this situation. Fräulein Kahled, I suggest we get started."

On the third floor Bassam Zwaiter waited with Jacob Wadud and a number of other Iraqis Roemer didn't recognize. They all looked spent. Wadud nodded at Roemer.

"Have your conference, Bassam," Whalpol told Zwaiter, "but be quick about it." He steered Roemer into the conference room.

The technicians from the communications van had set up their equipment at one end of the room. They listened with headphones. A soldier brought Roemer a mug of coffee.

Manning was at the long table studying the blueprints with Colonel Faulkner and Trautman, the plant engineer.

"We're going in after them," Whalpol said.

"You don't think Leila can talk him out of there?" Roemer asked.

"No."

"What the hell does he want, other than me?"

"Something about righting a terrible wrong."

"The killings of his parents and his wife. Both mother and wife were career women. They'd taken off their veils."

"Are you saying the man is going after women who remind him of his mother and his wife?"

"He's crazy."

They hunched over the blueprints and the BND major explained that one pond had already been drained, the sensors shorted out, and so far there had been no recognition from General Sherif's side. Colonel Faulkner's demolitions experts were standing by with the radiation suits, and the torch man was ready with his equipment to go in and cut the access plate in the pump room.

"We think there'll be a main firing line from the explosives to the control room," Whalpol said. "We'll attempt to find it and cut it."

"It might be radio-controlled," Colonel Faulkner said.

"That's our second option," Whalpol said. "We'll put two people into the crawl space above the control room. They should be able to see down through the suspended light fixtures."

"Well enough to pick off whoever is at the firing mechanism?" Roemer asked.

Whalpol nodded. "And keep anyone else from getting to it."

"For communications, we'll use ordinary police-frequency walkie-talkies. We'll keep it short and in code."

A radioman turned around. "They're asking for you again, Major."

"Any questions, Walther?"

"I'm going in through the water pipe."

"I don't think so."

"I started this, I'll finish it."

"Put on the loudspeaker." Whalpol went over to the communications gear. "Get Fräulein Kahled in here on the double. And no one tells the Iraqis with us what we're up to."

He took the microphone. "Basra Brigade, this is Abel One."

"Where's Roemer?" the speaker blared.

"Roemer's father is dead; Investigator Roemer is wounded and is receiving medical attention. As soon as he is able to move, we'll bring him over. Give me General Sherif."

"Request denied. We're giving you ten minutes. We want both of them at the outside gate. We are counting."

Leila and the other Iraqis came into the conference room. Whalpol motioned her over. She was pale. Whalpol handed her the microphone. "If your father and his people are willing to stand down, we'll guarantee their safe passage to Baghdad."

Leila closed her eyes. "Colonel Habash, this is Leila. I want to speak to my father."

The loudspeaker was silent.

Whalpol edged away from the communications table to Colonel Faulkner and Roemer. "Send your people through now," he whispered. "The torch man first, then your demolitions people. Roemer and I will take the control room ceiling."

"Stay out of this, Leila," Habash radioed.

Colonel Faulkner picked up his walkie-talkie. "Situation One," he said. "Situation One."

"Roger," the reply came.

"Father, if you can hear me, I want to talk to you," Leila persisted.

General Sherif's voice came over the speaker. "What are you doing here, little bird?"

"I've come to take you home. Jacob Wadud and I."

"Go home, Leila."

Jacob Wadud, his right hand in his pocket, blocked the doorway. Roemer stepped around the end of the table and confronted the Iraqi detective. He looked into Wadud's eyes. "Are you going to shoot us all, Jacob?"

"Whatever it takes. This is our project, remember?"

"I'm coming over there, Father," Leila said. "And then we're going home together. There is a plane at the airport waiting for us, and for your men."

"We want Roemer," Colonel Habash's voice boomed from the speaker. "Roemer!"

The radioman turned down the volume.

"What if they kill the hostages, Jacob?" Roemer asked.

"It's a chance we'll have to—"

Roemer grabbed his gun hand by the wrist, shoving the Iraqi out into the corridor.

Whalpol, Manning and Colonel Faulkner started toward the doorway at the same moment Bassam Zwaiter and the other Mukhabarat operatives drew their guns.

68

ROEMER RELEASED Jacob Wadud's wrist and stepped back, his hands away from his sides in clear sight.

Colonel Faulkner put his walkie-talkie to his mouth as Leila stepped around the communications table with a gun in her hand.

"If you call for help, I will kill you, Colonel," she said in a steady voice.

Faulkner lowered the walkie-talkie.

Two of the Mukhabarat agents trotted down the corridor to cover the elevator and stairs. The Iraqi Ambassador, ashen, stepped aside. Wadud with his pistol backed Roemer into the conference room. Zwaiter came in behind them and closed the door.

"You don't want to do this, Jacob," Roemer said.

"We're taking our general home with us," the Iraqi detective said calmly. He motioned toward the blueprints spread out on the long table. "We spotted what was going on at the holding pond. Our technicians figured it out immediately. They said it was risky, but it might work. Put your gun on the table, Walther."

Trautman, the plant engineer, wasn't armed. Zwaiter and the other Mukhabarat agent relieved the others of their weapons.

"Back in the corner," Wadud said.

Roemer and the others sat down at the far side of the room. Wadud spoke into the microphone. "Habash, this is Jacob Wadud. Let me talk to the general."

"That's not possible," Habash radioed. "Don't interfere, Wadud."

"Leila, Bassam Zwaiter and I are coming over there now. You are going back to Baghdad."

"Negative."

"The hostages can be released at the airport, or in Iraq, if you wish. But disconnect your explosives."

"Anyone coming within one hundred meters of our perimeter will be shot."

"I don't think so, Habash."

"We want Roemer!"

Wadud put down the microphone and switched off the radio. He faced the room. "We're going to leave here in a group. I am taking my general home."

"Don't be a fool," Whalpol said angrily.

"It might work," Roemer said. "But what happens if they start killing hostages?"

"You would be risking the same retaliation by trying to sneak into the place," the Iraqi detective said. He motioned toward the door with his gun.

The Mukhabarat agent opened the door and looked out into the corridor. Everyone else was gone. "It's clear."

"What if we refuse to go with you?" Manning growled.

"Then I'll shoot you," Wadud replied. Again he motioned toward the door with his gun. "They'll be getting nervous over there."

"Is this what you want, Leila?" Roemer asked.

She looked at him, painfully. "We can help him in Baghdad."

"You're willing to risk all of those lives?"

"He's my father!"

"Move it!" Wadud ordered.

Roemer and Manning led the group out. Most of the activity outside was directed toward the main gate, where all the newspeople were still being held back, and along the sandbagged barricade that established the one-hundred-meter perimeter

The helicopter was parked forty or fifty meters away. The crew stood by the machine.

"Walk directly to the barricade," Wadud said.

"Do you want me to come in with you?" Roemer asked Leila.

"No."

"His troops would kill you," Wadud said.

"Fanatics," Whalpol snapped. "The history of your people—"

"Yes," Wadud interrupted him. They headed across the parking lot to the barricade several hundred meters away. Generators roared, powering the floodlights illuminating the blockhouse.

"Keep it moving," Wadud said behind them.

Colonel Faulkner had already given the signal to his crew at the holding ponds. Unless the Iraqis had stopped them, the torch man would already be working his way through the narrow pipeline to the pump room, where he would cut out the access plate. The plan was for him and two demolitions experts to enter the R&D building first, decontaminate themselves and then stand by as an advance guard. If everything went well they would radio their code.

There was no telling, however, what General Sherif's troops would do once they were confronted by Wadud, Zwaiter and Leila. If they fired the explosives, none of this would matter.

One of Faulkner's lieutenants, seeing the group approaching the barricade, came over. "Has there been any further word, sir?" Then the young man spotted the Iraqis' weapons and reached for his own sidearm.

"No," Colonel Faulkner ordered. "I want you and your people to stand down."

"Yes, sir," the lieutenant said. The soldiers at the sandbags moved away.

Wadud turned to Whalpol. "As soon as we have the situation controlled inside, we'll radio you. We'll need a couple of transport trucks or a bus, and a clear route to the airport. If you don't interfere, no one else will get hurt."

"Do you know the general well enough to bet your life on it?"

"I do," Leila said. Before anyone could stop her, she shoved roughly past Manning and in broad strides leaped over the sandbags and headed across the hundred meters to the tall chain-link fence.

"Hold them!" Wadud shouted before Roemer could move. The Mukhabarat agents raised their weapons as Wadud and Zwaiter jumped over the barricade and went after Leila.

They got barely ten meters when a line of automatic weapons fire was laid down from three spots along the roofline. Zwaiter was hit several times, his body erupting in spurts of blood as he was blasted backward off his feet.

Leila stopped in her tracks, the bullets ricocheting off the pavement all around her.

Wadud raced in a zigzag back to the sandbags, the fire on his heels as he dove to safety.

Sporadic fire was being returned all up and down the barricade. Colonel Faulkner raced down the line, shouting the cease-fire.

Zwaiter lay facedown in a widening pool of blood. Leila, not hit, stared in horror at his body.

Except for the generators, a heavy silence descended over the parking lot.

"Leila," Roemer called from behind the barricade. "Come back. They won't fire on you."

She remained rooted to her spot, her eyes on Zwaiter's body.

"Leila!"

She walked toward the blockhouse gate.

Roemer started over the sandbags, but Manning yanked him back.

"Leila," Roemer called again.

She continued walking as if in a trance. No gunfire came from the blockhouse roof. Reaching the big gate, she took out her gun and fired at the heavy padlock.

"She can't crack the lock that way," Trautman muttered.

Leila fired again and again. Then she stepped back from the gate and looked up toward the building's roofline. "Father!" she shouted. "Father?"

Roemer could see no movement. They were up there, watching her, listening to her cries, but they were keeping out of sight. Fanatics, but disciplined.

"Father?"

"It's no use, Leila," Wadud called to her. "Come back."

She turned and gaped toward the barricade. Then she started slowly back.

"We'll do it my way now," Whalpol said.

"Roemer and I will go in," Wadud said. "We'll take a couple of Mukhabarat people with us."

"No way."

"He's right," Roemer said, watching Leila. "He and I, two Mukhabarat agents and two of Colonel Faulkner's people."

Leila reached Zwaiter's body, stopped and slowly bent down beside it.

Wadud jumped over the barricade and went across to her. He grabbed Zwaiter's arms and dragged him back to the barricade. Leila followed. An army ambulance was already racing across the parking lot.

Roemer reached for Leila, but she pulled away and headed toward the administration building. It was no use going after her.

"We'll go now," Roemer said.

"My torch man and demolitions crew are already on their way in," Colonel Faulkner said.

"Sherif's people will be wanting you on the radio," Roemer told Whalpol. "You're going to have to buy as much time as possible. Tell them we're all shook up down here. We need time to calm everyone down."

69

LEILA WAS nowhere to be found when they got to the administration building. Whalpol tried to radio Sherif's force at the blockhouse, but they did not answer.

The plant engineer, Trautman, quickly went over the blueprints with Roemer, Wadud and the two Mukhabarat agents who would go in with them, Abdul Salman and Hani Bouchiki.

"Our equipment truck is set up down on the Autobahn," Trautman said. "It's a couple hundred meters on foot up the hill and across a clearing to the holding ponds. You can't be seen from the R&D building because of the forest. But don't use any light until you are well within the tunnel, and even then it could be risky—a chance reflection through the opening."

"The radiation suits are in the truck?" Roemer asked.

Trautman nodded. "You'll have to carry your weapons and radios inside your suits so they don't become contaminated. Once you're decontaminated, there are three ways up to the reactor room. Two sets of stairs and the elevator. Colonel Faulkner's men will be waiting for you in the subbasement. They'll head up to the reactor and begin their search and disarming procedures."

"We're using codes," Colonel Faulkner said. "Situation

One was their go-ahead to enter the pipeline and cut their way into the pump room. Situation Two, they're in place. Situation Three means someone is in place above the control room ready to stop Sherif from triggering the explosives."

"Wadud and I will handle the hostages," Roemer said.

"Which leaves Salman and Bouchiki above the control room," Wadud said.

"Any questions?"

"Just one," Roemer said softly. "If it becomes necessary to kill the general, will you be able to do it?"

70

LEILA WAS gone. No one had seen her since she had walked away from the barricades after Zwaiter had been shot to death.

Rudi Gehrman and Colonel Legler stood with Roemer at the rear of a canvas-covered army troop truck.

"You don't have to do this, Walther," Colonel Legler said. "Leave this sort of thing to the army."

"I'm going to finish it."

"Don't be a fool," Gehrman snapped. "You're doing this because of Leila Kahled."

It was late and Roemer was very tired. It had been only a week since this had all started. It seemed like a lifetime. He supposed his old friend was right, but he had to do it this way. "She's missing just now, Rudi. Find her for me."

Gehrman grimaced in frustration. "And then what?"

"Get her away from here in case the reactor blows."

Wadud came out of the administration building on the run.

"We have to move now!" he shouted. "Whalpol reached Habash. They're blaming us for Zwaiter's death. Habash promises retaliation."

"They're going to kill the hostages?"

"Worse. They want you right now. I think they mean to blow the reactor."

"As soon as we're on the way in, Faulkner is going to clear this place."

"They'll touch off the explosives as soon as that starts happening."

"Then I'll turn myself over to them," Roemer said.

"The moment you showed up over there they'd set off the explosives anyway. Habash is as crazy as the general. You're the main issue now."

Colonel Faulkner came out of the administration building, Manning right behind him. "We just received a Situation Two; my people are in and decontaminated. They're waiting for you."

"What about the evacuation?" Roemer asked.

"Manning will get the civilians out, but I'm keeping my people here."

"We're going to hold them back from the airport to the north and the Siegburg exit to the south," Manning said.

"We're not screwing around any longer," Faulkner said. "Number-one priority is disarming the explosives. If it means killing General Sherif and every one of his troops, it will be done."

A helicopter came in low from the south.

"That's your father's body," Faulkner said. "It is up to you if you want us to use it as an . . . offering."

Roemer had turned numb. "Do it."

71

THE AUTOBAHN was already blocked off by the time the truck bearing Roemer, Wadud and the two Mukhabarat agents pulled up behind a tall van parked off the highway below the holding ponds. It was very cold, but the wind had died and the stars shone as brilliant points.

Trautman and two of his engineers waited inside the van with the silver radiation suits, in radio contact with Colonel Faulkner and Whalpol.

"The others are already in place," Trautman said as Roemer and the others pulled on the bulky suits.

"Any trouble getting in?" Roemer asked.

"Apparently not."

They climbed out of the van and started up the hill into the dark woods. They reached the holding ponds ten minutes later. The area was guarded by a tall chain-link fence topped with razor wire. Radiation warnings were posted around the perimeter.

A haze of vapor rose from the glistening, warm water, though ice had formed around the edges of the large, rectangular concrete ponds.

Trautman unlocked the gate and they went inside, climbed up over the earthwork ramparts and made their way to the pool that had been partially drained. Three large pipes were exposed. Two were blocked by a thick steel mesh; the third was open. An aluminum ladder led down to the pipe, three meters below the lip of the pond.

"It's nearly five hundred meters into the pump room," Trautman said.

They stopped above the open pipe. Roemer pulled out his walkie-talkie. "Situation Two?" he radioed.

No answer.

"Too much earth between here and there," Trautman said. "But we'll be able to hear you from the other side."

Roemer tucked the walkie-talkie inside his suit and sealed the jacket.

Trautman checked the water with his Geiger counter. "It's not bad," he said. "While you're inside the tunnel you won't have any radio communication with anyone."

They'd each brought an extra handgun to carry outside of their suits in case they ran into trouble before they were decontaminated. They would have to leave those weapons in the decontamination closet. Roemer stuffed his into an outer pocket.

"You each have sixty minutes of oxygen built into the suits, which will give you more than enough time, even if you do run into some trouble," Trautman said.

"We'd better get started." Roemer pulled on his hood. Trautman and his technicians made sure they were sealed in and their air supplies turned on; then they gave the thumbs-up.

Roemer started down the ladder first. Awkwardly, he felt for the lip of the pipe, and swung his legs inside.

He had to hunch over. His shoulders brushed the sides of the pipe.

Wadud came next, and then Salman and Bouchiki. As Roemer moved a few meters up the pipe, the darkness closed in on him. His knees bent, his left hand brushing the pipe ceiling as a guide, he moved on up the pipe.

Within seconds they were completely cut off from the outside. Inside the radiation suits, sounds were muffled. The cool bottled air had a metallic taste.

Fifty meters in, the pipeline angled steeply and the going became more difficult. Roemer began to sweat. He imagined that the demolitions team had been discovered and killed; Sherif's people were in the control room now, ready to throw the switch that would divert reactor water through this pipe. At least Leila was out of this. If she was still somewhere within the KwU compound, Rudi would find her and take her away. Zwaiter had been gunned down; she was burned out. There was a good chance she had returned to Bonn to get as far away as she could from whatever was going to happen to her father.

The angle of the pipe steepened again. Roemer had to bend into it, using his hands to keep from slipping back. Colonel Faulkner's people had made it up to the pump room, so he didn't think it could get much worse. But the going was tough.

The pipe seemed to go on forever. Once he slipped and Wadud stumbled up behind him.

"Are you all right?" Wadud shouted, his voice distant.

"Fine," Roemer shouted, and they continued.

He thought about his father. The pain had mostly gone, though he was glad he wasn't topside now to witness his father's body being offered up at the building gate.

Roemer figured they had been inside the pipe for about twenty minutes when he realized he could see. Ahead, a diffused light barely outlined the curve of the pipe.

They took out their guns.

Roemer continued quietly forward. A few meters from the circular opening he stopped to listen. He could hear machinery running, but nothing else.

Gripping his gun in his gloved fist, he looked through the opening into a large, high-ceilinged room crammed with machinery. Pipes ran in every direction.

On the far side of the room an open door led to a corridor. One of Faulkner's men, a German Army Gewehr 3A3 assault rifle at the ready, leaned against the door frame. He spotted Roemer and urgently beckoned for him to come out.

Careful not to rip his suit on the jagged edges of the torched opening, Roemer climbed out into the floor of the pump room.

The soldier spoke into a walkie-talkie as Roemer helped the others out of the pipe.

A second soldier appeared in the doorway. He pointed to the far end of the room. "Decontamination," he mouthed.

They trotted along the line of pipes into a large, white-tiled room and then into a long, narrow area with red arrows painted on the floor. Multiple shower heads lined the ceiling and walls.

ATTENTION, a notice read. ENTER DECONTAMINATION STALL FULLY CLOTHED. FOLLOW INSTRUCTIONS. SHOWERS ARE AUTOMATIC.

Roemer stepped in. Water mixed with foam spurted out of the shower heads, deluging him. Halfway through the stall, the water cleared and blow-dryers came on. Another notice advised him to wait for a Geiger-counter check. A red light would mean he had to go through the process again; green would mean he was decontaminated and could discard his outer clothing.

The light turned green. Roemer stepped out of the stall and peeled off his radiation suit.

Wadud appeared a moment later. He pulled off his hood and took a deep breath of fresh air.

"I'll be out in the corridor," Roemer said. "Hurry it

up." Trautman's men, sergeants Menzel and Brecht, were waiting at the far end of the pump room.

"Any troubles?" Roemer asked.

"Plenty," Menzel said, keeping his voice low. He glanced down the long corridor, at the end of which was a set of stairs leading up. "One of Sherif's glory boys is parked at the head of the stairs. We're not going to have a chance in hell of getting near the reactor."

"Can he be seen from the control room?"

"They can see him, all right."

Wadud came out of the pump room. "Salman and Bouchiki will be right with us. What's wrong?"

Roemer explained. Wadud pulled out his VP70 Hessler-and-Koch nine-millimeter automatic and Kevlar silencer, which he screwed on the end of the short barrel.

"I'll take him out. Hani can put on his uniform. It'll get us in."

"Any sign of the hostages?" Roemer asked Menzel.

"They're probably on the top floor," Menzel said. "The front stairs lead directly to the reactor room. If we can take out their man, we'll have a chance." He pointed the other way down the corridor. "The elevator is around the corner. But now the car is up on the third floor. We can get the door open and someone can go up the shaft. Unless they decide to bring the car down it should be okay. The back stairs are at the far end of the corridor."

"Have you checked them?"

"Only to the first floor. There's a steel fire door. Not wired. I'd say it probably opens on the reactor room main floor. In full view of the control room above."

"They're threatening to blow the reactor at any minute," Roemer said. "Which means we're going to have to do this right the first time."

72

AN AMBULANCE had drawn up to the helicopter bearing the body of Roemer's father.

Whalpol looked out the back of the communications truck as a white-shrouded bundle was unloaded from the helicopter. He shuddered.

Colonel Faulkner had been listening on the walkie-talkie. He nodded to Whalpol. "They're inside, but it's taking longer than we thought it would."

It was past midnight. Whalpol was tired. But it would be over with, one way or the other, very soon. "We give them Lotti Roemer now. It'll distract them for a few minutes."

"What about the evacuation?"

"Keep it going. Lieutenant Manning knows the drill."

"The media people are raising hell."

"Let them," Whalpol said.

The ambulance pulled away from the helicopter and drove slowly over to the communications truck.

Whalpol instructed the radioman to raise the R&D building.

Colonel Habash came back immediately: "You're running out of time."

"We have Lotti Roemer's body, Colonel Habash."

The radio was silent for a moment. Habash would be checking with the general.

"What about the son?" Habash radioed.

"He is on the operating table."

"How soon can you have him here?" Habash radioed. "Alive and awake."

"Three hours."

"You have thirty minutes, Major Whalpol."

"We'll try," he radioed.

"We want the body brought to within fifty meters of our gate, uncovered so we can see the face, and we want your ambulance to withdraw."

Faulkner looked at Whalpol.

"We're waiting," Habash radioed.

"We'll do as you say," Whalpol answered. "In the meantime we're evacuating all civilian personnel from the area."

"No."

"Oh, yes, you crazy bastard. If you want Lotti Roemer's body and Walther Roemer, you're going to have to give us this. Otherwise just go ahead and pull the fucking pin!"

Whalpol threw the microphone down in disgust. He felt dirty. He couldn't help thinking of Sarah Razmarah. Sherif may have killed her, but he himself had led her to Germany to her death.

At the back of the truck he passed Habash's instructions to the ambulance driver. "Just get it over with."

"Yes, *mein Herr,*" the driver said. He drove off toward the break in the barricade.

Whalpol watched through binoculars. The ambulance drove slowly through the barricade and swung around to a halt about fifty meters from the gate. The driver and the medic opened the rear doors and pulled out a wheeled stretcher, on which Lotti Roemer's body was strapped, and rolled it clear. Finally the medic pulled the shroud back, exposing the dead man's head.

They drove away in the ambulance, leaving the body lying out in the open.

A technician called from the truck. "Colonel Habash, sir. They say for us to keep our heads down, they're going to open fire."

"God in heaven." Whalpol brought the binoculars up to his eyes.

The night air was shattered by gunfire from the roofline of the R&D building.

The body came alive, dancing and jerking as bullets slammed into it. The wheeled stretcher tipped over, but still the firing went on and on.

Whalpol lowered his binoculars as he tried to control his nausea.

73

LEILA KAHLED hid in the woods near the KwU van from which she'd just stolen the radiation suit. She had started up toward the ponds when she heard voices. Plant engineer Trautman and two technicians emerged from the woods and crossed the grassy slope to the van. She had also stolen a police hand radio from the administration building and monitored the exchange between Whalpol and Colonel Habash.

Whalpol's lie about Walther being wounded was understandable. Habash's demand that Lotti Roemer's body be placed out in full view was insane.

Sounds of gunfire drifted over the hill on the light breeze. The firing went on for a long time, then stopped just as abruptly as it had begun.

Leila's heart hammered. The radio was silent, but she knew what had happened. Allah guide her, this was all insane.

Things her father had said and done in the months before they'd come here on this project made sense now. He had been adamantly against the reactor at first, but suddenly he had reversed himself and insisted that he be included.

It came to her, finally, that her father had planned this

very operation all along. But why? Even crazy people have reasons for what they do.

Trautman and the others drove off in the van.

Leila picked up the bulky radiation suit and the walkie-talkie and headed up the hill toward the holding ponds. At the fence, she wrapped the walkie-talkie in the radiation suit and heaved the bundle over. The oxygen pack went next.

She took off her coat and, holding it under her arm, scrambled up the fence. At the top she laid the coat on top of the razor wire, then climbed over it and dropped down the other side.

She crouched. There were no alarms. She was alone here.

Scooping up the suit and gear, she hurried across the top of the earthwork dam to the ladder, where again she stopped a moment to listen. They probably were looking for her. If Trautman spotted her car a few hundred meters up the Autobahn, they might put two and two together and try to stop her. But she would be inside by then.

She pulled on the radiation suit, the walkie-talkie inside. She opened the air supply control and pulled on the hood, sealing it.

She carefully climbed down the ladder and maneuvered into the pipe. A narrow trickle of water dribbled over the edge down into the pond. She crouched just within the pipe, staring into the impenetrable darkness. She wasn't particularly claustrophobic, but she did not relish the idea of burying herself so far underground in such a narrow passageway.

Getting a tight grip on herself, she started forward, her hands touching the sides of the pipe for guidance. Quickly she was in blackness, and she had to force down a rising panic as she hurried faster and faster.

74

KILLING THE guard would be risky. The man stood at the head of the stairs in plain view of the control room that overlooked the reactor floor.

Roemer ducked back around the corner where Wadud and the others waited. "There's enough machinery noise to cover a silenced shot. But if someone happens to be looking down when it happens, we'll be in trouble."

"What do you think, Jacob?" Roemer asked the Iraqi detective.

"One shot to the head," Wadud said. "With luck, no blood will get on the front of his uniform."

"I wish there was another way," Roemer muttered. He had no stomach for killing.

"So do I," Wadud whispered. "There are good men in there."

"We're going to have to make sure no one in the control room is watching," Roemer said. He turned to Salman, the Iraqi agent. "Go up the back stairs to the reactor room doorway. Check it and check the control room windows. When it's clear, check your walkie-talkie switch. When we hear it, Jacob will take out the guard."

Salman hurried off down the corridor. Wadud eased himself to the edge of the stairwell.

Bouchiki unstrapped his equipment belt and started to get undressed. The moment the guard was down he would change into his clothes and get back into view of the control room.

Roemer looked back down the corridor. Salman should be in position now. Roemer held his walkie-talkie up to his ear.

It seemed to take forever. Roemer was about to send Brecht back to check on Salman when his walkie-talkie clicked.

"Now," he whispered to Wadud.

The Iraqi detective stepped around the corner and fired two quick shots, the dull plopping sounds lost to the machinery noises.

The guard tumbled down the stairs.

Wadud leaped forward, Roemer right behind him. The right side of the guard's neck was blown away, but he was still alive. He clawed at the wound. Wadud smashed the butt of his pistol between the man's eyes, knocking him unconscious. A second later the man shuddered and was still.

Wadud looked up, pure hate in his eyes.

75

IRAQI AGENT Hani Bouchiki, wearing the dead soldier's combat fatigues and carrying his Kalashnikov slung over a shoulder, stepped into view on the reactor room floor, then nonchalantly leaned against the wall.

Their only problem now would come if anybody recognized Bouchiki as an impostor.

Menzel and Brecht came up with their demolitions-disarming kits. They were dressed in black. As soon as Bouchiki gave them the all-clear, they would make their way up the stairs and across the reactor room floor, where they could work around the Harwell spent-fuel element pool unobserved from above. Trautman suspected that the charges would be suspended within the pool itself, the wires leading out of the water, across the reactor room floor up to the control room.

Bouchiki held out three fingers behind his back—three of General Sherif's men were in the control room.

Roemer stepped back around the corner. "Three," he said.

Wadud looked up from the body and grabbed Roemer's arm, his grip like a vise. "Promise me we'll do everything within our power not to kill any more of those boys."

"I don't like this any better than you do."

"Insha' Allah," Wadud said softly.

Roemer looked at him for a long time. "Do you want me to take the control room ceiling? You can go after the hostages?"

"I'll be all right."

"You may have to . . . kill the general."

Wadud handed his silenced Hessler-and-Koch and a spare clip to Roemer. "Here, take my gun. I'll use yours. If I have to shoot, silence won't matter."

Roemer took Wadud's weapon and handed the Iraqi detective his PPK automatic and extra clip.

"Clear," Menzel said from the foot of the stairs.

Bouchiki was waving them up.

"All right," Roemer said. "As soon as you have the charges disconnected, give us the Situation Three code."

Menzel and Brecht scurried up the stairs and out of sight.

Roemer held his breath for several long seconds. Bouchiki gave the all-clear.

Wadud headed down the corridor toward the stairs at the opposite end of the building. Roemer followed him. They silently started up. On the first floor Salman was waiting for them, his gun drawn.

"Did Menzel and Brecht get into position?" Roemer asked.

"Yes, sir. They're behind some equipment next to the pool."

Roemer eased the door open a crack. An eerie blue glow from the spent-element pool illuminated the large room. Above the back wall were the tall glass windows of the control room. A man in battle fatigues had his back to the window; he was talking to someone. Below, crouched behind a computer console, Menzel and Brecht were pulling tools out of their kits.

Roemer could not see any wires leading from the pool.

It was possible that the explosives were equipped with a radio-controlled firing device. Then their only hope would be Wadud's ability to keep General Sherif and his men from actually pushing the button.

Roemer closed the door and stepped back.

"What's going on?" Salman asked.

"You and I are going after the hostages," Roemer said. "Jacob will take the control room ceiling. I don't want to make any big moves until we have the hostages secured, Jacob. When that happens I'll radio 'All clear.' Salman and I will try to join you. When you're in position, say 'Here.' "

They started up the stairs, keeping low and silent.

At the next level, the control room floor, they paused by the door. Salman wanted to open it, but Roemer held him back.

"He may have guards posted," Roemer whispered.

Wadud started up the next flight of stairs. Salman and Roemer followed him.

There were two floors above the control room. The first level contained offices for the engineers and scientists and a large drafting room. The floor in that room, according to the architectural drawings Trautman had shown them, was segmented in one-meter squares that could easily be lifted out of place, designed for access to the cable runs over the control room.

Wadud eased the fire door open and looked down the empty corridor, then stepped through. "I can make it from here on my own."

"Good luck," Roemer whispered.

Roemer looked up the final flight of stairs. The top floor contained the chief engineer's office as well as the executive cafeteria. From the cafeteria kitchen, there was access to the roof.

Whalpol and Colonel Faulkner had agreed that General

Sherif would have at least four men on the roof, one to cover each direction. Someone would have to be nearby watching the five men and two women hostages supposedly being held. They were the only KwU staff unaccounted for. There was a good chance that the hostages were being kept in the cafeteria.

There were no sounds from above. Roemer took out Wadud's silenced pistol; Salman took out his fifteen-shot, nine-millimeter SigSauer. They started up the stairs slowly, stopping several times to listen.

Roemer eased the door open. Halfway down the hallway was the cafeteria, but Roemer could see only the corner of one table inside.

They flattened themselves against the corridor wall and slowly worked their way to the cafeteria's open doors.

Someone inside coughed. Roemer heard an indistinct voice, a man speaking in German.

"No talking, I said," someone ordered just inside the door.

It was one of General Sherif's troops, just on the other side of the wall. How many others were in the cafeteria?

Roemer's walkie-talkie clicked and Menzel's voice came through, low but clear. "Situation Three impossible. Situation Three impossible."

The Iraqi suddenly appeared in the doorway. He fumbled to pull his Kalashnikov off his shoulder.

Roemer shot him twice in the chest at point-blank range, driving the soldier backward. He crashed against a table.

"Oh, God," a woman cried.

Roemer leaped into the room, low, sweeping his weapon around for another target as he ducked behind a table.

Salman slid behind a stack of chairs.

The hostages, one of them with a bandage around his

head, were seated together at one table near the stainless-steel serving counter. They looked terrified.

Someone shouted in Arabic from the stairwell in the kitchen.

Roemer frantically motioned for Salman to answer.

Salman hesitated a moment, then called out something in Arabic. There was silence. Salman sagged with relief.

Roemer held his weapon in both hands, aiming it at the door to the kitchen.

"It's all right," Salman whispered, moving closer. "He wanted to know what all the racket was about. I told him I tripped over my clumsy feet."

Roemer lowered his gun. The hostages watched them silently, not moving.

"Get them out of here," Roemer told Salman. "Menzel has evidently run into trouble disarming the explosives. Take them out through the pipeline. There have to be other radiation suits down there. Suit them up and get them the hell out of here."

"Yes, sir." Salman hurried over to where the hostages were waiting.

"God bless you," one of the women said.

There had been no Iraqi technicians working in the facility when General Sherif's people had taken over. For that, at least, Roemer was grateful. He went through the kitchen door. A narrow corridor led to the stairway that went up to the roof. There were at least four of them up there, he figured. It would be impossible for him alone to take them all out. If one of them happened to come downstairs and discover that the hostages were gone, the alarm would be sounded.

Roemer raised his walkie-talkie. Whalpol was monitoring this channel, so he must know that Menzel was having trouble. Roemer hoped that the BND major would be sharp enough to pick up the hint in his message, that they needed a diversion to hold the soldiers on the roof.

"Unit One, Unit One, something is going on up on the roof," he radioed. "You'd better get someone here right away."

"We understand," Whalpol's voice came over.

Roemer clipped his walkie-talkie back on his belt. He hoped like hell that Whalpol had understood and would be able to do something to help.

76

LEILA APPROACHED the opening of the pipeline with extreme caution. She had sealed her gun inside her suit, so she was unarmed until she could get through decontamination.

Carefully, she peered up through the hole, out across the pump room. No one was there.

She pulled herself through the opening and hurried down the long room to the decontamination chamber. She emerged a couple of minutes later with the green light. She peeled off her suit, tossed it on the pile with the others and went back across the pump room to the corridor. She'd been in this building many times, of course, but never down here.

She took out her Beretta. To the left, just before the stairwell, was a body, blood down its back. The dead man was clothed only in his underwear. What had happened here?

She recognized him as one of her father's troops.

She approached the dead soldier and bent down to touch his cheek. It was still warm.

She flattened herself against the wall and edged over to the stairwell. She caught a glimpse of a man in battle fatigues, blood down his back, at the head of the stairs.

He had to be the one who had come in with Roemer

and Jacob Wadud. They had killed one of her father's men and taken his uniform. Colonel Faulkner's demolitions crew was probably on the reactor room floor at this moment. Their next step would be to find the hostages.

She closed her eyes tight. What was she doing here?

Someone was coming down the stairs at the far end of the corridor. A lot of people!

Leila hurried back into the pump room, where she ducked behind some machinery. From where she crouched she could see the doorway, the decontamination chamber and the open pipeline as the first of the hostages came around the corner.

77

JACOB WADUD paused on the narrow catwalk in the maintenance space between the second and third floors. Below, through the grilles enclosing the built-in light fixtures, he could see the blue glow of the containment pool. The control room was another ten meters away.

He had been sent here to bring the general home alive. But now he felt like an assassin, stalking the man he had once proudly served.

He crawled forward a few meters so that he was directly above one of the fluorescent lights. From there he could look down onto most of the reactor room floor.

Hani Bouchiki, in the dead soldier's uniform, stood at the stairs. Faulkner's two demolitions people were crouched behind some equipment. They had radioed that the situation was impossible. So why didn't they get the hell out of there?

Wadud spotted the reason. One of the general's soldiers stood in the shadows beneath the stairs that led up to the control room. He must have just come down. If the light hadn't been so dim, he would surely have recognized Bouchiki as an impostor. But there was little doubt that he would spot Faulkner's men if they tried to move.

From this angle, Wadud did not have a clear view of the

control room windows. If someone was there, he would not be able to see the soldier below the stairs.

Wadud raised his gun and sighted the soldier. It would be a difficult shot. And the noise would alert anyone in the control room.

He could not risk it.

Something slammed into the back of his head, knocking him on his face. He fumbled with the PPK's safety catch as someone pulled him over on his back.

There were two soldiers dressed in battle fatigues. Wadud raised the automatic and fired twice, the first bullet catching the nearest soldier high in the chest, the second destroying the man's face.

The soldier reared backward into the second man, giving Wadud just enough time to get to one knee. He found himself looking into the barrel of a Kalashnikov, and he knew he was going to die.

He never heard the burst from the Russian assault rifle, but his body was blasted back over the catwalk's rail. He crashed through the thin acoustical tile of the ceiling and plunged into the pool.

78

SALMAN AND the hostages were in the decontamination chamber, suiting up. It was taking too much time. Leila started to edge away from her hiding place when shots were fired.

She started across the pump room. Salman, half dressed in a radiation suit, appeared at the decontamination chamber doorway. "What are you doing here?"

"There were shots, Abdul. Where are Roemer and Wadud?"

"Upstairs," Salman said. "In the false ceiling above the control room."

"What about the explosives?"

"Can't do anything about them. Hani is at the head of the stairs. Faulkner's demolitions people are on the reactor floor."

Leila's walkie-talkie clicked. Roemer came on. "We're all clear. Are you in position, Jacob?"

Leila started to raise her walkie-talkie but Salman motioned her to hold off. It wasn't possible Roemer could have missed hearing the gunfire. What was he up to?

"It's all clear," Roemer radioed again. "Are you in position, Jacob?"

"Jacob Wadud is dead," General Sherif's voice came from the walkie-talkie.

"Oh, God," Leila cried. "Get those people out of here now!"

"I want you here in the control room, Roemer," Sherif radioed. "Now."

Leila ran down the corridor to the stairwell.

"Roemer, in sixty seconds I blow the containment pool."

Leila took the stairs two at a time. Jacob Wadud was in the ceiling crawl space above the control room. Or at least he had been. Her father's troops had apparently positioned themselves up there to watch for an attack. Wadud was dead.

"Roemer!" General Sherif shouted.

79

ROEMER KEYED his walkie-talkie. "What do you want, General?" He needed time. It would take Salman and the hostages at least an hour to make their way through the pipeline and down the hill to safety.

"I want you." Sherif's voice was calm.

The elevator car was already on this floor.

"Are you going to kill me, General, is that what you want? Just like you killed all those others in Munich and Hama and South Yemen?"

"I don't know what you're talking about. You have fifty seconds, Roemer."

"Can you tell us why you did this . . . Michael?"

"You're insane, Roemer. Less than forty seconds."

"Do Colonel Habash and your soldiers know that you are the international terrorist called Michael? That you kill indiscriminately? Jews, Arabs, Muslims, infidels?"

A figure appeared in the cafeteria doorway. Roemer raised the nine-millimeter and snapped off a shot as he jumped into the elevator.

"Don't kill him," Sherif radioed. "Not yet."

Roemer punched the button for the pool floor. They needed just a little while longer. Whalpol, monitoring this channel, knew what was going on. He'd be speeding up the evacuation to minimize casualties in case this place went up. Roemer hoped Rudi had found Leila and gotten her out of harm's way.

"We're still counting," General Sherif radioed.

Roemer raised his walkie-talkie. "I'm on my way down, General. I'd like to hear your explanation."

If he could lure Sherif out into the open, and kill him, the general's troops might listen to reason.

Roemer pocketed his gun as the elevator stopped on the containment pool floor and the doors came slowly open.

A ragged hole had been torn in the ceiling; ripped wires hung down. Directly across from the elevator, less than five meters away, Menzel and Brecht were crouched behind a computer console. Bouchiki stood at the head of the stairs to the left, and across from the pool one of General Sherif's soldiers stepped out from beneath the stairs. He motioned for Roemer to come out of the elevator and move toward the pool.

Roemer stepped out slowly. He walked directly to the console so that he could look out across the dormant pool.

"This way, Roemer," the soldier called, his voice echoing.

Jacob Wadud's body floated facedown in the pool.

"I want to talk to General Sherif."

"Oh, you will, Investigator. You will."

General Sherif appeared at the control room window above.

"Sherif!" Roemer shouted. "General Sherif!"

Sherif stepped out onto the walkway at the head of the stairs. Colonel Habash and two soldiers came with him, their Kalashnikovs trained on Roemer.

"How did you get into the building?" General Sherif called down. "It was quite clever of you."

"Do you know why I am here?" Roemer shouted. "Do your men know why I have come?"

General Sherif said nothing.

"To arrest you for the murders of Sarah Razmarah and Joan Waldmann."

"Who would believe the son of a Nazi? Would you like to know what we have done to your father's body?"

"Have you told them, General, how you killed and raped those two young women?"

General Sherif started down the stairs.

"Have you told them how you raped one of the girls *after* she was dead?"

Sherif reached the bottom of the stairs and stopped. He was smiling, still perfectly in control. He pulled out his pistol.

"So the terrorist will strike again," Roemer growled. "Saddam Hussein will be proud of you. You have ruined all of this for him."

General Sherif pointed his pistol at Roemer's head.

"Kill me, General, but first tell me the truth."

Roemer figured the detonator was up in the control room.

"I told our president that Germany could not be trusted," Sherif said. "Not while you are in bed with the Americans. You have become worse than the Jews."

"I meant the truth about Sharazad Razmarah and Joan Waldmann. They did nothing to you, General. Nothing to harm Iraq. Why did you kill them?"

Sherif stiffened.

"They were nothing," he said in a reasonable tone. "They were whores. They deserved to die."

Colonel Habash flinched. The other two soldiers, half-way down the stairs, looked at their general in disbelief.

"Was it because they reminded you of your wife, or your mother?" Roemer asked.

General Sherif's face flushed. "They were both whores. Strumpets."

"But the Israelis killed them."

"I should have done it. I should have taken them to the desert and . . . taught them."

Roemer shook his head. "But it wasn't that way at all, General. Why else did you assassinate those people in Tel Aviv in 1957 except for revenge?"

80

LEILA OPENED the third-floor door and looked into the empty corridor. Access to the control room ceiling was through the drafting room floor. She'd seen that from Trautman's notations on the engineering blueprints in Administration.

Wadud had come this way. But he was dead. She'd heard every bit of it on the walkie-talkie. Death was all around, just like Beirut.

The drafting room was deserted. Two floor panels had been removed.

She went to the opening and got down on her stomach so that she could look all the way along the catwalk toward the control room.

There was someone down there, his back to her, his figure outlined against the blue glow from a jagged hole in the ceiling below, right over the reactor pool.

Leila eased herself onto the catwalk and started toward the crouching figure ahead. She could hear someone talking somewhere below. She stopped. It was her father and Roemer.

"The truth," Roemer said.

"Time to die," her father replied.

"No," Leila cried.

The soldier on the catwalk spun around, his Kalashnikov coming up. Leila fired three shots, the third catching the soldier in his right side.

The man cried out in pain, toppled over the rail and crashed through the ceiling into the pool.

Leila raced forward. "Father!" she screamed. "Father!"

81

LEILA'S VOICE from above echoed through the fuel rod room. Everyone looked up. Roemer pulled Jacob Wadud's gun out of his pocket and ducked off into the shadows.

The room erupted in a volley of shots, automatic weapon fire ricocheting off the concrete floor at Roemer's heels.

He dove behind a large steel cabinet.

Colonel Habash lay wounded at the foot of the stairs, and at least two of the Iraqi soldiers went down, but Sherif ran back up the stairs while Menzel fired at him from across the pool.

The soldier who had been beneath the stairs ran across Roemer's field of fire. Roemer squeezed off a shot. The soldier pitched forward on his face.

"Sherif!" Roemer shouted.

General Sherif fired from the top of the stairs; Menzel grunted and fell back. Bouchiki was gone from the head of the stairs, and Brecht, who had been beside Menzel, was nowhere to be seen. He'd probably been hit.

Sherif darted into the control room.

The detonator! Christ, the man was going to push the button!

Roemer dashed for the stairs as he popped out the spent

clip and rammed the fresh one onto the butt.

He flew up the stairs. At the top he crouched low and looked inside. Two soldiers were backed against a control panel. General Sherif, holding a small electronic device with a short antenna, stood in the middle of the room looking up at the ceiling.

82

LEILA WAS shaking, trying to hold her gun steady. She looked down through a light fixture into her father's eyes.

"Please, Father, don't do it."

General Sherif's eyes were wide, his nostrils flared, his face red.

"It's over, Father. The hostages are gone, most of your good soldiers are down, your position is untenable. There is no reason to continue. Let's go home. It will be okay."

"Leila?" he said softly. He could not see her.

Tears streamed down Leila's cheeks. "Father, please."

"They have to die," General Sherif said. "For what they did to us."

"They did nothing to us." Leila started to squeeze the trigger when one of the soldiers by the control room panel fired his Kalashnikov, the burst catching the general across his chest, knocking him back over a desk, blood spraying everywhere, the detonator falling to the floor.

No one moved. Roemer crouched outside the control room on the stairs. Leila stared at her father's body. Both the soldiers gaped at their general. Finally the young soldier who had fired dropped his gun, sank to his knees and wept silently.

83

If Chancellor Kohl had not personally asked him to remain with the BKA, Walther Roemer would have made good his promise to himself to resign. He didn't give a damn about the citation, about the BND's thanks, about the congratulations from Colonel Legler or the approbations from Chief Prosecutor Schaller and Ludwig Whalpol.

"What matters, Investigator," the Chancellor said, "is that we need you. Germany needs you."

Need, Roemer thought. Who needs who? Who belongs? For what purpose?

It was late, nearly ten, on a miserably cold, windy evening when Roemer left the Chancellor's residence on the Adenauerallee, climbed into his car and drove off.

He wore a tuxedo. He reached up and undid the bow tie and top button of his shirt, then lit a cigarette as he crossed the Konrad Adenauer Bridge over the cold, dark Rhine.

Three weeks had passed since the incident at the KwU plant. Incredibly, no outsiders had monitored the final walkie-talkie communications from the R&D building, a stroke of good fortune for them all. The media had been ruthlessly kept from learning the true extent of the threat. All they knew was that terrorists had taken over the R&D facility and had been stopped by a heroic BKA investigator.

The bodies of General Sherif and his soldiers had been removed in secret and flown back to Baghdad that very night. A brief press notice had announced the general's death a few days later, of heart failure in his home outside the capital. In the next days, Iraqi newspapers and television were filled with accounts of his bravery and the good deeds he had done for his country. Iraq still had its hero.

Over the past weeks Roemer had refrained from much thinking, but in the most recent days the loneliness had begun to catch up with him. The harsh reality was that no one really cared about him other than Rudi Gehrman and his wife.

Worrying about his father had occupied so much of his emotional energy that now a large hole was left behind.

Roemer had come to realize that his youth had been spent in the pursuit of survival, which left him in several ways stunted emotionally, incapable of trust.

Kata and Gretchen had not simply tired of him, they had been driven off by his aloofness, by his insensitive detachment.

Chancellor Kohl was correct: Roemer was a damned good cop. But there was this large lack in his personality: the ability to trust people who cared about him.

He turned off the bridge, but instead of heading up the busy Hauptstrasse to his apartment in the Oberkassel, he doubled back across the TEE tracks to the extension of the Rheinallee—the river drive. He parked his car below the bridge abutments, doused the lights and got out.

In the reflection of the city lights he could see the swift flow of the black water. For a second or two he had the bleak urge to climb over the retaining wall and leap down into the dark river and let it carry his body to the sea. It would be peaceful, free of loneliness.

There was an old peasant proverb: Life is unbearable, but death is not so pleasant either. He couldn't remember where he had heard it, but he suspected it was from his mother.

Headlights flashed across his car, and then him, as a Mercedes entered the parking area and pulled up. Someone got out.

Roemer stepped away from the retaining wall as the slight figure approached. Suddenly he didn't give a damn about the circumstances, the reasons, the motivations. He simply felt the chance that he might no longer be alone. There was still time to learn to trust.

"Walther," Leila Kahled said softly.

"I hoped you'd find me," he said.

84

ALL THE German engineers were gone and would not return. Saddam Hussein stood on a high balcony looking out across what was the greatest secret ever to be contained in this valley. Even greater, he thought, than the creation of mankind.

Muhammad had spoken of the Garden of Eden. It would happen again. Here in Iraq, in the Fertile Crescent.

Four hundred meters above, on the desert floor, work continued on the massive desalinization facility, but here, in the natural salt caverns formed millions of years ago, the real project—Iraq's real salvation—languished.

"But only for the moment, Mr. President," the man standing beside Hussein said.

"Your technology is not so good as the Germans', is this not so?" Hussein asked.

"We have more nuclear fuel," Nikolai Vasilevich Rogachev said. "President Nikolayev's new SALT proposal will mean that even more nuclear warheads will have to be dismantled. Plutonium makes a wonderful electrical generating fuel." The Russian grinned. "Did you know, Mr. President, that one half of a kilogram of fissioned plutonium is equal to ten *billion* watts of thermal energy?"

"That is interesting," the Iraqi leader answered. "But

tell me again about the financial arrangements and your security proposals."

"Of course, Mr. President," said Rogachev, who was a high-ranking officer with the new Foreign Intelligence Service.

It was too bad about Michael, Saddam Hussein thought as he and the Russian and the rest of their party took the elevator down to the main floor of the vast cavern.

But there were other Michaels. There were always other Michaels.